MW00426060

Catching the Bad Guy

Book 2 of the Janet Maple Series

The Janet Maple Series

Sign up for the mailing list at www.MarieAstor.com to be notified as soon as a new book comes out.

Catching the Bad Guy

Book 2 of the Janet Maple Series

By Marie Astor
Copyright © 2013 Marie Astor
All rights reserved.
ISBN-13: 978-1492953579

This book or any portion thereof may not be reproduced or used in any manner whatsoever without the express written permission of the copyright owner except for the use of brief quotations in a book review.

This is a work of fiction. Any resemblance to actual persons, places, event, business establishments or locales is entirely coincidental.

Author Contact
Website: www.MarieAstor.com
Facebook: Author Marie Astor
Twitter: @MarieAstor

Chapter One

"There is my favorite investigator." Dennis Walker sauntered into Janet Maple's office without bothering to knock. Dennis Walker never knocked. He simply barged in unannounced, the same way he had barged into Janet's life a little over a year ago, turning it upside down.

Her fingers tingling from furious typing, Janet looked up from her computer screen. "Today is the big day, huh?" Janet kept her voice cool, making a mental effort not to ogle Dennis's freshly tanned face. The man would look good even if he were pasty white, not that Dennis's silky-smooth complexion had ever been pasty white, not even in the dead of winter. But now he looked dangerously handsome. "How was your vacation? Puerto Rico, was it?"

"Turks and Caicos, and it was wonderful."

Janet nodded. She knew that. She had known the destination of Dennis's getaway ever since he had posted his vacation schedule on the department calendar two months ago, and she had spent weeks visualizing his trip: Dennis stretched on a lounge chair, sipping one of those resort drinks from a coconut with a dark-eyed lanky brunette lying by his side, or perhaps a blue-eyed blonde. When it came to women, Dennis had only one requirement: they had to be drop-dead gorgeous. Apparently, Janet Maple was not gorgeous enough for Dennis Walker.

"You look like you could use a break, Janet." Dennis's comment made Janet conscious of the dark circles under her eyes, which so far were her only reward for burning the midnight oil at work.

"Not everyone has the luxury of taking a week off before the most important case hearing of one's career."

Dennis's eyes locked on Janet's, his glance acknowledging their never-ending game of verbal tennis. "As I told my boss, I had scheduled my vacation months in advance; the case hearing had been moved three times. I have a life, you know, and I can't be at the Enforcement Division's beck and call."

"Can you believe the momentum the case has gained?" Janet steered the conversation away from the alarming subject of Dennis's private life, the details of which, despite all the hours she had spent pondering the subject, she wanted to know as little as possible.

"I know. We did all the groundwork and then every single regulator jumped on the bandwagon, including your former alma mater, the Manhattan District Attorney's Office."

Janet felt the usual sting of chagrin that the mention of her former employer never failed to trigger. Yes, her legal career had begun with a position of assistant district attorney at the Manhattan District Attorney's Office, but her promising start fizzled to a disappointing conclusion after she was downsized from the DA's office in the middle of an important case.

As if reading her thoughts, or more likely her expression, Dennis cleared his throat. "David Muller has wreaked enough havoc. It's high time he was brought to justice."

"I sure hope that's going to be the case."

Dennis frowned. "Why the hesitation?"

"For the very same reason you just mentioned: the case hearing has been postponed three times already."

"I guess we'll find out soon enough."

As if on cue, there was a knock on the door of Janet's office. The head of the Investigations department, Hamilton Kirk, stood in the doorway. "Dennis, Janet, may I speak to you a minute?" As always, Ham's facial expression was inscrutable, but the serendipity of his appearance made Janet look at her watch. It was after three p.m.: the Emperial case decision had to have been reached by now, and if the news were good even Hamilton Kirk would not have been able to resist the joy of announcing it.

"Of course, Ham." Dennis's tone was smooth, but not smooth enough for Janet to miss the hidden notes of apprehension in his voice.

Together, Janet and Dennis followed Ham into his office. Just why Ham had to insist on going to his office was beyond Janet. Although much smaller in size, her office would have provided sufficient privacy for their discussion, but then she had gotten used to not questioning Ham's idiosyncrasies.

The moment they reached Ham's office, Janet understood her boss's request. Hamilton Kirk had worked for various departments of the Treasury for over twenty years, during which he had acquired vast office paraphernalia—certifications and commendatory plaques, reference guides, and never-ending stacks of bulging folders that contained case materials—but now all of these items were neatly packed in cardboard boxes that lined the floor of Ham's office.

Both Janet and Dennis looked questioningly at Ham.

"I'm sorry, team," Ham paused to swallow. "As of today I'm retired."

"Retired? And you are springing this on us now, when you're already packed?" Dennis eyed Ham reproachfully.

Ham patted Dennis's shoulder. "I only found out this morning myself."

Janet had to make an effort to keep her jaw from dropping. "What do you mean?"

With a sigh, Ham stepped over the row of boxes and sat behind his desk. "Sit down, you two."

Mechanically, Janet and Dennis sank into the chairs opposite Ham's desk.

"I know that our job is not easy: we try to do what's right the best way we can with the few resources we have, and, let's admit it, on measly pay. I have worked in this place for over twenty years, and until this morning I still believed in such a thing as justice. But now I know that I have been a naïve fool." Ham shook his head. "They are kicking me out—"

"Who's kicking you out, Ham?" Dennis cut in.

Ham went on, ignoring Dennis's question. "Although I must say that the severance package is quite generous. Finally, my long-awaited dream of retirement has come true—the only funny thing is, is that now that it's here it doesn't feel nearly as good as I thought it would. In fact, it feels like being thrown out into a dumpster."

"Who is kicking you out, Ham?" Dennis repeated.

"My boss," Ham replied simply. "I've worked for the man for over ten years. This morning he calls me up from Washington. 'Ham,' he says, 'it's been wonderful to have you with us. In recognition of your stellar service, the most notable of which was your work on the Emperial case, your pension is now fully vested. Your retirement starts today.'" Ham shook his head. "He didn't even have the decency to give it to me straight."

"Give what to you straight?" Dennis demanded.

"Oh, come on, Dennis. If you plan to stay in this trade you've got to wise up or you'll end up an old fool like me. David Muller has friends in high places. As of this morning, the Emperial case has been dismissed by our Enforcement Division for lack of evidence. I am now retired, and next week your new boss will be coming in. His name is Alex Kingsley. He's some young hot shot from the DA's office."

"Alex Kingsley?!" Janet exclaimed.

Dennis shot Janet a sharp look. "Why, you know him?"

"Briefly," Janet replied, cursing her cracked voice and flushed face for betraying her agitation. "We've worked together," she added noncommittally. After all, she could not very well admit that Alex had been much more than her coworker at the DA's office. Janet had known Alex since they had met at Columbia Law, from which they had graduated in the same class. Alex had been her boyfriend for almost five years; he had been the man she had thought would be the one. And last but not least, not only had Alex taken credit for Janet's work on most of the cases that the two of them had been assigned to at the DA's office, he got a promotion that should have been Janet's. Then he put the icing on the cake by breaking up with her and suggesting that they remain friends. Needless to say, Janet had refused, and several weeks later she had been downsized.

"Who is this guy? Does he have the credentials for the job?" Dennis asked.

"Er ..." Janet's face grew warm. Her personal opinion of Alex was that he was not worth the ground he walked on, but then she was biased. Alex did graduate from Columbia Law, albeit only because Janet had contributed to that fact substantially by letting him copy her homework assignments and class notes, but who was counting, right?

"Dennis, listen to me," Ham snapped. "As far as the big men at the top are concerned, Kingsley's qualifications are irrelevant. The only thing that matters is that he's the man they want for the job, and I'm not." Ham looked away. "All the years of hard work down the drain ... If there's one thing I learned through this experience is that moral flexibility is paramount. If I had caved in when they told me, I would still have my job today."

"What do you mean, caved in?" Dennis asked.

"Our Enforcement Division had postponed the hearing three times. I should have gotten the hint."

"You mean they are in on it?" Janet blurted out.

"Hank Dooley, the chief of Enforcement, is a political shark. He's got his eyes set on Washington, and he'll do anything to get there—" Ham broke off, shaking his head. "There's no use talking about this now: what's done is done, and I don't intend to spend my time dwelling on the past. As much as I've enjoyed chatting with you young people, I ought to get going. I have a dinner date with my wife, and Neely doesn't like it when I'm late. Boy, she's going to be excited about the retirement package." Ham rubbed his chin, his eyes brightening up. "You know, I think I'm starting to warm to this retirement idea after all."

"We'll miss you, Ham." Dennis's voice was somber and sincere. "I'll miss you."

"I'll miss you too, both of you. This is not the way I expected my career to end, but when life slips you lemons the only thing to do is to try to turn them into lemonade. Make nice to the new boss. I hear he's been told to clean ship, so don't give him any pretext to do so." Ham rose from the chair and extended his hand to Janet. "The few months we've worked together have been a pleasure, Janet. I'm sure you'll have a stellar career, regardless of where it might be."

"Thank you, Ham." Janet tried not to read too much into the "wherever it might be" part.

"Dennis, I don't mean to sound patronizing, but you were truly like a son to me and you always will be. I know I busted your chops at times, but that was only because I wanted to see you reach your full potential. You are a damn good investigator, and if it were up to me I would name you as my successor. But, as things stand, it's no longer up to me. I hope there won't be any hard feelings."

"None, sir. Thank you, sir. It has been an honor and a pleasure to have worked with you."

Ham nodded. "Thank you, son. I'd better get packing: they want me off the premises by five."

"Goodbye, sir." Janet took one last look at Hamilton Kirk.

6

Unlike Dennis, she had not worked with the man for long, but in the brief time that she had known Ham she had grown to respect him greatly. Ham was honest, principled, and fair. These were qualities that were rare in any man and were certainly not among the traits that Alex Kingsley possessed.

Chapter Two

Janet Maple stared at her cup of coffee and untouched bagel. She did not have much of an appetite this morning, but neither would most people in her situation: having your ex as your new boss was not exactly a heart-warming prospect.

There was a knock on the door of her office. "Come in," Janet called out.

"Janet?" Ann Smith, Ham Kirk's former secretary, walked into Janet's office. Ann had worked for Ham for the past ten years. The shock of the previous day's events was written on her face.

"Hi, Ann." Janet was always glad to see Ann, but this morning she was especially so. She was about to say how horrible it was that Ham had been let go, but Ann interrupted her.

"Janet, Mr. Kingsley would like to see you." Ann's lips were drawn together and her eyes downcast.

The idea of Alex being addressed as Mr. Kingsley seemed preposterous. "But he wasn't supposed to start until next week."

"Apparently, his start date has been moved up," Ann replied matter-of-factly. "He said he wanted to see you right away."

Janet was about to ask her what it was about, but seeing the closed-off expression on Ann's face, decided against it. "Very well. Tell him I'll be right there."

After Ann left, Janet took a moment to collect her bearings. The thought of Alex—correction, Mr. Alex Kingsley—made her cringe. The man was positively evil: suave, ambitious, and pretentious beyond bounds. The pompous prick did not even have the decency to say hello. Instead, he had sent his secretary to do his bidding.

On her way to Alex's office, Janet stopped by Ann's desk and immediately understood the reason behind Ann's strange behavior: Ann's cubicle was filled with cardboard boxes. "Ann, I'm so sorry." Janet touched Ann's shoulder.

"I was offered a generous severance package, and I opted to take it," Ann replied evenly.

"But he can't just force you out! You've worked here for years!"

Ann looked away. "I believe that Mr. Kingsley will be hiring an assistant of his own choosing. My severance is conditional on the confidentiality agreement that I signed," Ann added.

Janet shook her head: it had not even been twenty-four hours since Alex's arrival but already he was reshaping the department according to his needs. "I understand. Good luck, Ann. I sure will miss you."

Alex's office door was open, but Alex was busy looking at something on his computer screen.

Janet knocked and waited for Alex to acknowledge her presence. In the few hours that Alex had been the occupant of Ham's old office, he had transformed the space into an unrecognizable state. Ham's modest office furniture had been replaced with an antique wooden desk and two plush armchairs that faced it. The chair that Alex sat on looked like a throne made of leather. The formerly empty walls were now lined with paintings in heavy frames. Next to Alex's desk stood a gigantic bookcase with glass doors; its shelves were filled with law tomes with brand new bindings.

"Janet, how wonderful to see you!" With his arms outstretched, Alex rose from his chair.

"Mr. Kingsley." Janet smiled brightly, extending her hand.

"Why so formal?" Alex exclaimed. "That's no way to greet an old friend."

Before Janet could say another word, Alex had her in his embrace. Janet's head spun from the onslaught of memories: his scent—he still wore the same cologne—along with the familiar sensation of his arms around her, transported her to a different time. A time during which she had been a happy fool, but happy nonetheless.

"You look wonderful," Alex remarked.

"Thank you." Janet noticed the stray grays on Alex's temples and the deepened lines on his forehead: all that climbing up the corporate ladder was beginning to take its toll on him. Still, she would be a liar to deny that Alex remained a very handsome man.

"So, how do you like your work here at the Treasury?" Alex asked. Nothing about his demeanor betrayed the least bit of discomfort.

Janet found Alex's poker face astounding. The man had to feel at least a little bit awkward: he had, after all, nearly ruined her life. But then it was also possible that Alex was incapable of remorse. "Great," Janet answered. "The work is challenging and rewarding. I'd be happy to walk you through the cases I've worked on."

Alex waved his hand. "There'll be plenty of time for that later. I'm going to cut right to the chase, Janet. You are the first person I called into my office, and the reason I did that is that I need an ally."

Janet waited for him to continue. Alex was even ballsier than she remembered. What on earth made him think that she would be his ally?

"Janet, there have been reports of employees of this office using questionable methods during investigations. Now, I'm always in favor of personal initiative, but the rules are the rules.

We can't have vigilante agents compromising the Treasury's reputation."

Janet gulped. She was fairly certain which employee Alex was alluding to: Dennis Walker did not always play by the rules. At times he liked to bend them a little. Like the time when Dennis and Janet had gotten Tom Wyman, who was a retained legal counsel, drunk on straight vodka martinis while their own martinis were made with olive juice and vermouth by a well-tipped bartender. While Wyman was out in a drunken stupor, Dennis had downloaded vital evidence from Wyman's laptop. That evidence had been the cornerstone of the Emperial case until the Treasury's Enforcement Division postponed the hearing, and finally rejected the evidence as inadmissible.

"I am asking you to be my eyes and ears, Janet." Alex leaned across his desk, his eyes locking on Janet's face. For a moment his face lost its well-composed mask. "Look, Janet, I know that you must have plenty of reasons to hate me. I wasn't exactly a prince. But a lot is riding for me on this job. If I do well here the sky will be the limit for me, and trust me, I will not forget you in my next move up."

Just like you didn't forget me before when you dumped me, alone and unemployed, while you were busy being the DA's superstar? Janet thought.

"I was sent here to clean house, and I need to know if you are going to be on my team. Do we have a deal?"

Janet's reasoning told her that she should say yes. She wanted to say yes, but as all the memories of Alex's betrayals flashed in her mind, her lips refused to obey her. "Alex, you may be charming and clever, but you are deceitful and dishonest. So far, you have been able to fool people into liking you but you won't always be able to do so. I'm sure that if you would have been in my place, you would have said yes. But that's just it: I'm not like you. I won't spy on my colleagues who have supported me and accepted me. We work as a team here, and you have a choice of either becoming a part of it or not." Janet rose from her chair. "Should you have any work-related questions, you can find me in my office."

Alex's face remained impassive, his smile growing ominously brighter. "You are forgetting one very important thing, Janet. I can fire the whole team, one by one."

"Not without cause, you can't. And the rest of us aren't retirement age, so you won't be able to get rid of any more people by offering them early pension packages."

Before she said more things she would regret later, Janet stormed out of Alex's office. She was so mad that she barely looked where she was going. There was a man walking toward her, and Janet bumped right into him. "Whoa, Janet. Are you all right?" Dennis Walker was standing only a few inches from her, his hands gripping her shoulders. "You almost knocked me over."

"Sorry, I just had a meeting with our new boss. I guess I'm a little rattled."

"He's here? I thought he wasn't supposed to start until next week."

"So did I, but apparently he's anxious to get a head start."

"What was the meeting about?"

"Dennis, I can't talk right now. I have a conference call." Janet used the first excuse that came to her mind.

Unlike her, Dennis would have taken advantage of the opportunity to ingratiate himself with Alex. Truth be told, Janet was now having second thoughts herself. Her bravado was beginning to evaporate, and she worried that she might have gotten both Dennis and herself into very hot water.

Chapter Three

Alex Kingsley watched Janet Maple storm out of his office on her long, shapely legs. Once the door slammed behind her, Alex leaned back in his chair, locking his hands behind his head. He did not care for people who crossed him, and he always made sure that the culprits learned not to repeat their mistakes. In this case, however, he could not help feeling guilty about his past with Janet. To say that he had wronged the girl would be an understatement of gigantic proportions, but then again it was not his fault that Janet never understood that you had to keep your superiors happy. Take this job, for instance: there was no way Alex would have been appointed as the head of the Investigations department had it not been for Cornelius Finnegan's glowing recommendation.

"Mr. Kingsley, Mr. Finnegan is on the line for you," Alex's assistant informed him through the intercom.

"Put him right through."

Even though Finnegan could not see him, Alex straightened up in his chair. "Mr. Finnegan?"

"Alex, my boy! How many times do I have to tell you to drop this Mr. Finnegan nonsense?"

"How are you, Cornelius?"

"I'm well, thank you. And how is your first day on the job?"

"It's going well, sir, thank you very much. Settling in; I'll be meeting with the staff shortly."

"Yes, that would be a very good idea. Make sure to keep an eye on that Dennis Walker character. Make sure that he doesn't pull any more stunts like he did with Wyman's laptop. It's a good thing Wyman didn't press charges—just imagine the liability!"

"I'll make sure that nothing of the kind ever happens again, sir."

"Good. That's why I recommended you for the job. Hamilton Kirk clearly was not up to it. At least the Enforcement Division had enough sense to reject the evidence and dismiss the charges against Muller. It was clear that Bostoff was the culprit."

"Yes, sir, I agree completely."

"I'm glad that you do, Alex. Tell me, is Janet Maple one of the investigators who helped Walker on this case?"

"Yes she is, sir," Alex replied laconically, thinking it best to omit the details of his earlier altercation with Janet.

"I remember her from when I was the New York County district attorney. She worked on the Borrelli Capital investigation, didn't she? A bright young thing. Too bad she got downsized. I'm glad to hear that she's doing well now. I understand that she, too, was involved in that whole Wyman escapade. You'll make sure that she doesn't get into any more trouble, won't you, Alex?"

"Yes I will, sir. You needn't worry about anything, sir."

"Oh, I'm not worried. It just pains me to see scum like Walker break the rules and think that he can get away with it. But even worse than that is the effect he has on other employees—it could be downright toxic. Before you know, you've got the whole organization going rogue. But look at me carrying on. I know that I've got nothing to be concerned about because I've got you there to put things back in order."

"Absolutely, sir. That's what I'm here for."

"I'm glad to hear that. Well, I've got to get going. We'll talk soon, Alex. You keep an eye on that Janet Maple girl."

"I will, sir." Alex hung up the phone. Just how was it that Janet always managed to get in the middle of it, was beyond him: first Borrelli and now David Muller.

Alex closed his eyes. Janet Maple. While most women were nothing more than a paragraph, or at most a page, in his life, Janet had been an entire chapter. They had started dating toward the end of his senior year of law school. At the time he had just broken up with another one of his girlfriends and needed a quick replacement. With final exams only a few months away and the tedious bar exam looming before him, he needed a girl with substance. When Alex took a second look at Janet's long chestnut hair, the luster of which could not be diminished even by the drab ponytail she usually trapped it in, her green eyes surrounded by full, long lashes that were lowered studiously, while her long, elegant fingers gripped a pen with furious determination and frantically scribbled every word uttered by their boring professor, he had decided that Janet Maple was the girl for him. They studied for all the exams together. Alex's grades soared, and he aced the bar exam.

After graduation, both of them got positions as assistant district attorneys at the New York County District Attorney's Office. The job did not pay much, but then it was mostly nine to five and Alex did not relish the idea of long hours that young lawyers were subjected to in private law firms. He would much rather try his hand at politics, and the DA job was the perfect launching pad for his ambitions. All he had to do was play his cards right.

He had kept his relationship with Janet secret at work. The DA's office did allow coworkers to date, but not in the same department, and he sure as hell was not transferring out of Investigations, which was the most prestigious department in the organization. Besides, he had liked being assigned to the same cases as Janet. The girl had killer instincts. She had cracked every single investigation that she and Alex had been assigned to. Alex was happy: not only was Janet great in the sack, she also did his work for him. All he had to do was report to his boss and wait to be noticed.

Jake Andrews, Alex's boss, had begun to take a real liking to him, often inviting him to drinks after work. Things had been going really well when Janet began investigating Borrelli Capital. Shortly afterwards, Jake Andrews had summoned Alex into his office. "Alex, you are now the lead on the Borrelli Capital case. It's imperative that you keep me in the loop on all the latest findings," Andrews had said.

Alex got the hint immediately. As per his boss's request, he reported each and every finding that Janet dug up.

Then one afternoon Alex was surprised to find Andrew's boss, Cornelius Finnegan, at the meeting. "Jake's been telling me about the wonderful job you've been doing on the Borrelli Capital case, Alex," Finnegan remarked.

Cornelius Finnegan had an oblong-shaped bald head and a hefty body that made him resemble a giant potato, but when Alex felt Cornelius's narrow blue eyes fix on him, he immediately understood that Cornelius Finnegan had not reached his position by being a dimwit. "Thank you, sir. I'm glad to be of service."

"I am glad to hear that." Finnegan rubbed his chin. "How would you like to have Andrews's spot?" he asked.

Alex shot a worried look at Jake Andrews: Andrews was still his boss. Andrews merely nodded benevolently.

"Relax, Alex," Finnegan grunted. "Jake and I have already discussed the matter. Jake is being promoted, and I need a man I can trust to take over his spot. What do you say? Are you the man for the job?"

"Yes, sir," Alex replied calmly. "As the head of the group, I will ensure smooth and efficient operations." He could barely contain his excitement: finally, he was graduating to the big leagues.

"And most importantly, you will keep your superiors appraised," said Finnegan. "Let's cut to the chase, Alex. We're going to close out the Borrelli Capital investigation with no action."

"And by the way, our budget has been reduced. We've been told to make cuts. You need to select one person to downsize," Andrews added. "As the new head of the group, the decision will be yours to make, Alex, but I hope that you will heed my input. My opinion is that we should downsize Janet Maple."

Alex felt his throat tighten. Yes, he was willing to sacrifice his principles to get to the top, but kicking Janet out would be a new low even for him. "Perhaps we could consider a warning or a performance improvement plan?"

Andrews shot a fleeting look at Finnegan.

"Alex," Finnegan said, placing his hand on Alex's shoulder, "I think that you're a very talented young man. You could have an excellent career here. Now, please don't make me think that I've overestimated you. Do you have what it takes to get the job done?"

As Alex looked into Finnegan's eyes, which had turned into mere slits, he knew that his prospects were hanging by a thread. This was his chance, but it could also turn out to be his undoing. Judging by the way Finnegan and Andrews planned to dispose of Janet, they would not think twice about doing the same to Alex. In an instant Alex made his decision. "Yes, sir, I most certainly do. I realize that ability to make tough decisions is part of being a manager, and I can make these kinds of decisions, sir."

The next day, Alex got Andrews's job. His first decision as the group manager had been to downsize Janet. At least he did not have to tell her himself: Human Resources did the dirty work for him. Getting to the top was not for the squeamish.

Several weeks later, Alex found out from Andrews that Nicholas Borrelli, the owner of Borrelli Capital, had given personal loans to half of Washington. Needless to say, Borrelli was getting off the hook.

Alex cracked his knuckles. For reasons he did not know and had no wish to find out, Muller had Finnegan's protection. Alex's task had been made clear to him. He was to ensure that the individuals responsible for the investigation were either frightened into silence or dealt with accordingly, meaning fired. Alex had already requested background files on all of his subordinates, and Janet Maple's file, along with that of Dennis Walker, were right at the top of the pile.

ಬಂಬ

Alex's handsome—yes, despite his base nature the man was handsome—face materialized before Janet's eyes: the magnetic look of his dark eyes that could morph from passionate to persuasive to humorous to impenetrable in a matter of seconds, the perfectly chiseled structure of his V-shaped nose, and the sensual curvature of his lips. Yes, Alex was a very good-looking man. From the taut musculature of his body to his confident stance, everything about him exuded an aura of success. The only trouble was that Alex was determined to succeed by any means possible. It had taken Janet almost five years of her life to learn this simple truth. By the time Alex was through with her, she was unemployed and alone.

Her job at the Treasury gave her a chance to turn over a new leaf in her life. But just as she thought that the past was safely behind her, all of her efforts were in danger of being vanquished by Alex's demonic hand. Yes, the man truly was the devil incarnate. Janet decided that this was going to be Alex's new nickname. But even devils could be exercised with holy water, and this time Janet was not going to surrender without a fight.

Janet's ruminations were interrupted by Dennis Walker poking his head through the doorway of her office. "Are you going to the staff meeting?" he asked.

"What staff meeting?"

"The staff meeting with our new boss. Don't you check your emails?"

Janet turned her attention to the computer screen and saw a slew of unread emails. One of them was a staff meeting request from Alex. The meeting time was five o'clock. What kind of a jerk would schedule a staff meeting for five o'clock? The answer was simple: Alex Kingsley. "Crap. I was hoping to get out of here early today."

Dennis's eyes narrowed. "Is there something you're not telling me?"

"What do you mean?"

"You've been avoiding me all day." Dennis took a seat in a chair that stood across from Janet's desk. "Now, are you going to tell me what's going on, or do I have to pry it out of you?"

"Nothing is going on," Janet snapped. She was not going to let Dennis Walker interrogate her. "We'd better hurry or we're going to be late for the staff meeting."

"Some thank you I get." Dennis shook his head. "Had it not been for me, you would have blown the meeting altogether."

"Thank you, Dennis." Janet rose from her chair and grabbed her notepad. "Now, can we please go?"

Dennis held the door open. "After you, my lady."

Staff meetings always took place in the main conference room, and, at least in this regard, Alex's regime was no different. When Janet entered the conference room she saw that most of her colleagues were already there. The conference room had one long, rectangular table in the middle with about fifteen chairs around it. These seats always became the spoils of those who arrived early and were, at the moment, all occupied. Normally, there were additional folding chairs placed against the wall but now they were nowhere in sight, leaving those who had not been sufficiently speedy in their arrival standing on their feet. "Great," Janet grumbled, leaning against the wall.

"Hey there, Janet." Peter Laskin nodded at her. "How is it going?"

Peter Laskin was the department's top analyst. Unlike Dennis, Peter rarely worked the field, but he was a whiz at analyzing data.

"Is that a new shampoo you're using, Peter?" Dennis cut in. "Your hair looks really bouncy today."

When Janet first met Laskin he had been bald and wore glasses. Then, after an extended leave of absence, Laskin returned with a full head of hair and glasses-free. This transformation became an endless source of jabs, which Dennis unleashed on Laskin daily. "Why thank you, Dennis. Yes, as a matter of fact it is," Laskin replied. "I think that people should never stop improving themselves, wouldn't you agree?"

"I agree completely." Janet could not help having a soft spot for Laskin: all those hair plugs must have hurt a great deal.

Their conversation was cut short by Alex entering the room. He was accompanied by a statuesque blonde with long legs and very large breasts who looked to be about twenty-five years old. She was dressed in a low-cut blouse and a black miniskirt.

Alex stood at the head of the table. As much as the sight turned Janet's stomach, she had to admit that Alex projected dominance. Instantly, voices quieted and complete silence filled the room. "Thank you all for meeting with me on such short notice," Alex began.

As if anyone here had a choice, Janet snorted inwardly.

"I would like to begin by introducing myself. As most of you already know, my name is Alex Kingsley. I am the new head of the Investigations department." Alex paused. "I know that Hamilton Kirk, the former head of this department, was greatly respected and loved by all of you."

There were several nods and excited yeses, which quickly faded under Alex's glare. "I have been asked to assume this post for several reasons: my experience at the DA's office and my management style. We've got a great deal of work to do, and it will require everyone's unwavering dedication." Alex paused, surveying the room. "I will be frank with you: there have been reports of questionable techniques being used during investigations. And I will tell you right now that I will not stand for rule infractions of any kind."

Alex's glance fell on Dennis and Janet, making Janet wish she could fall through the floor right then and there. "Now, I do not know how true these allegations are," Alex continued, "but I am determined to find out. I will be meeting with each and every one of you to review the cases that you have worked on in the past year. I expect your full cooperation in this process. My assistant"—Alex motioned toward the blonde—"Georgiana Russell manages my schedule and will be scheduling the meetings shortly."

I wonder what else she manages, Janet wondered, remembering how unceremoniously Alex had discharged Ham's former assistant, Ann. But then Ann was neither tall nor blond nor young, which were skills that Alex obviously considered to be vital in an assistant.

"That's all for today," Alex concluded. "Thank you all for coming."

As they filed out of the conference room, Janet caught Alex's sideways glance. She shuddered to think of the changes that Alex's reign would bring.

Chapter Four

Alex Kingsley leaned against the back of his luxurious leather chair and surveyed his new office digs. Not bad for a day's work, he thought. Alex had had the men working overtime, delivering furniture and hanging paintings. The place had been a dump and needed a complete overhaul. Just how had his predecessor managed to stand his crummy office surroundings was beyond Alex, but then his predecessor did not have the favor of the state attorney general.

Poor Hamilton Kirk. Alex smirked: he did not feel the least bit compassionate toward the former head of the Investigations department who had been so unceremoniously discharged. It was survival of the fittest, and those who did not possess keen political judgment were forced out. Ham Kirk had been a loyal and diligent servant of the Treasury, but just like Janet's principles had not gotten her anywhere at the DA's office, Kirk's diligence did not get him any accolades at the Treasury. On the contrary, it had gotten him sent out on early retirement. On the other hand, the chief of Treasury's Enforcement, Hank Dooley, was a much more reasonable man. Dooley had gotten the drift regarding the Emperial case right way and diligently postponed the hearings in response to Finnegan's directive. Now, it was rumored that Dooley could very well be destined for Senate or Congress.

Alex rubbed his hands in self-satisfaction. Finally, he was getting where he wanted to be in life. Finnegan trusted him, and Alex was certain that once he got the Treasury Investigations department under control, Finnegan would propel Alex to roles of much greater importance. Finnegan's name reminded Alex why he had been assigned to his new job in the first place. Today he would have his first meeting with that reprobate Dennis Walker. Alex had requested the background file on Dennis Walker and was surprised to learn that Walker was a former crook himself. A partner of a rogue hedge fund, Walker had been barred from the financial industry but had been spared further prosecution by the Feds for his cooperation. After that, Walker had been recruited by the Feds and had worked for them for several years until he was hired as a senior investigator by Ham Kirk.

Alex contemplated Walker's track record. Most people were motivated by either greed or ambition, some by both, and some, especially pathetic examples of human character like Hamilton Kirk, were motivated by a thirst for justice and truth. And then there were men like Dennis Walker who were most peculiar. One would think that after what Dennis Walker had been through, he would be the least likely person to be working as a white collar crime investigator. What drove him? Some twisted version of Stockholm syndrome? Perhaps it was desire for redemption? Whatever it was, Alex would find out.

"If you know the enemy and know yourself, you need not fear the result of a hundred battles," Alex recalled; it was his favorite quote from The Art of War, a book he perused frequently. While he fought his battles from behind his desk, they were just as vicious as those fought on the battlefield. Enough of this, Alex thought. There would be plenty of time to roll up his sleeves. Right now he was in a mood for some relaxation.

Alex pushed the intercom button. "Georgiana, would you come in here, please?"

"Right away, Mr. Kingsley."

A few moments later, Georgiana was standing in the doorway of his office. "Here's your morning coffee, Mr. Kingsley." Georgiana placed the coffee mug on his desk. Alex took a sip. The coffee was awful, but then he had not hired Georgiana for her coffee making or her secretarial skills.

Alex eyed Georgiana's ample breasts prominently displayed by the unbuttoned collar of her white blouse. "Close the door, will ya?"

Georgiana smiled slyly, swaying her hips left and right as she sashayed to the door and flipped the door lock switch. "Would you like me to take dictation, Mr. Kingsley?" she asked, tracing her finger along her full, parted lips.

"Come here, you."

Georgiana perched on Alex's knee. "I know shorthand."

Alex laughed at her cluelessness. "Nobody takes shorthand at the office these days, Georgiana. You've read too many detective novels."

"I think you'll like the kind of shorthand I have in mind." Georgiana placed her hand on Alex's crotch.

Alex kissed Georgiana's neck: this was exactly why he had hired her.

He had known Georgiana for over two years. At first she used to be his diversion from his relationship with Janet; after all, a man could not very well be expected to be confined to the affections of just one woman. A high-class escort girl, Georgiana had provided Alex with the excitement he yearned for. Georgiana told him that before she became an escort she had trained in gymnastics. When she turned fourteen, her breasts grew too large to fit into a leotard and were the reason why she had to leave the sport, but as far as Alex was concerned, Georgiana's breasts were magnificent.

Alex's promotion at the DA's office had given him additional income that he had been happily spending on Georgiana's affections. Soon, his rendezvous with her became

24

an addiction. It pained him to think of other men claiming Georgiana in his absence. He wanted to possess her completely, but he knew that his demands were impossible to realize. For one, Georgiana was a free agent, and for another, his salary made it impossible for him to be Georgiana's only client without filing for bankruptcy. If only he were higher up the food chain! Alex saw Finnegan and other top executives at the office charge their meals at expensive restaurants and bill exorbitant trips as work-related expenses. Finally, luck smiled his way.

When the job at the Treasury was offered to him, Alex saw his golden ticket. He carefully questioned Finnegan whether he would be able to select his own assistant, reasoning that Kirk's assistant would be unreliable because of her loyalty to her old boss. But Finnegan was no fool. He glanced at Alex shrewdly and laughed heartily, saying that yes, Alex could pick an assistant of his choice and that he could be quite liberal with the salary. There might even be room for a discretionary bonus. When Alex popped the question to Georgiana, she accepted his offer with delight, and now Alex had her all to himself.

His eyelids heavy with pleasure, Alex glanced at his watch. His next meeting was in twenty minutes. Georgiana would surely be done by then. After all, having sex in the office was one of the perks of a high-ranking government job. Even the president had done it. Alex slid lower in his chair and closed his eyes.

The ecstasy of Alex's climax was rudely interrupted by a knock on the door of his office. "Who is it?" Alex strained to keep his voice controlled.

"Dennis Walker. We have a ten o'clock."

"Just a minute." Alex motioned for Georgiana to get up as he hurriedly zipped his fly. That damn Dennis Walker was turning out to be an even greater nuisance than Alex had anticipated.

After he had made sure that he looked presentable, Alex whispered to Georgiana to open the door.

"Thank you, Georgiana. That will be all," said Alex as Georgiana ushered Dennis into the office.

Dennis's eyes shifted from Alex to Georgiana in an impertinent manner that Alex did not like at all. "Am I interrupting? I could come back."

"That's quite all right, Dennis. I was on a confidential conference call with the DA's office, but it's finished now. You can come in. We have a meeting at ten o'clock, don't we?"

"Yes, that's correct," Dennis confirmed with his eyes still fixed on Georgiana.

Alex found Dennis Walker's demeanor vexing. Of course Georgiana was not helping matters either, standing there like a transfixed idiot. Could it be that she fancied Walker? The mere thought made Alex's blood boil. "Thank you, Georgiana, that's all for now," Alex repeated.

"Yes, Mr. Kingsley." Georgiana finally got the hint and left the office.

"Now, let's get right to it, shall we?" Alex cracked his knuckles and motioned for Dennis to take a seat.

"Which case would you like me to start with?" Dennis asked. He had several thick binders under his arm, which he placed onto an empty chair next to him.

"Let's see here." On his desk Alex had a list of cases that had been assigned to Walker. The only case he really cared about was the Bostoff Securities / Emperial case. "Why don't we start with the Bostoff Securities / Emperial case?"

Dennis selected one of the heftier binders. "As the name of the case suggests, the investigation involved two entities, Bostoff Securities and Emperial hedge fund. Emperial hedge fund was one of Bostoff Securities' top clients. The Treasury Investigations department had been investigating Emperial hedge fund for several months when an opportunity for an undercover operation presented itself at Bostoff Securities, and I was selected to assume employment at Bostoff Securities as an undercover investigator."

"Had the court order for the undercover operation been obtained?" Alex asked sharply.

"Yes, all the supporting documentation is in the file." Dennis placed the binder on Alex's desk.

Alex pushed the file back in Dennis's direction. "Then perhaps you will be able to explain to me who at the Treasury sanctioned your drugging of Tom Wyman, Bostoff Securities' retained legal counsel, as well as abducting Wyman's laptop and stealing privileged and confidential documents from said laptop?"

"I am not certain which incident you are referring to," Dennis replied. "It is true that I was able to obtain documents from Mr. Wyman's laptop, but I was able to obtain said documents through the technology tools that I had as part of IT at Bostoff Securities. Gaining access to Wyman's files was part of the assignment."

Alex clenched his fists so hard that his knuckles turned white. That maggot Walker had some nerve! Not only had Walker been impertinent enough to interrupt Alex's pleasure that was being so expertly delivered to him by Georgiana, the bugger had the audacity to sit there and lie straight to Alex's face.

Alex placed his fists on the table and leaned forward. "Now, I think you know exactly what I'm referring to, Mr. Walker. I am going to cut right to chase here. I do not know what kind of operation the former department head was running here, but I will tell you this: there will be zero tolerance of protocol violations under my watch."

"With all due respect, sir—" Dennis began, but Alex cut him off.

"Precisely my point: I am your new boss and you will respect me. There will be none of that vigilante nonsense that you used to pull under the previous management. We are here to enforce the law, which means that we too are bound by law." Alex paused, studying the expression on Dennis's face. He had hoped to spot a glint of fear but came up empty. The man seemed to have nerves of steel. "Considering your past record, I can understand how you could think it justifiable to use unsanctioned means during an investigation. I will even give you the benefit of believing that you were acting out of your best intentions, but that does not absolve your wrongdoings. Because of the illicit manner in which the evidence was obtained, all allegations against Emperial have been dismissed."

Finally, Alex got a reaction out of Dennis. "But, sir, this is ridiculous. There is concrete evidence against Emperial. If you let Muller off the hook for what he did at Emperial, he will simply reopen another company to continue his fraud."

"Concrete evidence?" Alex raised his eyebrows. "I have already familiarized myself with the case, and the legitimately obtained evidence indicates that all of the infractions were the fault of Bostoff Securities." Here Alex had to struggle to keep a neutral face: compared to Emperial, Bostoff Securities was an exemplary firm, but unlike David Muller the owner of Bostoff Securities did not have the protection of Cornelius Finnegan.

"But sir, there are numerous records—"

"Listen to me, Dennis. Bostoff Securities was fined for its corrupt operations. The case is now closed. There is no legitimate evidence to support the allegations against Emperial or Muller, and I do not want you wasting the resources of this department on this matter any further. Is that clear?"

Dennis nodded. "Crystal."

Alex thought he detected freshness in Walker's voice, but decided to let it go for now. "Good. For our next meeting, I would like you to think about how you could better reallocate your time to be more involved in data analytics. More attention should be paid to the leads that we receive through our surveillances. I am very impressed with Peter Laskin's work. I'd like you to work more closely with him. There are many things you could learn from Laskin, like how to gather evidence the legal way. That will be all for now. Thank you."

Watching Dennis Walker leave his office, Alex could barely resist bursting into laughter. He had met with Laskin yesterday. Their meeting had been brief, but it had been long enough for Alex to understand that Laskin spent countless hours behind the computer screen, sifting through data, while Walker reaped all the accolades. Divide and conquer had been Alex's motto since he had been old enough to walk, and from kindergarten to college to law school to the DA's office, this strategy had never steered him wrong.

Chapter Five

Janet stared at her computer screen, doing her best to appear busy. Her mind was consumed with thoughts of Alex. Even though she had not seen Alex all day, she felt as though she could sense his noxious presence seeping through the walls of her office. The man she had hoped never to see again, was now in the same building, watching her, waiting for his chance to ruin everything she had worked for, just like he had done before.

Janet's thoughts were interrupted by Dennis Walker bursting through the door of her office. "We need to talk."

Dennis shut the door behind him and plunked himself into a chair opposite Janet's desk. "I need you to tell me everything that happened during your meeting with Kingsley."

"Hello to you too." Janet crossed her arms on her chest. She had not seen Dennis all day.

"Sorry. I didn't mean to be so abrupt," Dennis replied with mock politeness. "It's only that our new boss ripped me a new one this morning, and I would like to know why. Since you have a history with the man, I'd sure appreciate some insight."

Janet blushed. Her history with Alex had been extensive to say the least, but she certainly did not care to share it with Dennis.

"I tell you what," Dennis said, slapping his knee, "how about a drink after work? My treat. I think we could both use a night on the town."

Janet hesitated. A night out with Dennis Walker could lead to all sorts of risky outcomes.

"Come on, I know you want to say yes."

That was the trouble: she did want to say yes, just like she did every time Dennis asked her for a drink.

"All right," Janet replied brusquely. "It'll be nice to get out. Five thirty at the Bull and Bear?" She named the neighborhood bar where they usually went for a drink after work.

"Save the time, but change the venue," Dennis replied, eyeing her meaningfully. "How about The Vine instead? It's on Houston and Mercer in the Village."

"Meet you in the lobby at five?"

Dennis merely stared back at her, and Janet understood her mistake immediately. With Dennis Walker things were never simple. Apparently, he considered their meeting to be worthy of undercover protocol. "I'll meet you there," Janet corrected herself.

"I'll be waiting at the bar."

Great, Janet thought after Dennis had left her office, another meaningless pseudo-date with Dennis Walker. The man was a womanizer and a flirt, but somehow Janet's knowledge of Dennis's flaws did not make it any easier to resist him.

☜☞

At five twenty p.m., Dennis Walker was seated behind the bar stand of The Vine. As he waited for Janet, Dennis eyed the crowd, looking for pretty women. This was a habit of his, and even though at the moment his heart really was not into flirting, he thought the distraction would do him good.

His attention was drawn to an attractive brunette surrounded by four suits pawing for her attention like eager puppies. Junior associates, Dennis thought, probably marketing or consulting of some sort, but she's way out of their league—she's the kind of girl who goes for the top brass.

The brunette seemed oblivious to her companions' inept attempts at conversation:

"You nailed that account today, Roxanne."

"Hugh is going to be thrilled."

"I bet you're going to get an office soon."

Dennis's assessment had been correct. He spotted two middle-aged men making a beeline for the brunette siren. One was rail-thin with sour complexion, and the other had ruddy cheeks and a chubby stomach hanging over the belt of his pants. From the pompous and proprietary way the two carried themselves, it was clear that they belonged to that highly coveted club called Senior Executives.

At the sight of the older men, the puppies obediently dispersed their circle, disappearing into the background. The two old goats practically dribbled when the young beauty didn't reject their oily gazes.

The thin one droned on, "Yes, surely, teamwork is important, and today you have proved just how important it is, Roxanne."

"A job well done," the fat one chimed in.

The girl widened her eyes as though she was being imparted some great wisdom, looking at the two imbeciles with expertly crafted adoration.

Dennis was enjoying the spectacle so much that he forgot his usual reticence and stared openly, unwilling to miss a piece of this circus.

Sensing Dennis's glance, the brunette shot him a direct look and their eyes locked for a moment. If he had not been waiting for Janet, Dennis might have explored this highly enticing opportunity. As it were, he would have to pass. But then whom was he kidding? Ever since he had met Janet Maple, all the women he knew and any new women he met became just that: random women. Of course he knew that he had no one to blame but himself. Janet liked him; he was sure of it. The only problem was that he liked her too. The intense sensation he felt whenever he was in the presence of Janet Maple was an emotion that ran much deeper than mere attraction. Such emotions were against Dennis Walker's code of conduct. When it came to women, he liked to keep things simple, with no strings attached. Besides, Janet and he were coworkers, and no other combination had the makings of disaster written all over it like two dating coworkers.

Dennis had hoped that his latest conquest, Shoshanna, would free him from Janet. An heiress to a gym chain, Shoshanna was a twenty-seven-year-old voluptuous brunette. Dennis had met her in one of those swanky lounges. Surrounded by a pack of girlfriends, she was obviously bored by the types of men who were trying to gain her attention. Most men would have been intimidated to single out a woman surrounded by a fleet of girlfriends, but Dennis Walker was not most men. He had a gift when it came to picking up women in bars. A big part of this gift was his ability to guess a woman's favorite drink—a skill that mostly consisted of keen powers of observation and generous tips to the bartenders. After supplying the bartender with a twenty, Dennis learned that Shoshanna had been drinking lychee martinis all night. Just as her glass was about to become empty, Dennis had the bartender place another lychee martini in front of her. As Shoshanna's eyes lazily scanned the crowd for the source of this sign of attention, Dennis raised his glass to her from his corner of the bar. She smiled back, and within minutes Dennis was sitting next to her, chatting. That had been two months ago, and they had just returned from a trip to Turks and Caicos. The only problem was that Dennis had spent the entire vacation picturing Janet in a bikini.

"Hey there." Janet's voice brought Dennis back to reality. He flashed her a smile, hoping that his face was not betraying his thoughts.

"What will it be?" Dennis asked, drumming his fingers on the bar stand.

"A Bloody Mary."

"Sounds like a good choice. I think I'll join you." He gave the order to the bartender.

While they were waiting for their drinks, Dennis turned his attention back to Janet. She had taken off her suit jacket, unwittingly giving him a tantalizing view of her lovely breasts through the two opened top buttons of her blouse. It was more suggestion than an actual view, but Dennis enjoyed it when things were left to his imagination. Not wanting to be too obvious, Dennis quickly shifted his gaze to Janet's face. He was glad to see that tonight they were a shade of deep green, which meant that she was happy. The color of Janet's green-gray eyes always changed with her mood: when she was happy they were deep green, but when she was angry or upset, her eyes would turn almost gray. During the past few days, Janet's eyes had been a bleak shade of gray.

"Have you heard from Ham?" Janet asked, saving Dennis from the need to come up with small talk.

"No. I tried calling him several times but kept getting his voice mail. I gave up after my third message." Dennis sighed. Despite having occasionally butted heads with Ham, Dennis missed his old boss. And most of all, he was angered by the unceremonious manner in which Ham had been ousted.

"Maybe he's away on a trip or something," Janet suggested, but the look on her face made it clear that she did not really believe her own suggestion. "Or maybe he doesn't want to be reminded about everything that happened."

"I can't say that I blame him. If I were in his place, I wouldn't want to hear from any of us either. And that pompous prick they sent in to replace Ham!" Dennis clenched his fingers into a fist. "Do you know that he had the nerve to tell me that the evidence we obtained on Wyman was inadmissible and was the reason for the case being shut down? Does he take me for a complete idiot?"

Janet hastily looked away, busying herself with her drink.

"I, for one, am not giving up that easily. Kingsley reeks of foul play, and I intend to find out whom he's working for." Dennis fixed his eyes on Janet. "What exactly do you know about the guy? Please, I need to know."

Janet shook her head. "I don't want to talk about it, Dennis, okay? It won't make any difference anyway."

Dennis halted. Ever since Kingsley became the new department head, Janet seemed constantly on edge. She said that she had worked with Kingsley at the DA's office, and Dennis intended to find out just what was it that Janet knew about their new boss, but he had to tread lightly. On several occasions he had tried to get Janet to talk but she had snapped at him, which was incredibly uncharacteristic of her. There had to be a reason for Janet's reaction, and Dennis was determined to find out what it was. At the moment, however, it was difficult for Dennis to concentrate on the task at hand. It had been a while since he had been out with Janet alone. Usually, whenever they went out for drinks after work either Laskin or Ham Kirk would join in. But now, alone with Janet, Dennis was suddenly as nervous as a schoolboy. Objectively speaking, this was not a date at all, but this knowledge did not stop Dennis from wishing that it were.

Dennis forced himself to focus. "Come on, Janet. Don't you want to get back at the guy? If not for our sake then for Ham's? We can't let Kingsley destroy everything we've worked for. Granted, some of the evidence was not exactly procured by the book, but until Kingsley came into the picture no one gave a rat's ass. And now, all of a sudden, all the blame's been put on Bostoff, Muller's been exonerated, and we're being told to shut up. Don't you want to know who's behind all this?"

Janet downed the rest of her drink in one long swallow. "Fine, I'll tell you, but if you hate me afterwards, blame yourself."

After she had finished the account of her relationship with Alex, Janet felt Dennis's searing eyes upon her. "You dated the guy, and you're just telling me now? Don't you think it would have been prudent to tell me ahead of time?" Dennis glared at her.

"I didn't think that my personal life was any of your concern," Janet snapped, wishing she could disappear. It was not her fault that Alex had dumped her and while he was at it had taken credit for her work, but for some inexplicable reason she felt like someone stung with social leprosy. But then she knew the answer why: Alex was the victor and she was the loser. Alex's career was soaring, and from the smug, cocky way he carried himself, Janet guessed that he was doing equally well in the personal life department. By comparison, Janet's fortunes were bleak. The direction of her career was once again uncertain, and the status of her personal life was equally nebulous. A fact that was made painfully obvious by her spending Friday night in a bar with a coworker. A very handsome coworker, but still only a coworker.

"Your personal affairs do not concern me," Dennis replied coolly. "But when it comes to work matters, I think that professional courtesy behooves you to keep me in the loop."

Janet felt her face burn. So there it was: she was of no concern to Dennis Walker.

"I'm sorry," Dennis retreated. "I didn't mean for it to come out the way it did."

In spite of herself, Janet's heart quickened. Did that mean that he really cared? Could it be that he too, just like her, yearned for them to become something more than whatever it was that they were to each other?

Dennis finished his drink and signaled to the bartender for another round. "Janet, don't you realize the importance of everything that you just told me? Alex is a crook, and what's worse, he is working for even bigger crooks."

"Yes, but what's to be done?" Janet struggled to hide the disappointment in her voice: Dennis only cared about work after all.

"Don't you see it?" Dennis asked.

Oh, I see it, Janet thought. It's crystal clear. You only need me when it's work-related. Like when you got me to get all that evidence on the Bostoff case.

"Alex sabotaged your work on the Borrelli case because his superiors told him to do so, and he got promoted in return. Now, the same thing is happening with Emperial. David Muller must have friends in some very high places," Dennis continued, oblivious to Janet's mood. "But this time"—Dennis paused, placing his hand on Janet's arm— "you've got me by your side. I won't let Alex destroy everything we've worked for."

Under the direct gaze of Dennis's eyes, Janet felt something inside her shift. He looked so sincere, so concerned. But he didn't care about her; work was the only thing that mattered to him. Work and one night stands. Part of her wanted to storm right out of there, but she knew that she had to finish her story since Dennis was bound to find out anyway. "Dennis, I haven't told you everything." Janet gulped, anticipating another outburst from Dennis.

Instead, his voice softened. "What is it, Janet?"

"During my meeting with Alex he asked me to be his eyes and ears ... He wanted me to snitch on you."

"It seems that I'm rather high on Kingsley's list. I presume that you agreed? This is going to be fun," Dennis added, rubbing his hands.

"What do you mean agreed? Of course not."

"You refused?"

"Yes," Janet mumbled. Not only had she refused Alex's task, she had told him exactly what she thought of him, which was not much.

Dennis fixed his eyes on her. "Janet, tell me exactly how the conversation went."

Janet took a long sip of her drink. "I told him that I wasn't going to spy on my colleagues, to which Alex replied that he had the power to fire the whole team, one by one. And I told him that there wasn't anyone else left of retirement age on the team, so he wouldn't be able to bully people into retiring like he did with Ham and Ann."

Janet braced herself for Dennis's indignation; instead, she saw a smile on his face, and what looked like a glint of awe in his eyes. "Janet Maple, you've got guts." Dennis squeezed her arm. "Don't get me wrong, I think it was very brave of you to tell Alex off that way, but perhaps—"

"Perhaps it was not the smartest thing to do?"

"Look, I'm not here to criticize you. If anything, I'm grateful. You could have taken Alex up on his offer and not told me anything about it. But instead you warned me. Thank you for that."

Their eyes met, and Janet thought she saw a flash of something far stronger than gratitude in Dennis's gaze. But then it was probably nothing more than her wishful thinking. "So you're not mad at me?" Janet blurted out, cursing her own sheepishness. As if Dennis Walker had any right to be mad at her. If anything, it should be the other way around.

"No, I'm not mad at you, Janet." Dennis squeezed her hand this time, moving in closer. "But I hope that you'll consider my suggestion."

"What is it?"

"I understand how you feel about Alex, but if you want to get back at the sucker, you'll have to put your emotions aside. Do you think you could do that?"

"What do you have in mind?" Janet asked. A suggestion coming from Dennis Walker could never be simple.

"Go into his office on Monday and apologize. Then do what he asked you to do."

Janet crossed her arms on her chest, flaring with indignation. She was not apologizing to Alex. "Why don't you do it yourself, Dennis? What's stopping you from sucking up to the new boss?"

Dennis shook his head. "Janet, you really need to learn how to cool it if you want to outmaneuver a man like Alex. And for your information, I would gladly suck up to him, but the prick hates my guts. He's been sent here to shut me up, and there's no way on earth I can ingratiate myself with him. But you, on the other hand," added Dennis, eyeing Janet appraisingly, "have all the necessary equipment."

Janet tightened her arms around her. "If you're suggesting—"

"I'm suggesting that we expose that hypocritical bastard Kingsley for the slime that he is, and in order for us to do that we'll both need to swallow our pride. Please, Janet, just trust me on this. Together we can outmaneuver the dirtbag."

"Fine," Janet sighed. She didn't like Dennis's idea in the slightest, but then she didn't really have much choice. At least this way she would have a fighting chance with Dennis standing by her side.

Chapter Six

Janet paced the floor of her office, clasping and unclasping her hands. The prospect of apologizing to Alex turned her stomach, but she had promised Dennis that she would and there was no going back now. How many women ended up having to apologize to their ex-boyfriends? Not many, but she was one of the lucky few. There was no use grumbling about it. She might as well get the humiliation over with.

With leaden steps, Janet walked down the hallway that led to Alex's office. She was about to knock on his door when the sound of a female voice stopped her. "Do you have an appointment to see Mr. Kingsley?"

Janet turned around and saw that the question had come from Georgiana Russell, the flashy blonde Janet remembered Alex introducing as his assistant. "Hi, Georgiana. No, I don't, but I was hoping I could see him."

"I am in charge of Mr. Kingsley's schedule," Georgiana replied, pouting her pink lips for emphasis. "I will check if he is available."

Before Georgiana had a chance to attend to her task, Alex's door opened and the man himself stood in the doorway. "Janet! What a pleasant surprise. Come in, come in."

"Thank you, Alex."

Alex leaned against the door, holding it open with his shoulder. "Please, have a seat," Alex offered, motioning at the chair that stood across from his desk and closed the office door.

Janet sat down and crossed her legs, her skirt hiking up a few inches above her knee. When they had been together, Alex had often told her that he loved the shape of her legs. She might as well use every weapon in her arsenal.

"Alex," Janet started tentatively, "I wanted to apologize for speaking out of turn during our meeting last week." She lowered her eyelashes for added effect and then looked up at him again. "I don't know what came over me. I'm not like that at all. You are the head of this department now, and I want to assure you that I will diligently carry out any task that you choose to delegate to me. I can't tell you how sorry I am and how badly I feel about what happened."

"No need to apologize, Janet," Alex assured her, waving his hand magnanimously. "I understand completely. We are all human, and we all can be guilty of overreacting at times."

"I am so glad that you understand." What a pompous prick Alex had become. He was so full of himself he could not see past his own nose.

"And I am so glad that we have an understanding, Janet. I promise that you will be well-rewarded for your cooperation."

"So, is there anything in particular you'd like me to do?" Janet asked.

"For now, I just want you to keep a real close watch on Dennis Walker. I tell you, Janet, the senior management is none too happy with the stunt he pulled during the Bostoff / Emperial investigation. He won't get away with those kinds of antics on my watch. Not him, not anyone else for that matter. If you see anything that doesn't look right, you let me know immediately."

"I will, Mr. Kingsley."

"Now, Janet, such old friends as us hardly need to bother with formalities, wouldn't you agree?"

"Thank you, Alex."

"Thank you, Janet. I'm so glad to know that I have a friend in you."

"Of course, Alex. I'd better get back to work." Janet rose from her chair and moved toward the door.

"And Janet?"

"Yes?"

"Let's grab a drink after work one of these days."

"Sure. I'd like that." Janet hurried to leave before Alex would come up with a place and time.

෨෬

"So, how did it go?" Dennis looked at Janet across the table. They were having lunch in a pub several blocks away from the office. Dennis had specifically chosen a table that was facing the door to survey any new arrivals.

"I think he bought it."

"Told you so. Aren't you glad that you listened to me?"

"I'll be even gladder when we nail the bastard."

"Boy, I wouldn't want to cross you, Janet. So, what does the boss want you to do?"

"Oh, nothing other than spy on your every move and report to him immediately any suspicious activity."

"Sounds like you're going to have your hands full."

"Oh, and he also mentioned that he might want to have drinks sometime."

"Oh?" Dennis's eyebrows rose. "Look, Janet, I wouldn't want you to do anything that you're not comfortable with."

"Relax, Dennis. I'm a big girl. I can handle Alex," Janet's voice was playful, but inside she was sizzling with delight at Dennis's reaction. The man was definitely jealous.

"I just meant that I wouldn't want thing to get too far out of hand."

"They won't. I wonder if I'm the only one Alex asked to spy on you. I wonder if he spoke with Laskin at all. Do you think we should ask him?"

"Oh, I don't think we should. He might get overexcited. He's great at muckraking in Excel spreadsheets, but when it comes to undercover work he can't handle the stress. He might blab us out to Alex."

"This is hardly undercover work, Dennis." Janet shook her head. Male vanity never ceased to amaze her. It was not enough for Dennis to know that he was far better looking and charming that Laskin, he had to stomp on the poor chap every time he got the chance.

"Sure it is. It's internal undercover work," Dennis retorted.

"I just thought it might be nice to have Laskin on board, but suit yourself."

"I'm not saying that it's a bad idea, but I think it's too early for that, that's all."

Chapter Seven

David Muller motioned to the waitress for another round of drinks. A few moments later, a pretty blonde brought two dirty martinis to the table. The service at Delmonico's was top-notch. David was a frequent patron, and the waiters practically fell over themselves in order to please him.

"To fortuitous outcomes," said David as he raised his drink, smiling at his lunch companion, Tom Wyman.

"Cheers." Wyman took a long swallow of his drink. "I must admit that I thought it was going to be touch and go for a while," Wyman added, popping an olive into his mouth.

"For a while," David conceded, "but not for long." Wyman deserved much of the credit for the happy outcome, but that did not give him the right to rub it in. Had Wyman not introduced David Muller to Aileen Finnegan, David would not be celebrating his exoneration, but that was where Wyman's contribution ended. David did the rest of the work himself and would have to continue doing it for the foreseeable future. The authorities had built what seemed like a bulletproof case against David Muller and his hedge fund, Emperial; the broker David conducted his dealings through; and Bostoff Securities, along with its owner, Jonathan Bostoff. Fortunately, however, there was no such thing as bulletproof evidence—not when one was dating the daughter of New York's attorney general. Aileen

Finnegan was far from being a beauty, but her father's political clout more than made up for her physical shortcomings.

"Aileen sure has fallen for you. But then you were always quite the ladies' man."

David downed the rest of his drink, refusing to dignify Wyman's remark with an answer. Wyman had been in just as much hot water as David. The services that Wyman had performed for Jon Bostoff and Bostoff Securities were egregious enough for Wyman to lose his law license and would have cost him a huge fine and possible jail time. David had been the one to take the bullet for both of them. It just so happened that Aileen Finnegan fancied David's British charm. Despite his last name, David Muller had little to do with Germany except for his ancestors who had left their homeland for Great Britain somewhere in late eighteen hundreds. Not that David cared: his was not a pedigree worthy of a family crest. But while his Essex accent placed him solidly in the middle-class in his homeland, to Americans he was bona fide English nobility.

"You are aware that Cornelius Finnegan is expecting you to propose marriage to his daughter, right? He already thinks of you as his son-in-law." Wyman would not relent.

David flinched at the reminder of the hefty price he had agreed to pay for his and Wyman's freedom.

"They hung all the blame on that dope Jon Bostoff, but the decision could easily be reversed if additional evidence were discovered," Wyman added.

As if David needed reminding just how much additional evidence could come to light. He had devised the scheme himself, and he had hired Tom Wyman to help him execute it. Bostoff Securities was struggling financially, and Jonathan Bostoff, who had just taken over the company management after his father, was the perfect mark. Hungry for profits, he was dumb enough to go along with David's plan. David sent stock prices plummeting while reaping ginormous profits from his scheme, but legally Bostoff was on the hook. All of David's orders had been sent through Impala Group, a Cayman Island-based company that Wyman had registered in Bostoff's name. The scheme seemed impenetrable until an undercover Treasury investigator managed to get Wyman drunk and steal company documents from him, exposing David's elaborate cover-up. Cornelius Finnegan's mighty hand had made the evidence inadmissible, but David understood that his fortune could easily change if he lost Finnegan's protection. "I wonder what the statute of limitations is on the case ..." David mused.

Wyman placed his glass on the table and stared at David. "Listen to me, David, and listen well: Cornelius Finnegan is not a man to cross. He takes his family matters close to heart. If you were to so much as harm a hair on his daughter's head, the man would make sure that you never saw the light of day again."

"Yeah, you're not the one banging her, Tom." Now that the deal had been struck, David felt that he had exchanged the threat of physical prison for a figurative one. The prospect of years of making love to a woman one abhorred seemed a sentence too wicked even for the most inventive prosecutor to assign.

"I would gladly do the honors, but she picked you. Get some Viagra for crying out loud!"

Normally, David would have been insulted by Wyman's words, but as the image of Aileen's fleshy thighs and udder-like breasts materialized in his mind, Viagra started to sound like a very good idea.

"Get off your high horse, David," Wyman continued. "Let's look at the facts: yes, you've made good money, but as far as the big timers are concerned, it's small change. With Cornelius Finnegan backing you, you could play in the big leagues and no one would as much as dare lay a finger on you."

"Fine, you've convinced me. Now, let's order," David snapped. A good steak was just what he needed to lift his spirits.

An hour later, David Muller exited Delmonico's in a much better state of mind. He declined Wyman's offer to split a cab under the pretext of wanting to walk off the heavy dinner.

Once he saw Wyman drive away in the cab, David signaled for another taxi. He might be required to deliver sexual pleasure to Aileen Finnegan for the foreseeable future, but that did not mean that Aileen would be the only woman receiving his attention.

David checked his watch: he was right on time. In a few minutes, Mila Brabec would be in his arms. A look of longing came over David's face as he thought of Mila's long, slinky legs and the way she wrapped them around his shoulders when the two of them united in all-consuming passion. Mila's blue eyes were like deep pools of water, not tiny slits like Aileen's, and Mila's breasts fit gracefully into the palms of David's hands instead of sloppily spilling over like Aileen's. Mila's skin was unblemished ivory, as opposed to Aileen's never-ending freckles that were splattered over her face and her forearms, and Mila's long hair was as dark and smooth as onyx, not at all like Aileen's frizzy red mop. Until he had met Mila Brabec, David Muller had been proud to say that he had never really been attached to a woman. But now he knew that all those years of idle sex were meaningless. At the age of thirty-nine, he had fallen in love for the first time.

He had started seeing Mila when his scheme with Bostoff Securities had been in full swing. At the time, David's world had seemed complete: he was rolling in dough and bound to make more of it. David bit his knuckles. Just when things seemed to be going your way, life turned the tables on you and spat you right in the face. He dreaded the thought of Aileen and the many nights and days he would have to spend with her. In a way he felt sorry for the girl: a twenty-nine-year-old virgin! The idea seemed ridiculous but in Aileen's case it had been true. Had a different woman been involved, David might have been flattered, but with Aileen he was merely reminded of how dire his circumstances had been. Apparently, no man had considered Aileen to be a worthy conquest. Still, as much as he griped, he knew that being sentenced to Aileen was better than being sentenced to jail. He had bartered his freedom to achieve his aims before.

David's father was a shopkeeper, but he had wanted more for his son. He made David a deal: David did not have to work in the shop after school as long as his grades were good enough for him to make it into top colleges; if he failed, he would have to work off his allowances retroactively, with interest. David did not need a greater encouragement and was accepted into Cambridge. With a Cambridge degree in hand, David had been able to secure a position in London working for a U.S. investment bank. A few years later, he had convinced his supervisor to send him on an assignment to New York.

From the moment that he had arrived in New York, he knew that he wanted to make this splendid country his home, and not just in any of its cities but the city: New York. There were none of the stuffy class distinctions of his homeland; the air felt freer, lighter, with opportunities lurking behind every corner. There was, however, just one problem: unless David found a means of obtaining legal documentation to stay in the U.S., his presence in New York would be at the mercy of his employer. He had been in his mid-twenties at the time, which was far too young for marriage, but David knew what had to be done. Girls fell all over him, but he was careful in his choice. He was not marrying for love but for a purpose.

He picked the most easygoing of the contenders for his affections: Linda Johnson was an accountant at a major accounting firm and was as bland as her name. The two of them led a fairly happy marital existence, which was helped by the fact that both worked long hours. Of course, David's late "work" hours included activities other than work, but Linda either remained blissfully oblivious to the fact or simply did not feel the need to object. Five years later, David became a citizen

of the United States. A month later he moved out of his and
Linda's apartment and filed for divorce.

He had come a long way from a hopeful wannabe to his
current station in life, and he was certain that a man as
enterprising as himself would not be currying Cornelius
Finnegan's favors forever. Yes, most likely he would have to
marry Aileen, but that did not mean that he would have to stay
married to her forever. Despite Tom Wyman's cautionary
words, David knew for a fact that no human being remained
powerful indefinitely—politicians especially so.

ಬಿಂಕ

In her ground-floor, Lower East Side studio apartment, Mila
Brabec was busy finishing her makeup. After applying the last
coat of mascara, Mila examined her reflection in the mirror. She
was wearing David's latest gift to her, a black lace teddy with
black lace stockings, both from La Perla. The man sure loved
giving her lingerie, but as far as Mila was concerned these gifts
were for David: she could just as easily bang him in a T-shirt.
They had been seeing each other for a while now. It was high
time for more generous gifts; jewelry would be a good start. But
what she really wanted was a better place to live. She was sick
and tired of this dump. The windows of her sunless apartment—
if a two-hundred-fifty-square-foot hole could be called an
apartment—were facing the pavement, and the bathroom was
out in the hallway and had to be shared with three other tenants
on her floor. At least she did not have to walk up the rickety
stairs, which made the ground-level location of her apartment a
major plus. It was not the Upper East Side, but it was far better
than the apartment Mila shared with her parents and grandfather
in Prague.

She had dreamed of becoming a model, thinking of the
women from her country who had made it big: Petra Nemcova,

Daniela Pestova. These glamazons too had been hopeful girls once, vying for their place in the limelight. There was no reason why Mila Brabec should not find her own spot under the sun. Boys and men had been lavishing her with their attention ever since Mila turned twelve. In Prague, men threw wistful glances at her every time she walked down the street, but in New York beautiful women were an everyday occurrence. It had taken a little over three months to rid her of her illusions. After canvassing every modeling agency in town, Mila learned that at twenty-two she was considered too old as she was competing against nymphets of fifteen, and her perfectly normal weight of one hundred twenty pounds on a five-nine frame was deemed to be borderline elephantine. So, no modeling contract for her but she kept her spirits up. The way she saw it, she had a year in New York: that's how long her visa was for, and she might as well use it. Who knew? She might meet an American prince tomorrow and have her fairy-tale ending. After all, her cousin Ania had managed to find her prince charming, and Ania was not nearly as good-looking as Mila.

It was because of Ania that Mila found herself in New York. Cousins through their fathers, Ania and Mila had never been close back in Prague. The five-year age difference between them was partly to blame, but more so was the difference in their temperaments: Ania had always thought Mila to be too wild, and in exchange Mila was irked by Ania's timidity. But when Ania had snagged her American documentary producer husband and established herself in their Upper East Side penthouse residence, she was compelled to boast her new lavish lifestyle to her relations, which led to her extending an invitation to Mila. Mila did not have to be asked twice. There was nothing holding her back in Prague. She had just received her degree in finance and was slated to start work as a teller in the local bank. The day after she received Ania's invitation, Mila informed her future employer that she would not be commencing her employment. The way she saw it, there would always be time enough to go back to Prague and get a job as a bank teller or a secretary, which was all one could hope for even with an A average from the best university in Prague, at least not without influential connections paving one's way. And with her mother working as a secretary and her father employed as a factory worker, Mila did not have anyone to help her but herself.

A month after Mila's arrival, Ania started asking questions about Mila's plans. Determined to milk her stay at Ania's luxurious digs for as long as possible, Mila avoided concrete answers until Ania started dropping forceful hints about Mila moving out. Sure, she was happy about Mila extending her visa, but newlyweds Ania and Daniel needed their privacy. As if a six-bedroom penthouse lacked privacy. But Mila had no choice but to start looking for a place to live. When the ground-floor apartment in the crappy Lower East Side building became available, Mila moved right in. At least, no matter how small the place was, she did not have to share it with clothes-and-food-stealing roommates. Ania had been kind enough to co-sign the lease for her, and Mila had just enough savings from her college summer jobs to pay the first month's rent and one month's deposit. Then, she got a job as a waitress.

Six months ago Mila's luck finally changed. She met David Muller at one of those late-night fashionable lounge bashes the girls at her job were always fluttering to, and things started to look up. When she first heard David's British accent, Mila had been wary. What use would dating another foreigner be to her? But once she learned that David had lived in New York for almost twenty years and had his citizenship, she relaxed: as far as she was concerned, David was as American as Washington. Still, she had to play her cards right. Her U.S. visa was only good for another five months. If she did not get David to commit, off she would go, back to the motherland.

Not that Mila's attention was committed exclusively to David. With his busy work schedule, David saw her no more than three times a week, which left her plenty of time to fish, but so far David had been the most attractive catch Mila had secured.

The sound of the ringing doorbell brought Mila back to reality. It was time to go and rock David Muller's world.

Chapter Eight

"I will see you later, honey pie," David Muller whispered into Mila's ear.

"Do you really have to leave now?" Mila pouted.

As David's eyes traveled along Mila's long, shapely legs, graceful arms, the valley of her abdomen, and her lovely breasts, he was tempted to stay. But he knew that he was in no position to cancel his dinner with Aileen. At least for now, Cornelius Finnegan held way too much clout over him.

"Yes, baby, I do," David whispered, tracing the outline of Mila's long neck with his lips.

"If you're not in too much of a rush …" Mila's hand slid down his stomach.

David glanced at the clock on the nightstand: it was a quarter after seven, and he had to make it to Long Island by eight p.m. to pick up Aileen. "No can do, baby. Sorry, I've got to run. But I will take a rain check." David nibbled Mila's breast.

"Ouch!" Mila squealed with mocked hurt. David knew that she loved him using his teeth on her when they made love. "I'll hold you to it."

"You won't have to. I'll be here to collect."

David rose from the bed and wondered if he should shower before leaving, but decided against it: there simply was not enough time. Besides, it was not as though he planned to take

Aileen back to his place tonight. After making love to Mila it would be simply impossible.

"Honey bear?" Mila pouted.

"Yes, baby?" David felt himself melt with tenderness toward her. He loved it when she called him honey bear. It was a nickname Mila had invented especially for him.

"Oh, nothing," she murmured, lowering her eyes. "I know you're in a hurry. We'll talk later."

He rushed toward her. "What is it, Mila? You know you can tell me anything."

She looked up at him, her eyes pleading. "It's just that I was thinking of renting a different apartment, and I was wondering if you could help me find one. Would you know of a good real estate agent?"

David understood the hint at once. How could he have been so pigheaded? He had been seeing Mila for months, and aside from a rich assortment of lingerie, she was none the better for it. Sure, he wanted her to love him for himself, which was why he had been cautious. But now that she had stuck by him, he could become more generous. Besides, it would be nice to be able to see Mila in surroundings that matched her looks.

"Say no more, baby. I'll have my agent find a nice place for you." David kissed Mila's hand. "I've got big plans for us, baby. You just wait and see."

With that, David put on his jacket and headed for the door. With any luck he would make it to Aileen's on time.

⊰⊱

Aileen Finnegan sat down at her vanity table and took out her makeup kit. There had been many times in the past when she would feel discouraged to go on with the process, confronted with her pasty white, freckle-splotched skin, thin lips and small eyes ringed by short, pale eyelashes, and stringy red hair. Even as a girl she had always known that she would never be beautiful. Why was it that some women were beautiful and some not at all? Shouldn't there be some fairness when it came to divvying up good looks? Aileen often wondered. But when it came to good looks, genes and luck determined the outcome.

Even in her middle age, Aileen's mother was a graceful blonde with long, lanky legs and alabaster-smooth skin, and as a young woman she had been a knockout. One would think that Aileen would have inherited at least some of her mother's beauty, but no such luck. From her face to her stocky body, she was the spitting image of her father. Aileen loved her father to death, but she thought that being the replica of Cornelius Finnegan's features in a female form had to be the cruelest joke of all times. The only thing Aileen had in common with her mother was the color of her eyes, but even there she had been gypped: the deep blue color was wasted on the small, narrow shape of Aileen's eyes. At family gatherings Aileen had always felt like an ugly duckling as she tried to fit in with her pretty cousins from her mother's side. Often after looking at family photo albums she would be on the verge of tears. Why her? Often when applying mascara to her short lashes, Aileen felt like flinging the mascara brush at the mirror—what was the use? But not today.

Aileen applied powder to her face, eye shadow to her lids, and a coat of mascara to her eyelashes. She puckered her lips and drew pink lipstick over them. She pulled up her hair and pinned it up in loose knot, letting wisps of hair hang loosely by her temples and neck. Then, she leaned back and examined the result. Yes, the dreadful freckles were still everywhere on her skin, including her forearms and neck, her nose still resembled a small potato, and her eyes had not gotten any wider, but there was a new spark of happiness in them that lent a glow to her entire demeanor.

David Muller's presence in Aileen's life brought her confidence that she had never possessed before. True, she was no beauty, but the fact that she had managed to commandeer the attention of a man as handsome and charming as David Muller meant that she did have some appeal. Otherwise, why would he be interested in her? Of course the naysayers would be quick to provide a different answer, and Aileen was not naïve enough not to realize it. During those nights that she was alone in her bed without the reassurance of David's presence to soothe her worries, she tossed and turned, unable to fall asleep and wondering whether David's interest in her was driven by her father's stature and connections.

But tonight Aileen was too happy to dwell on these dark thoughts. For the first time in a very long time she actually felt pretty. The wrap dress she had on hugged her curves attractively, and the Spanx she had donned did a good job of keeping her midriff in place. She had lost a total of fifteen pounds over the last few months, which greatly contributed to the overall improvement in her appearance. There was no need for her to drown her sorrows in food now that she had David Muller to look forward to.

Lately, Aileen had been contemplating implementing other changes as well. Perhaps it was time for her to get her own apartment. At twenty-nine she was too old to be still living in her parents' house in Great Neck, Long Island. With ten bedrooms there was plenty of room, and the wing where her bedroom was located had complete privacy from her parents' wing, but it was still her parents' house. And now that she finally had someone to bring home, she wanted a place of her own.

Aileen checked her watch. It was almost eight o'clock. In a few minutes David would be here. She felt her heart flutter with anticipation as she thought of David's arms around her. She had never imagined that being with a man could feel that good.

Aileen thought back about the first time she had met David. It was at a thousand-dollar dinner fundraiser her father had organized. As Aileen later learned, her father had needed to fill table seats, and David, along with his friend Tom Wyman, had agreed to buy tickets. Lean and muscular, with his stylishly cropped blond hair and piercing blue eyes, David had looked so incredibly sharp in his tuxedo and bowtie that Aileen had literally felt her legs grow weak. Her heart was in her mouth when she saw that they would be sitting at the same table. Her breath caught as she tried to think of a pretext to talk to him. What would she say? She was almost ready to give up. With his James Bond looks, why would a man like David Muller be interested in her anyway?

"Aileen. Aileen Finnegan?" David had said, interrupting her ruminations.

Aileen had nodded, smiling pleasantly, as she dug her nails into the palms of her hands. Calm down, she had thought. It's now or never. You can try to get this man, or you can die a spinster who lived her entire life in her parents' house.

Chapter Nine

Mila Brabec was having lunch with her cousin Ania. As usual, Ania had insisted on dragging Mila all the way to the Upper East Side. They were seated in a pretentious but rather shabby café a few blocks away from the Metropolitan Museum of Art.

"Don't you just love the museum mile area?" Ania shrugged her shoulders self-indulgently.

"Yes, it is lovely," Mila replied, trying not to sound envious. Ania had light blond hair, deep blue eyes, upturned nose, and plump, rosy cheeks. With her broad hips, strong thighs, and double-D breasts, Ania looked like she belonged on a farm milking cows and baking bread. Instead, she had received a degree in art history and had worked as a tour guide, conducting daily tours of Prague's rarities for tourists. By an unbelievable stroke of luck she just happened to be guiding a city tour when Daniel Bauer of Upper East Side was visiting Prague in search of the next subject for his documentary.

"It's too bad that you have to rush for your shift at the restaurant. We could have stopped by the Metropolitan Museum. They are having the most fascinating exhibition on the origins of Egyptian art," Ania continued.

"That would be nice, but I have a date with David tonight."

"Oh, I just assumed that you'd be working. Aren't Friday and Saturday nights best for good tips?"

"You are certainly correct there, but I took tonight off to spend it with David."

"How is that going? Any signs of him getting serious?"

"I am working on it," Mila replied evasively. For now, she did not want to tell Ania about David's promise to relocate her into a new apartment. They were supposed to meet with the real estate agent tonight. David had told her that he had found the perfect love nest for them.

"I certainly hope that it will work out," Ania remarked judiciously. "You've got about six months left on your U.S. visa, correct?"

"That's right." Mila knew that Ania would love to see her running back to Prague in defeat. As annoyed as Mila was at her cousin, Ania did have a point: the time on Mila's visa was ticking, and if she planned to stay in New York she'd better find the means to do so.

"How's Daniel doing? Does he have any new friends you could introduce me to?" Mila asked without much hope for a positive response. In the beginning she had hoped that Daniel might introduce her to some of his friends: rich people always hung out together, and if Ania had managed to capture Daniel's heart, Mila was bound to become an overnight success, too. But Mila's hopes had failed to materialize. While Daniel had many friends, most of them were trust fund leeching types who lived under the heels of their mothers. Afraid of being disinherited, these men–boys were wary of getting seriously involved with any woman not handpicked by their mothers. Some of these boys were plenty willing to go for a fling but, as Mila subsequently learned, that was all they were willing to go for.

Ania blotted her lips with a napkin. "I thought you were serious with David. Besides, all of Daniel's friends are married or involved in serous relationships."

Serious relationships with their mothers who control their allowances, Mila sneered inwardly. "You're right. Besides, most of Daniel's friends are much older than I am anyway."

This was not entirely true and, even if it were, the statement would be nullified by David's well over ten-year age difference with Mila. But Ania did not know how old David was, and Mila was desperate for a snappy retort. "Look at the time." Mila consulted her Guess watch, making a mental note to extort a more prestigious watch from David. "I've got to run and get ready to meet David."

"Have fun." Ania reached for her wallet to pay the tab.

"I sure will." As payback for Ania's snootiness, Mila did not even bother offering to pay her share of the bill. After all, she had only had a cup of coffee and house salad while Ania had gorged on lamb chops. And Ania had already secured her prince charming; Mila still had to marry hers.

Two hours later Mila was rushing to meet David in SoHo. They were supposed to look at an apartment in a recently erected luxury building.

Mila's heart quickened when she spotted David waiting for her. He was always so immaculately dressed: clad in a closely tailored sports jacket, black slacks, and a dark violet collared shirt, he was the image of sharp elegance. So what if he was nearing his forties? David's lean physique, youthful face, and, most importantly, his bank account made it very easy for Mila to fall in love with him.

"Hi, honey," Mila greeted David and wrapped her arms around his neck.

He responded by locking his lips with hers in a long, deep kiss. "Mmm, you smell sooo good, baby. I've been thinking about you all day."

"I don't believe that!" Mila pouted playfully. "You must have plenty of important things to occupy your mind with during the day."

"That being so, none of them are more important than thinking of you," he countered, wrapping his arm around her waist. "Shall we go upstairs?"

"I thought we were supposed to meet the realtor."

"He's waiting for us upstairs."

David nodded at the doorman who held the lobby door open for them. "It's this way," said David, steering Mila toward the elevator hall.

Mila did her best to maintain her composure. The building lobby shone with modern chic opulence. Sure, the lobby of the Upper East Side building where Ania resided with her husband was impressive, but it was also dated and was starting to show signs of wear. Here, on the other hand, everything shone with newness and lightness.

The elevator door swung open, and David ushered Mila inside. "Up we go," he said, pressing the last floor button.

Once the elevator doors opened, David took off his tie and placed it over Mila's eyes. "No peeking," he said.

"But, David, I could slip!" Mila protested. She was after all wearing four-inch Louboutin heels that she had borrowed from her friend at the restaurant.

"Not with me guiding you," David whispered, placing his hands on Mila's hips.

After several confusing steps, she heard the sound of a key in a door lock. Then, she felt herself being lifted into the air as David swept her up into his arms.

"Now, you can look," David announced, as he placed her back on the floor and took the blindfold off her eyes.

The first thing Mila saw was the giant floor-to-ceiling windows. The room seemed to be endless in size, and the ceilings were enormously high. The furnishings were light and elegant: an Italian designer sofa, arm chairs and coffee table. A luxurious cowhide rug covered the floor. "David! This is incredible!" Mila pressed her hands to her mouth.

"Go on, take a look around."

She tiptoed into the bedroom and saw that it was furnished with a vanity table, an armoire, and a king-sized bed that was already lined with satin sheets.

"You haven't seen the best part," said David as he swung open the closet doors. The space inside was almost the same size as Mila's current apartment. Only this was meant for dresses and shoes, with long rows of hangers and racks.
"David!" Mila squealed.

"And don't forget the bathroom."

David walked into the hallway and swung open the door. "Voila!"

Mila nearly had a heart attack. The only time she had seen a bathroom like this was in advertisements for luxurious hotels, not that she had ever stayed in one. There was green marble everywhere, with a sunken giant bathtub taking center stage. "The bathtub is also a jacuzzi," David observed casually. Mila was merely able to gasp by way of response.

"So, do you like it?"

"I love it!"

"Good. Because I've signed the lease. Now, why don't we try out the new bed?"

About an hour later, after he had made love to Mila in every possible position imaginable, David exhaled contentedly. His eyes feasted on Mila's lean, graceful body. Her head rested against his shoulder, and he buried his face in her hair. Everything about this woman was electrifying: her body, her face, and even her smell—especially her smell. The only problem was that he could not get enough of her.

David grabbed his watch from the nightstand. It was almost seven p.m., and he had an eight-thirty dinner with Aileen. He did not want to but he had to get moving. Tonight's dinner was made that much more important by the fact that Cornelius Finnegan would be meeting David for drinks beforehand and joining them for dinner afterwards. Eventually, David might work up the courage to cancel a date with Aileen, but he wouldn't dare to cancel on Cornelius Finnegan. At least not yet.

"I've got to get going, baby." David carefully disengaged his shoulder from Mila's lovely head.

"Don't you want to stay over?"

"I wish I could, baby, but I've got a business dinner."

"On a Friday night?"

"Money never sleeps," David quoted Gordon Gekko. The words took him back to 1987, the year the movie Wall Street had been released. David had been a teenager at the time, full of hungry dreams, and when he saw Michael Douglas as Gordon Gekko on the silver screen, he knew that he too would find his fortune on Wall Street. Funny how things looked different in retrospect: the kind of trading Gordon Gekko perpetrated in Wall Street seemed like mere child's play to David now.

Mila said nothing and rose from the bed to gather her things. David could sense her annoyance. "But, baby, will you keep our nest warm for me? You can move in tomorrow." David placed the apartment key in Mila's hand.

Her eyes lit up. "Really, David? Tomorrow?"

He nodded. "As far I am concerned, this place is yours. And here is some cash in case you want to pick up a few things." David placed a bulging envelope on the vanity table.

"Thank you, sweetie," said Mila, linking her warm, full lips with his.

Reluctantly, David pulled himself away. He could not very well show up for a date with Aileen with a boner. "I really have to get going, baby."

David stepped into the shower and turned on the coldest water possible. He would not have bothered to shower for Aileen, but he wanted to look spick and span for Cornelius Finnegan.

❧❧❧

Half an hour later, David walked into Keens steakhouse. Had it been up to him, he would have opted for a more modern venue, but Keens was Finnegan's favorite place, and David knew better than to contradict Finnegan. David took a seat by the bar and waited for Finnegan to arrive.

He did not have to wait long. Always punctual, Finnegan appeared in the doorway at exactly eight o'clock. "Hello, David."

"Cornelius."

"How is my daughter's favorite fellow doing?" Cornelius slapped David on the shoulder. "You know, you're all Aileen talks about these days."

"Thank you, sir. But I'm sure you're exaggerating. In fact, I think it's the other way around," David managed, praying to God that his compliment sounded convincing. Were it within his power, he would prefer never to hear a word about Aileen.

"Huh. You smooth talker," Cornelius chuckled. "Let's go get a table. There's something important I want to talk to you about before our girlie gets here."

David could feel his apprehension rising. He sincerely hoped that what Finnegan had to say would not have anything to do with the Emperial investigation.

"Well now, that's much better," remarked Finnegan once they were seated in a private dining room. The wood-paneled room only housed a few tables, all of which were empty at the moment. "I've asked them for some privacy," Finnegan added, eyeing David meaningfully.

David took a small sip of his scotch. He wanted to keep his head clear when talking to Cornelius.

"Aren't you going to drink your drink?" Finnegan asked.

"I'm just trying to cut down on liquor, but tonight certainly warrants an exception," David agreed and took an obedient swallow.

"Good. I wouldn't want to see you turning into one of those health-obsessed vegans or whatever they call them." Finnegan finished the rest of his drink and signaled to the waiter who was standing by the far side of the room. "Bring us another round of Macallan, Johnny."

CATCHING THE BAD GUY

Uneasy under the direct stare of Finnegan's tiny, glinting eyes, David finished the rest of his drink.

"So, I trust that those dogs at the Treasury left you alone?" asked Finnegan.

"Yes, Cornelius. I'm most grateful for your influence on the matter."

"I'm only glad to be of help. After all, my future son-in-law can only be a law-abiding citizen," said Finnegan, slapping David on the shoulder.

The side door opened, and the waiter walked in with their drinks. "Set them down here, Johnny," said Finnegan. "And then leave us alone. My daughter will be joining us later in the evening. Please let us know as soon as she arrives." The waiter placed the drinks on the table, bowed and left the room.

Finnegan sipped at his scotch. "The old department chief at the Treasury was very much set in his ways—not the kind of man one could do business with. But the fellow I got there now used to work at the DA's office, and he knows how things really work, so I don't think you'll be hearing from them anymore. And now that we have the Treasury under control, there is another matter that I'd like to discuss with you."

David swallowed apprehensively. Would Finnegan be blunt enough to press him for a proposal date for his daughter?

"A childhood friend of mine has just been elected to the board of directors of a very prominent company. Let's say this friend of mine were to come into some valuable information"— Finnegan paused, twirling his thick thumbs—"would there be a way for us to capitalize on it?"

A wave of relief washed over David. Now, there was a topic he was more than happy to discuss. "Certainly, as you know, information is the ultimate form of currency," David spoke slowly, eyeing Finnegan meaningfully. "The regulations around insider information are strict, but there are a number of structures that could be formed in order to maintain anonymity."

"Like the setup you strung together for Emperial?" Finnegan's tiny eyes glinted. "Look, David, I hold the post of New York State attorney general, and before that I was the Manhattan district attorney. I know all about rules and regulations and, best of all, I have the contacts to make sure the regulators keep their noses out of our business." Finnegan raised his glass to his lips. "Now you, David, are said to have the trading expertise to get the thing done."

"Yes, sir," David replied evenly. Did the old man really have to rub David's nose into it?

"Now, Muller, I hope you didn't take me the wrong way. I was just busting your chops. I want us to be partners, and I want us both to make money while doing it. So, how about you open up a new hedge fund and we get to work?"

"Certainly, I could do that. What kind of trading volume are we talking about?"

"David, do you really think it's going to be just us? There are people I need to include to insure that our interests are protected. You are not the only one who wants to get rich."

David stifled a smile: the regulators were even more corrupt than the rogues who were trying to get around the rules.

There was a light knock on the door and the waiter entered the room. "Sir, Miss Aileen is here," he announced.

"Thank you, Johnny." Finnegan wiped his face with a napkin. "I think I'll be going now."

"Aren't you going to dine with us?" David asked, half elated, half alarmed. The thought of not being subjected to Finnegan's scrutinizing eyes was a relief, but the prospect of being alone with Aileen's passion was alarming.

"Not tonight." Finnegan rose from his chair. "I believe that we've discussed everything we needed to discuss. Let me know as soon as you have everything up and running. And David, I trust that you will keep Aileen out of this? There's no need for her to be troubled by any of this."

"Of course, sir."

At that moment the door swung open and Aileen was ushered into the room by the waiter. "Hello, girlie!" Finnegan exclaimed and kissed Aileen on both cheeks. "You're looking mightily swell tonight," he added.

"Oh, daddy!" Aileen blushed, glancing at David coquettishly.

Here, even David could not help feeling moved. Aileen was trying so hard for him: she had been losing weight and even though she was still plump, tonight she looked almost cute. She had put a lot of effort into her look. Her flared skirt concealed her wide hips and her freckles were almost invisible under expertly applied foundation. Her red hair was expertly pulled up and her eyes were shining with the happiness of seeing him. But no amount of mascara or perfume would ever make Aileen come close to Mila's beauty.

"Hello, lovely," David slipped into his British accent as he often did around Aileen. What could he do? The girl was a sucker for Jane Austen.

"I'll leave you two lovebirds alone," Finnegan grunted.

"Aren't you staying for dinner, daddy?"

"What would two young folks like you want with an old goat like me? No, I'm heading home to keep Mrs. Finnegan company. Goodnight you two. David, I look forward to hearing from you."

"What was that about?" asked Aileen after Finnegan had left.

"Oh, nothing important. Just a few investment ideas your dad asked me to look over." David smiled with self-satisfaction. A plan for getting out of Finnegan's hold on him was slowly beginning to form in his head.

Chapter Ten

Janet walked into Delmonico's where she was meeting her childhood friend Lisa for lunch. Lisa was already sitting by the bar.

From grade school to adulthood, Janet's friendship with Lisa had been tempestuous to say the least, but somehow it had managed to make it through even the roughest of trials.

Lisa smiled and waved, quickly slipping off the bar stool. "Janet!" Lisa opened her arms for a hug.

"It's great to see you, Lisa," said Janet, returning Lisa's embrace.

The hostess showed them to their table.

Janet leafed through the menu. She was not very hungry, had not been hungry ever since Alex became her new boss.

Lisa opened the menu. "I'm starving. I think I'll have a burger."

"Burger sounds good," Janet replied. She was not about to bother Lisa with her work troubles, not when Lisa was only a month away from tying the knot with Paul Bostoff.

"That's right. To hell with the wedding diet," Lisa cheered.

"You don't need a wedding diet. You look great."

"Thanks. It's the wedding preparations. We're just so happy. Paul's marketing company is doing really well. Jon is doing well too. He opened a white collar crime consulting business. Believe it or not, already a ton of clients have signed up."

"I believe it." Jon Bostoff certainly knew the subject matter firsthand.

Lisa reached across the table and squeezed Janet's hand. "Thank you, Janet."

"For what?"

"For putting an end to that madness that Jon got us all in." Lisa halted. "I've never really spoken to you about this, but I know that I should have. I had my head in the clouds, or to be more specific, up my ass. Had it not been for you, things could have turned out really badly for all of us."

"Do you really feel this way?" Janet asked. She was not sure how she herself would have reacted had she been in Lisa's shoes. Lisa had been the general counsel at Bostoff Securities, and it was Lisa who hired Janet after Janet had lost her job at the DA's office. Shortly afterwards, Dennis Walker had entered the picture. Janet had been torn between her loyalty to Lisa and Dennis's offer. Dennis had promised immunity for Lisa but not for Paul Bostoff, Lisa's fiancé and the company's chief operating officer. The affairs of Bostoff Securities looked grimmer by the minute, even if neither Paul Bostoff nor his older brother, Jon Bostoff, realized it. The Treasury was not the only regulator investigating the firm: Dennis had warned Janet that the SEC and FBI were hot on the trail. In the end, Janet decided to accept Dennis's offer. She had spent months agonizing over her decision, but, surprisingly, they had all survived, and even more surprisingly, Lisa and she were still friends.

"Yes. Jon had gotten himself into such a mess with that snake David Muller! Jon was so desperate for the firm to make money that he was willing to do almost anything for it. The whole thing was headed for disaster. But then why am I telling you this? You are the one who discovered it all in the first place."

Janet shook her head. "I didn't do it on my own."

"Yes, you did. But then I guess you do have a point. If I hadn't dragged you into Bostoff Securities in the first place you would have never had to deal with the mess that was going on there. And there I was, thinking that I had done you a great favor, while it was you who saved me."

All this praise made Janet feel uncomfortable. In the light of recent developments, she did not really feel like a hero. Janet frowned. What was the use of hiding the truth? Muller's exoneration would become public soon enough. She might as well tell Lisa now.

"What's wrong?" Lisa asked.

"The case against Muller has been closed due to insufficient evidence."

"What?"

Patiently, Janet recounted everything that had happened at work since Alex became her boss.

"The Alex Kingsley?" Lisa asked.

Janet bit her lip. "There is only one, as far as I know."

"This reeks of foul play. You've got to figure out who is behind all of this."

"That's what Dennis is saying, but I just don't know. Alex must have the backing of some really powerful men, and I just don't think that Dennis and I will be able to bring them down."

"You're not going to give up without a fight, are you? You can't let Alex repeat what he did to you at the DA's office. You've got to stand up to him."

"I don't know if I can."

"Sure you can. You've always been the one talking about justice and fairness. I used to make fun of you for that, but now I know that you were right. You have to make things right—if not for yourself, then for Jon and me."

Janet lowered her eyes. She had spent the majority of her career chasing after the bad guys. Granted, her chasing did not involve any actual running or gunfights. Her job was mostly done behind the desk, raking through rows of data. But the crooks she was after could do just as much damage as those with guns, like the Ponzi scheme crooks who had stripped her grandfather of every penny he had ever earned, sending him into fatal cardiac arrest. "Muller will not get away with it, not if I can help it."

"Good. Oh, I almost forgot to tell you, can you believe that he had the nerve to RSVP for the wedding?" Lisa exclaimed.

"You mean you invited him in the first place?"

"Long before the whole ordeal began, Jon had asked to include Muller on the guest list. Somehow, his name was never taken off and an invitation was sent to him. Still, I can't believe that he actually accepted." Lisa narrowed her eyes. "But now that I think about it, it might be a blessing in disguise."

"How?" Janet stared at her.

"Have you picked your date for the wedding?"

"I ... um ...," Janet stammered. In a fit of unchecked optimism, she had selected the "plus one" option when sending her reply to Lisa's wedding invitation. At the time, she had genuinely thought that she would have a date, and that Dennis Walker would be that date.

Lisa was too excited to pay attention to Janet's love life. "You have to bring Dennis as your date."

"What? Why?"

"Don't you see? It will be an excellent opportunity to get close to Muller. Dennis will weasel the information right out of him."

"What makes you think so?"

"Isn't Dennis supposed to be this top notch sleuth? He certainly managed to pull the wool over everyone's eyes when he was masquerading as an IT engineer at Bostoff Securities. David Muller should be a piece of cake. You told me that neither you nor Dennis had actually met Muller face to face, right?"

"That's right," Janet confirmed, none too happy with where the conversation was heading. "The Enforcement staff questioned him. We never met with him in person."

"So it's perfect! Ask Dennis to take you to the wedding, I'll arrange the seating chart so that you'll be at Muller's table, and the rest should be a piece of cake."

"There is just one problem. I don't think that Dennis will agree to be my wedding date. He is seeing somebody," Janet blurted out. Sure, she wanted to help Lisa, but the thought of asking Dennis Walker out, even for a purely professional reason, literally made her stomach cringe.

Lisa stared at Janet. "I don't care about Dennis Walker's social life. We've got to play every card in the deck, and I'm not taking no for an answer. After everything the two of you put the Bostoffs through, you owe it to them and to me to make things right."

☜☞

Janet lingered in the hallway section that led to Dennis Walker's office. It shouldn't be that hard to ask a man out on a date, should it? she thought. And it's not even a date; it's an opportunity to find out what David Muller is up to. No need to get worked up about it; just two coworkers joining forces on an undercover assignment—an undercover assignment with romantic possibilities ...

Janet braced herself; she had promised Lisa to get Dennis to come. The door to Dennis's office was half ajar. Janet was about to walk in when she heard the sound of Dennis's voice. He was on the phone. She hesitated; she was not one to eavesdrop, but when presented with an opportunity it was hard to resist.

"Yes, baby," Dennis's voice, slick with suaveness, carried past the doorway. "Of course I missed you. I told you that I've been busy at work. Of course I want to see you. Yes, tonight would be great. My place or yours?" Dennis purred suggestively. "Of course we'll have dinner first. Yes, Buddha Bar sounds great. I'll make a reservation. See you soon, honey boo."

Honey boo. Janet's face burned. What an idiot she had been to even think about asking Dennis Walker out. In her defense, she was going to ask him out for work-related purposes, but Dennis would have surely considered her invitation a flirtation. And the truth of the matter was that it would have been.

Ducking her head in embarrassment, Janet rushed down the hall.

"Janet! How is it going?"

Startled, Janet looked up. Peter Laskin was standing a few inches away from her. If he had not called her name she would have stumbled right into him. "Peter!" Janet aimed for a smile but ended up with a scowl. "Everything is great. How are you?"

Laskin shook his head. "Come on, Janet. You can't bullshit a bullshitter."

Janet felt a shiver run down her spine. Could it be that Laskin had seen her eavesdropping on Dennis?

"It hasn't been great for anyone here since Ham was let go. Oh, excuse me," Laskin coughed, "I meant to say 'left for early retirement.'"

Janet smiled with relief. "I couldn't agree more. I'm just trying to stay positive, you know?"

"I know." Laskin scratched the spot on his head that used to be bald before he got the implants. "I'm trying to hang in there as well. What's that you got there?"

"Oh, this ..." Janet glanced at Lisa's wedding invitation that she still had in her hand. Suddenly, she had an idea. There was no way in hell she was asking Dennis Walker out, but she had no objections to asking Peter Laskin. So what if Laskin hardly ever worked the field? Two pairs of eyes would be better than one; besides, she did need a date for the wedding. "It's funny you should ask," Janet replied, lowering her eyes demurely. "I was just going to see you about it, actually. Would you accompany me to my friend's wedding?"

Laskin's eyes flashed with surprise. "Why, yes, I'd be delighted. On second thought, let me just check my schedule to make sure." Laskin fumbled with his Blackberry. "When is it?"

"It's on a Saturday three weeks from now." Janet hoped that Laskin would not turn her down. Just how much mortification could a girl endure?

Laskin traced his finger along his Blackberry screen. "I'm wide open," he confirmed. "It'll be my pleasure, Janet."

"Good, that's all settled then."

"Actually, I was wondering if you'd like to grab a drink after work this Thursday?"

"Sounds like a great idea," Janet stalled. "But I've got so much work to catch up on. I'll let you know later in the week, all right?" Her worst fear was becoming a reality: Laskin had misunderstood her invitation as actual interest in him. To be fair, he could not very well be blamed for his reaction. Normally, when a girl asked a guy to be her date, to a wedding nonetheless, the guy would be safe to assume that the girl was at least somewhat attracted to him. But Janet's life was anything but normal, so Laskin would just have to suck it up.

Chapter Eleven

At five thirty p.m., Janet closed the door of her office. She would have liked to go home but she was meeting her law school friend Katie Addison for drinks. Katie was also in Lisa's wedding party, and Katie had insisted that they meet to discuss some last minute wedding details.

"Janet." At the sound of Dennis's voice, Janet's finger froze halfway to the elevator button.

"Hey there, Dennis. How is it going?" Janet tried to sound as relaxed as possible, lest he suspect how upset she was at him having other love interests in his life—love interests that were not her.

"I'm fine, thanks." Dennis scratched his forehead. "Do you want to grab a drink after work? If you could just wait a minute while I grab my jacket ..."

Why don't you ask your honey boo? Janet wanted to snap. The man's cockiness was unbelievable. Did he really expect her never to have any plans?

"I'd love to, but I can't. I have a previous engagement." Janet pressed the elevator button.

"How about tomorrow then?"

"I'm not sure. I'll have to check my schedule."

"Oh, all right. Let me know tomorrow morning then. I found this really funky bar that I think you'd like."

He's already assumed that I will say yes, Janet bristled inwardly. But then she knew that she was the one to blame for Dennis's attitude. In all the times he had asked her for a drink after work, even when the invitation was last minute, she had never refused. She had hoped that these outings would lead to something more, but they never had. As far as she was concerned, she was done with plugging the gaps in Dennis Walker's schedule.

If only she could come up with a snappy remark, but her mind had gone blank from her hurt pride. Mercifully, the elevator doors opened and she jumped right in.

"So I'll call you tomorrow?" Dennis poked his head in the elevator, the tone of his voice a pitch higher.

Janet merely smiled. Sometimes silence worked better than words. She had had it with Dennis Walker and his charm.

When Janet got to the bar where she was supposed to meet Katie, Katie was already seated by the bar stand with a drink in front of her. "Sorry I'm late," Janet apologized. She was still wired up from her earlier encounter with Dennis.

"Oh, that's okay. Swamped at work?"

"Yeah. It's getting to be really bad." Janet grabbed the cocktail menu. "What are you drinking?"

"A cranberry margarita."

"I'll have the same," Janet said to the bartender, "with an extra shot of tequila, please."

"What's gotten into you?"

"Dennis Walker," Janet blurted out before she could stop herself. Talking about Dennis Walker was probably not a good means of putting the man out of her mind, but then she really could not help herself.

"Oh, that old story. What happened?" At least Katie had the decency not to roll her eyes, but the tone of her voice produced the same effect.

Janet sighed. "Nothing happened. That's exactly my problem. Why can't I just forget about him?"

"The man is cute, so I can't blame you there. He is charming, and there is definitely chemistry between the two of you. Palpable chemistry."

"You are not helping."

"Look, Janet, if you like the guy, just tell him so. Who knows, maybe he's thinking the same thing? Maybe underneath his bravado, Dennis is just shy and he's afraid to ask you if you'd like to take your relationship to the next level."

"Really? Somehow I just don't think that's the problem. And we don't have a relationship."

"I beg to differ. In my book routinely mooning over a man and jumping at his every beck and call, abandoning all prior commitments, is a relationship. A slightly warped one, but a relationship."

Janet sighed. There had been one occasion when Dennis had asked her for a drink after work, and she had cancelled her night out with Katie because of it. "I've already apologized to you like a million times, and I bought you dinner to make up for it!"

"I'm not mad at you. I was just saying it to make a point, and the point is that you never break your commitments for anyone but you did it for him. You really like the guy, so just go for him."

"Do you think that Dennis Walker really needs any encouragement when it comes to asking a woman out?"

"Fine, maybe he doesn't. I'll admit that he doesn't seem like the shy type. But maybe he just doesn't know that you'd like him to ask you out. I mean really ask you out."

"In that case he is either deaf, dumb, or blind. Or perhaps all three, and he's found a really good way to hide it. But I highly doubt it." Janet finished the rest of her drink. "At least you'll be glad to know that I'm not jumping at his beck and call anymore."

"Oh yeah?"

"Yeah. He wanted to grab a drink after work tonight, but I told him no. Then he asked me if I can meet him tomorrow, and I didn't commit to anything either."

"That's a good way to start—give the guy the cold shoulder."

"Oh, come on! Don't I get a break? First you say that I jump every time he snaps his fingers, and now you're saying I'm giving him the cold shoulder? What was I supposed to do, stand you up instead?"

"No. But you can meet him tomorrow and just flat out tell him how you feel about him. Have a couple of drinks and then just kiss the bugger. There are only two possible outcomes: either he kisses you back, takes you to his place where the two of you proceed to make wild, passionate love, and you live happily ever after; or he doesn't and, yes, there will be some embarrassment there, but at least you'll get him out of your system."

"There is also a third possibility where he takes me to his place where we make passionate love for one night, and then he never calls me again. Only it will be really awkward because we will keep seeing each other at work."

"Is that why you're so afraid to take things further with him?"

"Maybe." Janet shrugged. "Let's face it: I don't have the best track record when it comes to dating coworkers."

"Is this about Alex again? That was over a year ago. Why can't you just forget about him?"

"Because now I see him every day, reminding me of my failure, and I don't want to risk repeating the same experience with Dennis."

"At least we've gotten to the bottom of this. I think I should have become a shrink instead of a lawyer," Katie concluded. "Look, Janet, I'm not a relationship expert, but I do know one thing: when you want something or someone, you've got to go all in. I know I'm happy that I did."

Katie was right. For about two months she had been happily dating one of the partners at her law firm.

"How are things with Adam?" Janet asked. A handsome, young attorney in his mid-thirties, Adam Lewis was a transfer from the Washington office, and Katie had been assigned as his associate. At first, the idea of anything more than a professional relationship with her boss had seemed impossible, but then one night, when they were both working late, their mutual attraction had taken over.

"Great. Just great." Katie's eyes lit up. "The firm is fine with it; they reassigned me to a different partner, and we are officially a couple. He's taking me to meet his parents next weekend. And he is going to be my date for Lisa's wedding. I was worried that he might get spooked—you know how guys are about going to weddings—but he said that he'd love to take me."

"Katie, that's wonderful! That means he's really serious."

"Dennis could be serious too. All you have to do is ask him."

"If you must know the truth, I was going to ask him to be my date for Lisa's wedding."

"And?"

"He is seeing someone."

"How do you know? Did you ask him?"

"I didn't need to. I overheard him speaking to her on the phone. He called her honey boo."

Katie crossed her arms on her chest. "That doesn't mean anything. Do you really expect a man like Dennis Walker to be single? So he's dating, but that doesn't mean it's serious."

"And what makes you think that he wants to get serious with me?"

"I don't know if he does or doesn't, but I do know that unless you go out of your comfort zone, you'll never find out. So who's your date for the wedding then?"

"Peter Laskin."

"The dude you told me about, the one with the hair plugs? Since when do you have a thing for him?"

"Not everyone has been blessed with Dennis Walker's good looks. There's nothing wrong with improving one's physical appearance," Janet snapped. "Besides, attraction has got nothing to do with it. It's more of a work assignment."

"Lisa's wedding is a work assignment to you? Just wait till she gets a load of this."

"She knows. She's the one who told me to invite Dennis in the first place and not because she was trying to get him and me together. Remember David Muller?"

"Of course."

"As you know, he got off the hook while Jon Bostoff was made a scapegoat, and Lisa is not very happy about that."

"So she wanted you to bring Dennis to the wedding so that he could apologize to the Bostoffs for the botched up investigation?"

"Would you just listen? Turns out Muller had accepted his invitation to the wedding."

"You mean to tell me that after everything that's happened, they still decided to invite him?"

"They didn't mean to. His name had been on the original guest list, and somehow it was never taken off, so when the invitations were sent out, his went out by mistake. Still, I can't understand how he could have accepted it. Lisa wanted me to bring Dennis along, thinking that Dennis might be able to get close to Muller and get some information out of him."

"Doesn't Muller know that Dennis works for the Treasury?"

"He might know his name, but not his face: they had never actually met. Dennis did all the prep work, but he was not part of the deposition proceedings; that part was handled by the lawyers in the Enforcement Division."

"I see. So you chickened out and instead of asking Dennis you asked Laskin?"

Janet nodded. "At least that's better than going alone. Besides, Laskin is sharp."

"From what you told me, he sounds like an ace."

"Be nice."

"Not if it's going to stand in the way of your happiness. In fact, I'll be as mean as possible to get you off your butt and into Dennis Walker's arms."

ജാ

David Muller entered the swanky interior of the Carlyle hotel on the Upper East Side. "How may I help you, sir?" The head waiter hovered by David's elbow.

"I'm meeting John Francis," Muller gave the alias that Cornelius Finnegan had told him to use.

The head waiter nodded. "Right this way, sir."

David followed the head waiter through the dimly lit carpeted lobby into the restaurant. It was a little after six in the evening, and the dining room was mostly empty. David prided himself on patronizing New York's most distinguished restaurants, but the Carlyle had escaped his attention until now. In his mind the establishment was obsolete. Only someone as socially unrefined as Cornelius Finnegan would choose a place like this for a meeting. But then again, unrefined or not, Finnegan's powerful connections could not be underestimated.

"Here we are, sir." The head waiter opened the heavy curtains that hung across the entrance into the private dining room, then quietly left.

David immediately saw Finnegan's hefty frame behind the round dining table, but the primary object of his attention was the man seated next to Finnegan. The two made the most incongruous pair, with Finnegan resembling a giant spud, and his companion being as willowy as a reed.

"David, there you are!" Finnegan's brogue filled the room.

"Good afternoon, gentlemen," David replied in the crispest American diction he could master.

"David, I'd like you to meet my good friend Kevan Magee. Kevan, this is David Muller, a very capable and smart young man who also happens to be my daughter's soon to be fiancé."

David did his best not to wince at the introduction. If things went according to plan, there was a good chance that Finnegan would soon abandon his patronizing ways toward David. He brushed his hand against his jacket pocket, thinking of the brilliant plan he had devised to get rid of Finnegan and his homely daughter. Now, all he had to do was get Kevan Magee to talk.

"It's a pleasure to meet you, Kevan," said David and offered his most open smile.

Kevan extended his bony hand. "Any friend of Cornelius's is a friend of mine," he said in a voice that was as thin as his physique.

"What do you say we eat first and talk later? I'm starving." Finnegan patted his ample stomach.

"Sounds good to me," Kevan agreed.

"What will you be drinking, David?" Finnegan asked.

David glanced at the glasses that stood opposite Magee and Finnegan; he did not even have to guess what was in those glasses: eighteen-year-old Macallan was the only drink that Finnegan favored. "I'll have a gin martini with a lemon twist," replied David. He was not speaking out of spite; it was simply that the smoky smell of Macallan gave him a headache.

Finnegan burrowed his nose in the menu, licking his lips as he always did in anticipation of a meal.

David eyed the menu with indifference. Food was the last thing on his mind: he was hungry for far more important things. With the help of his lawyer, Tom Wyman, David had spent the past two weeks setting up a network of companies through which he could conduct the kind of trading activities that Finnegan had been hinting at—insider trading to put it bluntly.

Wyman's help did not end with a network of companies; he had given David a wonderful idea on how to end Finnegan's clout over him once and for all. David patted his jacket pocket: inside it an iPhone was recording each and every word that was being uttered by Finnegan and Magee.

"So, Kevan, Cornelius tells me that the two of you go back a while," David probed after they had placed their orders with the waiter.

Kevan nodded, pressing a napkin to his lips. "Yes, indeed."

"We went to the same Catholic school up in the Bronx, St. Simon's," Cornelius cut in. "Kevan was the brain and I was the muscle—we made a damn good team."

"Yes, those were good times indeed," Kevan agreed.

"There's nothing like sharing childhood reminiscences," David remarked. By the looks of him, Kevan seemed to be much more suited to a religious vocation than that of a corporate board member, and David was beginning to have serious doubts whether Kevan would in fact be able to deliver the valuable information that Finnegan claimed his friend had access to.

"Remember the time when you had the brilliant idea to put a cockroach into Sister Myra's chalk box?" Finnegan elbowed Magee. "The darn thing nearly got away, but I got it in there. It was right before the math test, too. I thought our math teacher was going to have a heart attack: there she was, reaching for some chalk, and the cockroach crawled right over her hand. Needless to say the math test was cancelled."

"And the best thing was that we never got caught," added Magee.

This time David's laugh was genuine.

"And the time we put glue on Sister Agnes's chair?" Finnegan's ample frame quivered with laughter. "I tell you, David, there are enough stories to fill a book. Ah, the food is finally here—it's about time." Finnegan cast an impatient glance at the waiters.

Kobe steak was placed in front of Finnegan. David had opted for seared grouper, while Magee had ordered soft-shell crabs. "You call this a steak?" Finnegan eyed the waiter with indignation. "I can barely make it out on my plate!"

"I apologize, sir, but this is our portion size for kobe steak. Would you like another piece?"

"Oh, forget it," Finnegan waved his fork. "Just bring me another plate of mashed potatoes and put some gravy on them."

"Would pommes mousseline be all right, sir?"

"Whatever you call it. Oh, and bring us a bottle of Macallan so we don't have to call for you every time our glasses go dry."

"Certainly, sir." With a bow, the waiter departed to execute Finnegan's order.

"That does it, Kevan. Next time we're going to Keens." Finnegan cut into his steak. "Chewy like a piece of rubber," he muttered between bites. "How's your dish, David?"

David's grouper was tolerable, but before he could respond, Finnegan switched his attention back to Magee. "What's that you ordered, Kevan? Reminds me of the cockroach I put into Sister Myra's chalk box." Finnegan looked genuinely pleased with his joke.

Magee, who had been gamely attacking his dish, contemplated the last remaining soft-shell crab on his plate. "Indeed, there is a slight resemblance, but I would imagine that soft-shell crabs are much tastier than cockroaches although I have to admit that I never chanced to eat a cockroach."

Finnegan chuckled. "That's Magee for you: he's always got a comeback for every line."

David smiled in agreement. Indeed, his impression of Magee had undergone a complete transformation: there was much more to this Magee fellow than he had thought.

After they were finished with their main courses, Finnegan ordered a slice of cheesecake, while David and Magee limited themselves to coffee.

"So, Kevan, I think now is a good time to tell David about the purpose of our little get-together," said Finnegan, licking the last bit of cheesecake from his fork.

Magee nodded, taking a sip of his coffee. "David, Cornelius has told me a lot about your financial expertise, but I hope that you will allow me to ask you a few questions."

"By all means." David did his best to put on the most genial expression.

"Let's say a certain public company, let's call it company A, is in merger talks with another public company, let's call it company B. What do you think would happen to the shares of these companies if the merger were to go through?"

David suppressed his irritation. Was Magee questioning him on the rudimentary principles of financial markets? "Typically, once the merger is announced, the stock of the acquiring company would decline in price, while the stock of the company that is about to be acquired would appreciate in price. Of course, that depends on the conditions of the merger. If the company is being bought at a discount—"

"It's being bought at a premium," Magee interrupted, "and a handsome one at that. And what would you do if you were to know about such information several days before the merger was to be announced?"

"I'd buy call options on the stock of the company that's being acquired. This would require a smaller financial commitment than buying actual shares of the company and result in a much greater gain. Of course, I'd have to be sure that the information is reliable," David added.

"It is ironclad, which is why it is imperative to proceed with great caution."

"Oh, calm down, Kevan." Finnegan poured himself another drink. "David is not a novice. He knows what he's doing. Besides, as New York attorney general, I've got everyone covered."

"I do not doubt you, Cornelius, but I do remember a certain investigation involving Bostoff Securities and Emperial hedge fund, the latter of which, if memory serves me correctly, David was the owner."

Magee's black, button-like eyes burrowed into David's face; in them, David saw ruthless shrewdness. If anything were to go wrong, Magee would not hesitate to cut anyone's throat, including Finnegan's, in order to save his own neck.

"Like I told you, Kevan, I've got your back, just like I've got David's. Who do you think put the kibosh on the Bostoff investigation?"

"I do not doubt your abilities, Cornelius. I am merely anxious to ensure that everyone's interests are protected."

"I know that, Kevan, and I give you my word that we can trust David. I trust the man with my daughter. Is that not enough for ya?"

Here, David felt a pang of guilt, as he thought about the microphone in his jacket pocket.

Magee took a sip of his scotch. "It is, Cornelius. The question is, is it enough for you?"

Noticing the exasperated look on Finnegan's face, David decided to intercede. "Kevan, I understand that we just met, but I hope that Cornelius's word will suffice until we become better acquainted. In the meantime, please feel free to ask me any questions you may have about my background or professional experience."

Magee nodded. "David, I hope that you will not take me the wrong way. I do not have any doubts about your knowledge or trustworthiness. I am merely concerned for the safety of everyone involved."

Finnegan grunted. "We understand that, Kevan, but from what you told me, this deal is going to come down soon, and unless you've got someone else in mind to trade for us, you'd better tell David what it is he needs to do."

An hour later David left the Carlyle, smiling like a cat that ate a canary. Even better than the prospect of making a hefty profit from Magee's information was the knowledge that David now had Finnegan and Magee—the maggot, as David had nicknamed his new acquaintance—by their balls. Even Finnegan's connections would not save him from the scandal that would unleash if David were to release the recording of their conversation. Finally, his luck was turning around. David signaled to an empty cab that appeared by the curb—more evidence of his newly found luck—and gave the driver the address of Mila's new apartment. Soon he would be able to see Mila as frequently as he wished.

Chapter Twelve

Alex Kingsley checked his schedule for the day. He had a one-hour space between meetings, which would give him plenty of time for a quickie with Georgiana. This was truly the perfect job. Alex was about to buzz his assistant in when her number rang on his telephone. "Mr. Kingsley?"

"Georgie, you must be psychic. I was just going to call you. Get your hot behind in here."

"But Mr. Kingsley, I have Mr. Finnegan on the line for you."

Alex gulped, his desire draining right out of him. "Put him through please."

"Cornelius? How are you?" Alex's shoulders tightened with apprehension. Why was Finnegan calling him now when Alex had just given him a report two days before?

"Hello, Alex. How's the job treating you?"

"It's going well, thank you, sir."

"Any new developments?"

"Not that I am aware of, sir."

"Perhaps you'll be interested to learn that Jon Bostoff has started a consulting company: a white collar crime consulting service, to be precise."

"I see." Alex wondered what Finnegan was driving at. It was not uncommon for former crooks to offer consulting services, Frank Abagnale being one of the most famous examples. Why couldn't Bostoff do the same?

"Do you?" Finnegan added meaningfully. "Reformed sinners can be very dangerous. We wouldn't want Bostoff in his new capacity to start digging under Muller."

"I understand, sir." Alex could have kicked himself for being so dense. He knew personally what a pest a reformed sinner could be: Dennis Walker was the perfect example. With Muller let off the hook, Bostoff would be out for blood, and if he was anywhere as good as Walker was, both Finnegan and Alex would have to watch their backs.

"Perhaps I should remind you that Bostoff has been barred from the financial industry for three years. I think that it is the responsibility of the Investigations department—and by that I mean it's your responsibility—to ensure that this sanction is enforced."

"I understand, sir. I will take care of it."

"Make sure that you do."

Before Alex had a chance to utter any more assurances, Finnegan hung up.

Alex stared at the phone. He had made the decision to trust Janet as his eyes and ears at the office. Yes, she had put up resistance at first, but he had attributed her initial refusal to scorned pride: what woman did not hold a grudge against her ex-boyfriend? Still, that did not mean that the two of them could not look past their differences and become allies. The past weeks had proved that Janet had finally learned to adapt: she had provided Alex with detailed reports on her colleagues' activities. Alex had specifically instructed Janet to notify him of all the developments related to the Bostoff and Muller case, and she had repeatedly told him that there were no new developments. Was the bitch lying to him? He would find out right now.

Alex picked up the phone and dialed Janet's extension. "Janet, please stop by my office immediately," he barked and hung up.

‌ဧာမ

As she headed toward Alex's office, Janet wondered about the reason behind her summons. She had been feeding Alex with fake reports ever since the commencement of his tenure at the Treasury. Could it be that he was on to her?

"Janet!" Laskin's voice made Janet stop dead in her tracks.

"Hey there, Peter."

"How's it going, Janet? Boy, I tell you, either you're really busy or you've been avoiding me because I haven't seen you all week."

Avoiding running into Laskin, and when failing to do so coming up with excuses not to meet him for drinks or any other of the outings that he so tirelessly suggested, had become Janet's routine in the past few weeks. "You guessed it—it's the first one—I've been really busy." Janet hoped she sounded convincing. She only had to keep up her charade a few more days until Lisa's wedding, which was on Saturday.

Laskin eyed her dubiously. "So you haven't been avoiding me?"

"Come on, Peter, you know better than that! Why would I be avoiding you?"

"Oh, I don't know ... For the same reason you've been blowing me off every time I ask you out for a drink."

Janet widened her eyes, feigning a hurt look. "Me, blowing you off? I've just been real busy, that's all."

"So we're still on for the wedding?"

"Of course we're still on for the wedding. You're my date, remember?"

"What's all that wedding talk about?" Alex's Kingsley's voice made Janet freeze with her mouth agape.

"Good morning, Alex. I was just on my way to your office with my report," Janet rattled off.

"And you were doing that by chatting idly in the hallway?"

"Actually, sir, we were just discussing one of our latest leads," Laskin cut in. "I think we might be on to a tax evasion scheme."

"Tax evasion, huh?" Alex smirked. "So what's tax evasion got to do with a wedding?"

"Oh, that sir, absolutely nothing sir," Laskin replied coolly. "Janet needed a date for her friend's wedding, and I agreed to accompany her, that's all. We were just confirming the details since the wedding is this Saturday."

"I see. Excellent. Carry on Peter. I sure would like to see a report on that tax evasion scheme you mentioned."

"I'll get it on your desk as soon as I have all the details, sir. See you later, Janet." With that, Laskin left Janet alone with Alex.

"Shall we?" Alex motioned toward his office.

"Of course." Janet followed Alex into his office.

"So, what's the department been up to this week?" Alex asked after he took a seat in his chair and propped his feet on his desk.

"We've had a very large number of alerts this week," Janet began, "and we are still going through all of them to select positive leads."

"Sounds promising, but I've got something more important that I'd like you to focus on. Apparently, Jon Bostoff has returned to the financial industry, this time in the capacity of a white collar crime consultant. Were you aware of this development?"

What is he after? Janet wondered. Of course she knew that Jon Bostoff had started his own business, and judging by the look on Alex's face, he suspected as much. Her choices were to lie and appear clueless (and if Alex knew anything about her it was that she was not clueless) or tell the truth and take her chances. She chose the latter. "Yes."

"And you didn't think it important enough to bring it to my attention?"

"No. I didn't think there was anything wrong with Bostoff's new company. Is there?"

Alex frowned. "You are aware that Bostoff signed a settlement that bars him from the industry for three years, and here he is, violating the very agreement that saved him from going to jail."

"Alex, with all due respect, Jon Bostoff is not conducting any financial operations. He is merely advising companies that are concerned about white collar crime."

"Sounds like you know a lot about what Jon Bostoff is up to. Oh, that's right, I almost forgot—that friend of yours, Lisa, she was involved with Jon's brother, wasn't she? Are they still together?"

"Yes, they are getting married this Saturday."

"So that's the wedding Laskin is taking you to?"

"Yes."

"I see. Wish all the best to the bride and groom for me."

"I will." Janet rose to leave.

"And Janet, I'd like you to keep an eye on Jon Bostoff. Once a crook, always a crook. You wouldn't want him to be on the loose again, would you?"

"Of course not. I'll get right on it." Janet rose from her chair. "I'll see you later, Alex."

ജാരു

After Janet left his office, Alex wondered if she was telling him the truth. Did she really not think it important enough to tell him about Jon Bostoff's new business venture? Maybe she did but he was still not convinced, and he could not afford to take any chances.

Finnegan had made it clear that he wanted Bostoff erased from the map. Now Alex had to come up with a pretext to do so. Too bad that he had only just learned about Janet's invitation to

Bostoff's wedding; he would have certainly liked to be the one to accompany her to that interesting get-together.

Alex glanced at the calendar on his computer screen. Today was Wednesday, which left plenty of time until Saturday. Move over, Laskin, Alex thought, Janet Maple is about to get herself a much more suitable date for the Bostoff wedding.

Chapter Thirteen

When Janet got home, Baxter's excited barking erupted from behind the door while she fumbled with her keys. At least there was one male who was always happy to see her, and the fact that this male just happened to be a Jack Russell terrier did not make his welcome any less enjoyable. "Hey there, Baxter. Did you miss me?" Janet asked as Baxter jumped up and down excitedly, making it clear that his answer was affirmative.

"Do you want to go for walk?" The question was rhetorical: usually, whenever she knew she would be home late, Janet asked her neighbor Mrs. Chapman to stay with Baxter, so Janet knew that Baxter had already been walked. Still, she could use a walk tonight, and she knew that Baxter never minded a chance to get outdoors again, which he confirmed by barking excitedly. "Come on, then. Let's go." Janet secured the harness of Baxter's leash around his chest. "Come on!"

Minutes later they were exiting the lobby of Janet's building. Usually, Janet chose Carl Schurz Park as the destination for Baxter's walks, but tonight she wanted to have the buzz of the city around her, so she simply headed down Second Avenue.

A few moments later she heard footsteps trailing her. She was about to hasten her step when she felt a hand touching her shoulder. The sensation was so unexpected that she shrieked, freezing in place. "Janet, it's me, Alex. Sorry, I didn't mean to scare you."

Surprised, she turned to see Alex Kingsley standing in front of her. "What are you doing here, Alex? You scared me to death!" Baxter growled and barked in reinforcement of her words.

"I'm sorry to have scared you. I happened to be in the neighborhood and I just thought I'd say hi."

"Were you visiting friends?" Having recovered her presence of mind, Janet eyed Alex suspiciously. What was Alex doing hanging around her building?

"Sort of," Alex replied evasively. "Hey there, Baxter. How are you doing, old friend?"

Alex was about to lean down to pet Baxter, but instead jumped back as Baxter unleashed a wave of loud barks. For their relatively small size, Jack Russell terriers have very impressive teeth, and now Baxter was demonstrating this characteristic with abandon. Janet barely managed to yank Baxter's leash to keep him from pouncing on Alex.

"Easy there, fella," Alex said, attempting a laugh, but Janet could tell that Alex had been frightened. She sent a mental thank you to Baxter. "Do you mind if I walk with you a bit?" Alex asked.

A low, menacing growl erupted from Baxter. "Calm down, Baxter." Janet gently tugged on Baxter's leash. "Sure, by all means." She was not exactly thrilled about the idea, but Alex was still her boss, so at least for the time being she had to play nice.

When they reached the next block, Alex halted. "Janet, I have to be honest with you: I didn't just happen to be in the neighborhood tonight. I came here because I wanted to see you."

"You did?"

"Yes, I did," Alex's voice was grave. "The past few weeks brought back many memories. Janet, I've made many mistakes, the gravest of which was treating you the way I did. There hasn't been a day that I haven't regretted it."

Janet stared back at Alex in mute awe. Did he really think that he could wipe away all the hurt he had caused with one lame apology?

"I guess what I'm trying to say so ineloquently is that I would like to ask you for a second chance."

Janet was too stunned to speak. Did she have the word pushover written on her forehead? Apparently, the answer was yes. With Dennis expecting her to drop everything at the snap of his fingers, and Alex thinking that he could just waltz back into her life, it simply had to be the case.

"And I can't think of a better way to embark on this new path than to be your date for the Bostoff wedding," Alex continued.

Immediately, Janet's ears pricked up with suspicion. "The Bostoff wedding?"

"Yes. A wedding is a special occasion. Janet, I hope that you'll give me a chance to be by your side, so that we could perhaps begin the journey of rekindling the feelings we once had for each other. Feelings that are still very much alive for me."

Janet barely resisted a snort. She'd be damned if she would let Alex use her as an admission pass to the Bostoff wedding. "Oh, Alex, I can't believe you actually feel this way." Janet pressed her hand to her chest. "It means so much to me. But the Bostoff wedding ... you see, I've already asked Peter and it simply wouldn't be right to cancel on him at the last minute."

"I'm sure that Laskin would understand."

"He very well might, but that's not the kind of person I am. When I make a commitment, I keep it. But I sure hope that you'll think of other ways for us to reconnect," Janet added, not wanting Alex to get overly worked up.

"I would like that," Alex replied. "And do let me know what happens at the wedding."

"Oh, I will Alex."

"Good night, Janet."

Just as Alex turned to leave, Baxter yanked his leash out of Janet's loosened grip and lunged at Alex's leg, tearing off a chunk of his left trouser. "That damned dog!" Alex jumped back, holding his leg.

"Oh, Alex, I'm so sorry! Did he bite you?"

"He almost did. This is a thousand-dollar suit! You nasty rat of a dog!"

Alex towered over Baxter. Baxter growled, exposing his teeth, between which he was still holding a piece of Alex's trouser.

"Baxter, down boy, down," Janet commanded Baxter in a quivering voice. She had never seen Alex this angry.

Noticing her reaction, Alex backed away. "I'm sorry for losing my temper, Janet. I think I'd better call it a night."

"Good night, Alex. I'm sorry about Baxter. I don't know what's gotten into him."

As Janet turned toward her building, a smile was playing on her lips. "Well done, Baxter," she whispered. "Well done."

⑊④⑧

Tucking his hands into his pockets, Dennis Walker sped up Second Avenue. At least now he knew why Janet had been blowing him off—her schedule was filled with much more important matters, like a rendezvous with Kingsley. Dennis wanted to kick himself for being such an idiot. To think that he had been about to break the major covenant of his life code for Janet while she was out and about canoodling with their lowlife of a boss. Seeing Janet walking Baxter with Kingsley felt like being punched in the gut. It reminded Dennis of a similar evening when he had been the man walking next to Janet. He had longed to kiss her then but instead, scared of what he might feel, he had chickened out. Ever since then, his attraction to

Janet only seemed to grow stronger, becoming an indelible part of his existence.

Granted, Dennis had no right to make any demands on Janet. It was not as if he had made his feelings for her clear to her. He himself had indulged in the company of random girlfriends in his efforts to put Janet out of his mind. All of them, including his latest liaison, Shoshanna, had been a complete wreck. No woman wanted to play second fiddle to another, and despite the fact that he hated admitting it, Janet Maple occupied Dennis's mind completely.

So much for keeping things simple, Dennis thought. In his defense, he had not always been this way. There had been a time when he was capable of having feelings for a woman, even committing to one. But ever since his former fiancée, Vanessa, had walked out on him during the most difficult time of his life, Dennis had vowed never to get close to another woman: there just didn't seem to be any point in such a complicated arrangement. Dating was fine, but he was not prepared to commit to anything further.

It seemed that his past was forever catching up with him. The memories of his life as a trader sprang up in his mind. During his first year at Vitaon hedge fund, Dennis had reaped the largest bonus of his career. The day after he got his money, he proposed to Vanessa with a ten-carat diamond ring from Harry Winston. Dennis still remembered the shock he felt when he discovered Vitaon's fraud. The hedge fund might have been booming, but it was most indiscriminate as to the sources from which its investors' money came, including terrorists and drug cartels. Dennis was shocked to discover that all of the fund's managers knew about the fraud. As a thank you for his remarkable performance, Dennis was promoted to partner and let in on the secret. Joy was not the emotion Dennis felt after his promotion. With his new title, he would be liable for the fraud that was taking place at Vitaon.

Dennis knew that he had to get out, but before he could circulate his résumé on the street, he was approached by the Feds. They were onto the whole scheme, and they were willing to offer Dennis a deal if he agreed to aid in the investigation. Dennis would have to give up all the compensation he had made at Vitaon and he would be barred from the industry, but he would not be prosecuted further. Should Dennis pass on the chance, the offer would not be extended to him again.

Terrified, Dennis had said yes. For several months he wore a wire to work and downloaded hundreds of emails and documents to aid the Feds in their case. In return, he got to keep his freedom, but lost his livelihood.

The biggest blow was when Vanessa left him. At least she was decent enough to give him back the engagement ring. As much as it had hurt him, Dennis knew that he would need every penny he could scrape.

Since then, Dennis had rebuilt his life from scratch and become a top-notch white collar crime investigator. His career in fighting white collar crime began after the Feds had been so impressed by the information Dennis had procured for them during the Vitaon hedge fund investigation that they offered Dennis a contract. After several years of working for the Feds, Dennis went to work for Ham Kirk at the Treasury Investigations department. Ham had taught Dennis a great deal, for despite the fact that Ham had spent the last two decades of his career behind the desk as a department head, he was still as sharp as a whip. Although Ham could be tough on his employees at times, he was impressed by Dennis's work and had hinted on several occasions that he saw Dennis as his successor. Not that Dennis had any plans to rush Ham's retirement, but it pleased him to know that one day he would take Ham's place. Not because he wanted to oust Ham from his job, but because it was a great honor and it made Dennis feel that he had managed to make something of his life after all. The fact that Dennis had earned recognition from a man as upstanding as Ham Kirk meant that redemption was still possible. And who knew, perhaps one day Dennis might even earn back his right for a woman's true affection—a woman like Janet Maple.

But now all of Dennis's hopes had been shattered by one man, and that man's name was Alex Kingsley. Not only had Alex forced Ham into early retirement, took over Dennis's dream job, and undermined all the work Dennis had done on the Emperial case, but somehow Kingsley had also managed to reclaim Janet Maple's affections.

Revenge is a dish best served cold, Dennis thought. There was nothing like a well-worn cliché to get one's spirits into a fighting mode. Dennis rolled his hands into fists, feeling the skin tighten over his knuckles. He would make Kingsley pay and then some for everything the man had done.

Chapter Fourteen

Janet took a deep breath and massaged her temples. It was the day of Lisa Foley's wedding.

Janet eyed her reflection in the mirror. She was wearing a green emerald silk sheath, with a matching chiffon scarf around her neck. Black pumps and a small emerald silk clutch completed the ensemble. Emerald was the theme of Lisa's wedding for two reasons: green was Lisa's favorite color, and green also symbolized a new beginning.

A little over a year ago, Paul Bostoff was chief operating officer of Bostoff Securities, a boutique brokerage firm that had been started by his father, Hank Bostoff. Paul's brother, Jon Bostoff, was the company president. The firm was struggling financially but Jon was determined to turn it around. He brought on new clients, the largest of which was Emperial hedge fund, owned by David Muller. What Jon kept hidden from everyone was that his plans to revive Bostoff Securities' balance sheet involved catering to hedge funds that made their returns through illegal trading schemes. At first, things seemed to be going well. The company revenue grew, but unbeknown to the Bostoffs their world was about to change. Treasury had launched an undercover investigation of Bostoff Securities, planting Dennis Walker as Dean Snider, IT engineer, his alias at the time.

At the thought of Dennis, Janet bit her lip. She had been unable to resist her attraction to him from the first time she laid her eyes on him when he was fixing—which she later found out was really bugging—her computer. From that time on, Dennis Walker, or Dean Snider as she knew him then, kept running into her everywhere. Whenever he saw her, his blue eyes radiated warmth that sent Janet's heart fluttering. How could she have known that the charmer she was foolish enough to confide in would turn out to be an undercover investigator from the Treasury? Even Baxter had been fooled by Dennis's charm.

"The case against Bostoff Securities has been in the making for a long time," Dennis had said. "You can help the investigation or go down with the sinking ship. Bostoff is small fish anyway. It is Emperial we want. Naturally, you will get immunity in exchange for your cooperation." At Janet's request, the Treasury agreed to grant Lisa protection. Janet had asked for Paul's immunity as well, but was told that any of the Bostoffs were out of the question. The only thing that had kept Janet from going crazy with guilt while she helped Dennis obtain the evidence he needed was Dennis's assurance that Emperial was the true target of the case. Little did she know that Jon Bostoff would be made into a scapegoat, and David Muller would walk away without so much as a slap on his wrist.

Here was her chance to set things right. Muller was going to be at the wedding, and Janet was determined to find a way to get close to him. Granted, if Dennis were with her, this task would seem a lot less daunting. Perhaps she had been wrong to let her personal feelings for Dennis affect her judgment. Hell, she knew she had been wrong, but it was too late to do anything about it now. She would have to face the brilliant—granted twisted and corrupt, but still brilliant—David Muller on her own. Initially, she had thought that Laskin would be there to help her, but now she was not sure. It was all her fault too. Her dodging Laskin's invites to lunches and after-work drinks must have offended him because when she tried to meet him to tell him the actual reason for their going to the Bostoff wedding, Laskin blew her off. She had hoped to speak to him earlier in the day, but Laskin was late, and now she was no longer sure if he was going to show up at all.

There was a faint rapping on the door. "Janet, it's me, Katie."

Janet opened the door. "Is it time?"

"Almost. Your date is here."

"Finally! He's late. I've got to talk to him."

Katie cast a side glance at Janet. "Chicken."

"What's that supposed to mean?"

"You know very well what that means. You were supposed to come with Dennis. Instead, you have a date who looks like he's wearing a squirrel on his head."

"He does not! You're only saying that because I told you about the hair plugs."

"Fine. He does not have a squirrel on his head. Actually, he is kind of cute, but Dennis Walker is positively dreamy."

Don't I know it, Janet thought. She had spent too much time daydreaming about Dennis. It was time to get back to reality. "This isn't a real date anyway. I'm here on an assignment, remember?"

"Yes, I remember. You're supposed to get close to the infamous David Muller."

"That's right. Here's his picture in case you spot him before I do." Janet pulled a copy of a Forbes magazine article titled "Movers and Shakers." The article had been written before Emperial hedge fund was investigated for market manipulation, and David Muller's confident, smiling face was prominently displayed in the middle of the text.

"Isn't it the cardinal rule of all undercover officers to burn the mark's picture?"

"I'm not an undercover officer, and Muller is not a mark. I'm not here to shoot him; I'm just going to try to get close to him." Janet stuck the picture into her green silk purse.

"Fine. So what's your plan?"

"My plan?"

"Yes, your plan. You and Laskin must have a plan."

"We do, which is why I have to go and talk to him immediately."

"There's no time to talk to him now. The ceremony is about to begin."

Janet checked her watch. "That's right. Silly me! I almost forgot."

Katie put her hands on her hips. "There is no plan, is there?"

"Yes there is. The plan is to get close to Muller," Janet lied. She would just have to wing it until she got a chance to talk to Laskin.

Twenty minutes later, Janet was standing by the altar. The two bridesmaids were next to her: Katie was one of them, and Daphne, the fiancée of Janet's law school friend Joe O'Connor, was the other one. The groom, Paul, and his best man and brother, Jon, stood in front of the altar next to the justice of the peace. The groomsmen were gathered on the other side of the altar and included Paul's two best college buddies and his nineteen-year-old nephew, Tyler. For the wedding photo session that took place earlier in the day, Katie and Daphne had been paired up with Paul's married but age appropriate groomsmen, while Janet had been paired up with Tyler. Broad-chested and blond, Tyler was a stud, but that did not alleviate the fact that not only did Janet not have a real wedding date, she could not even get a man of her age to stand next to her in Lisa's wedding photos. This seemed grossly unfair as both Katie and Daphne had men in their lives who not only served as their dates during social occasions but also loved them during ordinary days, and Janet had no one.

Out of the corner of her eye, Janet caught a glimpse of Peter Laskin who was seated in the far left corner of the third row. Why couldn't she fall in love with Laskin and forget about Dennis Walker? It would make things so much simpler. At an average height of five foot ten, with a straight nose and average-sized mouth, Laskin was, well, an average-looking man. Some women might even consider him to be on the attractive side, but by no means was he as charming or as good-looking as Dennis. Janet felt a stab of guilt: this was supposed to be Lisa's moment, and there Janet was, indulging in self-pity instead of being happy for her friend.

The bridal march started, and everyone's attention turned to the bride. Escorted by her father, Lisa walked down the aisle. She wore a beautiful formfitting dress of white silk with a slit in the front. Her short hair was adorned with tiny white roses, completed by a shoulder-length veil. Paul's face beamed with happiness as he watched Lisa walk toward him.

Janet noticed movement in the last row. Her disapproving eyes darted to the source of commotion—there was nothing tackier than being late for a wedding reception. She was about to redirect her attention back to Lisa, who was now approaching the altar, when Janet noticed that the man who had just arrived was David Muller. He was dressed in an expensive black tuxedo. Next to him stood a plump redhead. Her hair was pinned in an elaborate updo; she wore a chiffon dress of pale blue. Janet wondered about David Muller's date. She had seen pictures of him in gossip columns linking him to models and starlets, and while it was obvious that Muller's redhead had taken great care in her appearance, she did not even come close to the glamazons that Muller usually dated.

❦

David Muller thought that there was nothing worse in the world than wedding ceremonies. But there he was, stuck in an uncomfortable chair, sitting next to Aileen, listening to sappy wedding wows. His discomfort was made even greater by the fact that he was a guest at the wedding of the family whose business he had destroyed. David cast an irritated glance at Aileen. Normally, he was careful to camouflage his emotions during his interactions with her, but he knew that he was safe now: Aileen's eyes were glued to the front of the room. Her face was a mixture of joy and tears. With one hand she was tightly clutching David's hand, and with the other was dabbing her moist eyes with a tissue .

The justice of the peace droned on, "A wedding is more than a celebration of love. It reaches into the future and asserts the bride and groom's intentions for that which tomorrow shall hold. The promises and vows that the bride and groom make this day shall guide them into their common future. I will ask you now if you are prepared to make these promises."

David felt Aileen's clasp tighten and resisted the urge to move his hand away. His only hope was that this ridiculous spectacle was not filling the silly creature's head with crazy ideas.

"Lisa, have you come here today of your own free will to take Paul to be your husband, that you may live together as equal partners sharing all that life has to offer?"

"I have," David heard the bride respond. As if there could be a different answer? he wondered. It was only in the movies that brides ran away from the altar. By the looks of it, this wedding had cost a pretty penny, and in David's mind no one walked away from the deal once the cash had been put up.

"Will you love him, comfort him, honor and keep him all the days of your life?"

Blah, Blah, Blah. David was about to roll his eyes, but stopped just in time when he noticed Aileen's head turning. She shot him a dramatic look and squeezed his hand, then returned her attention to the ceremony.

"I will," Lisa's voice carried through the room.

"Paul, have you come here today of your own free will to take Lisa to be your wife, that you may live together as equal partners sharing all that life has to offer?"

"I have."

106

"Will you love her, comfort her, honor and keep her all the days of your life?"

"I will."

Oh brother, David groaned inwardly, wishing the spectacle would be over with already. He could barely resist the urge to strangle Aileen with both hands, metaphorically speaking of course. He might not be the most moral of human beings, but he still did not consider himself to be capable of murder, although Aileen's behavior certainly warranted such an action. David had already resigned himself to spending the weekend with Aileen. After the blissful Friday afternoon he had spent with Mila, the prospect loomed gloomily before him, but was made utterly intolerable when Aileen announced that they had a wedding to attend.

"What wedding?" David had asked, fearful of a family gathering: the last thing he needed was to meet more of Aileen's relatives; his acquaintance with her father was all he could handle at the moment. Or worse, perhaps one of Aileen's best friends was to walk down the aisle, a spectacle that would undoubtedly fill Aileen's head with thoughts of matrimony. As bad as his suspicions were, Aileen's answer literally knocked the wind out of him.

"Don't you remember?" Aileen puckered her lips in what she probably thought was a playful pout. "It's the Bostoff wedding. The invitation had been lying on your desk since forever, so I answered it. I left the RSVP card on your desk, but I also wrote down all the details just in case."

David frowned. He had lots of papers on his desk, but he always took care to sort out the important ones and toss out the junk, and he was fairly certain that he would have classified the invitation to Paul Bostoff's wedding as the latter. In fact, now that he thought about it, he was certain that he had tossed the invite into the wastepaper basket. "I had no intention of going to that wedding. Where exactly did you find the invitation?" Was

Aileen sifting through his garbage? The crimson blush that was creeping down her cheeks confirmed his suspicions.

"I, oh, like I said, honey, it was on your desk, and I thought that you wanted to go, so I answered it. Weddings are such happy occasions, and this one is taking place in a really lovely part of Long Island. Don't you think it would make a wonderful outing? I've already booked a room at the bed and breakfast, and we can make a weekend out of it. We could go antique shopping on Sunday or do a winery tour."

A weekend with Aileen was bad enough; a weekend with Aileen, trapped in some crappy bed and breakfast in the middle of nowhere, would be nightmarish. David rattled his brain for a possible escape. He was certain that the Bostoffs had been as unpleasantly surprised by his RSVP card as he was to learn that Aileen had accepted the invitation on his behalf. He wondered why he had been invited in the first place. It had to have been a clerical error; or perhaps the Bostoffs planned to execute their revenge on him for walking away from the investigation with hardly a scratch while Bostoff Securities had been decimated. In either case, the occasion promised to be awkward to say the least. That was it, he had had it. Aileen might have a powerful father but that did not give her the license to yank David around like some marionette."Aileen, I am not happy about this in the least. The invitation was addressed to me and you should have consulted me before responding. I hope that it isn't too late to cancel."

"Cancel? But I've already bought the dress, and I've made an appointment for my hair to get done tomorrow morning."

"I'm afraid you'll have to cancel it, and I hope that you've kept the receipt for the dress, so that you can return it." David was mentally rubbing his hands in delight. Every cloud had a silver lining, and Aileen's idiotic behavior had just given him an excuse to play the hurt lover; he would punish her by cancelling his weekend with her altogether. Already he was thinking of the time he would spend with Mila; he had told her that he had to work through the weekend, but he would call her now and tell her that his weekend had opened up.

"Return it? Cancel my hair appointment?" Aileen's lips quivered.

"Yes, darling, I'm afraid so. In the meantime, I'm going to try to reach out to the Bostoffs and apologize for this confusion, and of course I'll send a check as well. Hopefully that will be enough to make amends. This is really no way to behave, Aileen. I did not expect this from you. You'll excuse me but I'm going to leave now. This weekend will give you plenty of time to reflect on your behavior." A few weeks ago David would not have dared to address Aileen in such a tone, but he had already gathered plenty of dirt on Finnegan, so David decided to begin the gradual process of reducing the amount of attention and time he had until now been obediently devoting to Aileen.

"To reflect on my behavior?" Aileen's voice acquired a menacing ring to it. "Very well then. I'm sure I'll have a great time reflecting with my parents. Daddy had said that he wanted to have a family weekend, but I told him that you and I would be going away. I'm sure he'll be glad to know that our plans have been cancelled."

David stared at Aileen with newfound respect. Up until now she had never used her father as clout. At times David wondered whether Aileen was daft enough to think that he was dating her out of pure affection, but now he knew better. Very well, he would have to swallow his pride and accompany Aileen to the Bostoff wedding. Soon he would be free from Finnegan's yoke, but for now he still needed the old man, and Aileen would get whatever Aileen wanted.

"Do you, Paul, take Lisa to be your lawful wedded wife, to love, honor and cherish her through sickness and in health, through times of happiness and travail, until death do you part?" asked the justice of the peace.

"Yes."

Of course he does, David bristled inwardly. Otherwise, he wouldn't be standing there, you oaf.

"Place this ring upon her finger and repeat after me: 'With this ring I thee wed and forever pledge my devotion.'"

The groom mumbled on as he was told.

"Do you, Lisa, take Paul to be your lawful wedded husband, to love, honor and cherish him through sickness and in health, through times of happiness and travail, until death do you part?"

"Yes."

"By the act of joining hands you take to yourself the relation of husband and wife and solemnly promise to love, honor, comfort, and cherish each other so long as you both shall live. Therefore, in accordance with the law of New York and by virtue of the authority vested in me by the law of New York, I pronounce you husband and wife. You came to me as two single people and you will now leave as a married couple, united to each other by the binding contract you have just entered. Your cares, your worries, your pleasures and your joys, you must share with each other. The best of good fortune to both of you."

"Wasn't that beautiful?" Aileen whispered, her pudgy fingers squeezing David's hand so tightly he barely suppressed a yelp.

"Very," David managed. So far he rated his experience at the Bostoff wedding as akin to the pain of matches being stuck into one's eyes—not that David had ever been subjected to such a horrid torture, but he had a vivid imagination and he feared what was to follow.

Aileen dabbed her eyes. "Aren't you glad we came? I have a feeling that the reception is going to be wonderful."

"I am sure it will be," David confirmed, hoping the he would be spared the awkwardness of running into the groom's brother, Jon Bostoff.

Chapter Fifteen

"You may now kiss as husband and wife."

As the justice of the peace uttered the concluding words of the wedding ceremony, Paul Bostoff drew Lisa into his arms, and the two locked their lips in a long, passionate kiss.

Applause and cheering erupted from the audience. While she clapped, Janet's eyes surveyed the back row. She was relieved to see the blond of Muller's hair. Not that Muller's presence elicited any sort of positive emotion in Janet, but she owed it to Lisa and Paul to set things right, and Muller was the key. Whether it was the emotional rush from the ceremony, the pent-up anger from the blatantly unjust way in which the Bostoff Securities and Emperial case had been handled, or a combination of both, Janet felt empowered by a surge of boldness. Who did this Muller character think he was, anyway? Just because he wore swanky suits and dated supermodels did not mean that he was superhuman. And the latter bit was not even true anymore: Muller's current date did not look anything like a supermodel, proving that Muller was just an ordinary human being after all. An exceptionally corrupt human being, but a human being nonetheless, one who had to obey the law just like the rest of the mortals, and Janet would make sure that he would not escape it. Which brought her to her next point: aside from the fact that Lisa had arranged for Muller to be seated at the same table as Janet and her date, Janet still did not have a plan for getting close to Muller. She needed to talk to Laskin so that they could come up with a strategy before the reception began.

"Shall we?" Tyler Bostoff offered his arm to Janet.

"Thank you, Tyler." Janet leaned on Tyler's arm and followed him, along with the flow of the guests who were now headed toward the reception hall. Once they reached the front row, Janet spotted Laskin and disengaged herself from Tyler.

"Peter," Janet called to her date in a hushed whisper.

"Janet! At long last! I was beginning to think that I would never get to spend any time with my date." Laskin cast an askance glance at Tyler.

Janet ignored Laskin's pointed remark: now was not the time for ego stroking. "Actually, I wanted to talk to you about that. Let's go in here." Janet grabbed a hold of Laskin's arm and drew him into the guestroom that had been reserved to store the wedding gifts.

"Wow, Janet, if you were that eager to see me, we could have arranged something sooner."

Janet shut the door behind them. "Look, Peter, I have to come clean. I invited you as my date because I need your help."

"You mean to tell me that you are not attracted to my sexy looks or my charm and wit?"

Janet stared back at him, wondering how she was going to work her way out of this one. Then she noticed a smile on Laskin's lips.

"Relax, Janet. I may be a little slow on the uptake at times, but I'm not dumb. One doesn't need a PhD in human behavior to know that you and Dennis have the hots for one another, so when you asked me to be your date I knew that romance was not your motivation. I've tried to get you to tell me exactly why you needed me to be here with you, but you blew off all my attempts to do so. And then when you finally had time to meet, something had come up and I couldn't make it."

112

Janet blushed at her own vanity. So far, it seemed like Laskin's investigative instincts were much keener than her own. "I'm sorry, Peter."

Laskin waved his hand. "Forget it, Janet. Now, do you want to tell me why you asked me to come with you? I suspect it has something to do with the Bostoff case."

How did you know? Janet merely blinked, restraining herself from uttering the question that was on her lips. The groom's name was Paul Bostoff, and one did not have to be Sherlock Holmes to figure out the rest.

"I am familiar with the case," replied Laskin, as though having read her thoughts. "After all, I did do all the analytics for Walker while he romanced you in the offices of Bostoff Securities under the pretext of an undercover assignment."

"There was no romancing—"

"Save it, Janet. I've worked with Walker long enough. Now, are you going to tell me why you asked me to be your date for the wedding?"

Janet opened her mouth and then closed it. There was no use trying to fool Laskin. Her embarrassment made her speak in formal, contrived language as though she were making a statement during a deposition. "There is concrete evidence indicating that David Muller, owner of Emperial hedge fund, had orchestrated a market manipulation trading scheme."

"I know about that too, Janet. While Bostoff was guilty in accepting the trades, Muller was the mastermind behind the operation. But then, low and behold, Muller walks away and Jon Bostoff takes all the blame. Not to mention that our boss gets fired, and both yours and Dennis's careers now seem to be headed for the crapper, so you can skip the background and cut right to the chase."

"You never leave anything out, do you?" Janet held her breath, wondering if Laskin also knew about her long-standing and painful history with Alex, but to her relief Laskin remained quiet. At least he did not know about that.

Laskin reddened. "I didn't mean to sound so harsh. With our new boss, all of our careers are headed for the crapper. Now, what's your plan? Because if you have one, I sure want to hear it. I don't like Kingsley any more than you do."

"I want to get Muller," Janet said simply. "I thought that together we'd be able to get close to him and see what he's up to. You probably know this already, but the bride is a very good friend of mine and—"

"Obviously," Laskin interrupted. "You are the maid of honor."

Janet shot Laskin an irritated look.

"Sorry, I couldn't help that one. Spending too much time behind the desk makes me snippy."

"I can see that. So, a few weeks ago, Lisa told me that David Muller had accepted his invitation to the wedding."

By the surprised expression on Laskin's face, Janet was glad to see that the man did not know everything after all.

"The Bostoffs invited Muller to the wedding? I would think that they would hate his guts."

"And they do. Lisa was just as surprised as you are. Muller's name was on the original list of the invitees, but somehow it was never taken off and an invite was sent to him. Now, I have no idea why, but not only did he accept, but he has actually showed up."

"Muller is here?"

"Yes. He was a few minutes late to the ceremony, so he sat in the last row." Janet opened her purse. "Here, this will help. This is a picture of him from a magazine article published before the investigation. I think he's keeping a lower profile now."

Laskin took the paper from Janet's hand. "You're not supposed to carry the mark's picture with you."

"We're not spies, Peter. I'm pretty sure that I didn't breach any security codes by carrying an article about Muller in my purse." Janet snatched the paper back from Laskin and put it in her purse. "Did you memorize his face?"

"I sure did. Now, what's your plan?"

"Lisa has arranged it so that we are sitting at the same table with Muller and his date. We'll have a few drinks, strike up a conversation, and then we'll try to find out what Muller is up to these days."

"That's your plan?"

"You've got a better one?"

"Not at the moment, but I could have come up with one if I had had fair warning."

Janet cast a dubious look at Laskin, convinced that he was just showing off.

Laskin scratched his ear. "Before we go in there, we've got to have a story to tell. Okay, I got it. We can't say that we're married since we don't have wedding rings. That would have been a nice prop, had we had more time to plan this ..."

Inwardly Janet admitted that Laskin had a point, but she was not about to admit it out loud. "Lots of married people don't wear wedding rings."

"You mean lots of men don't wear wedding rings. But when it comes to formal occasions such as weddings, wives watch their husbands like hawks, making sure that they have the gold band on their fingers."

"If you say so."

"I know so. Weddings are prime dating ground, for both men and women, and you know how territorial women can be."

Janet did not necessarily agree, but at the moment she was not particularly interested in hearing Laskin's argument on the matter, so she decided not to contradict.

"So, we are going to say that we are boyfriend and girlfriend, and that we've been dating for a year—long enough for the woman in the relationship to expect an engagement, but not too long for it to be hopeless. This way you can whine to Muller's date about how you can't wait for me to propose."

"Good one," Janet agreed.

"And I can gripe to Muller about not wanting to pop the question." Laskin patted his chin. "Do you know if Muller smokes?"

"I don't think so, but I'm not sure. Why?"

"Because if we knew that he was a smoker, I would have brought cigarettes. There's hardly a more conducive environment for men to share confidences than a cigarette break, especially during a wedding. At the same time, there is nothing more annoying than someone you've just met bumming a cigarette off of you, so regardless of Muller's preferences we are going to have to pass on this option."

"I'm sorry. You are so much better at this than I am." Janet felt like an amateur. Clearly, she had been too busy obsessing over her hatred for Alex and her unfortunate attraction to Dennis instead of focusing on nailing Muller.

"It's all right, Janet. The last few weeks haven't exactly been a walk in the park for any of us. I didn't mean to make you feel bad. I was just letting off steam, but now is not the time to do that. We've got to get our game on. So, we've been dating for a year. I'm in information technology and you're a teacher. How does that sound?"

"Sounds good, Peter." Janet paused. Laskin did have a good head on his shoulders. "I'm glad that you're going to be my partner on this."

"I'm no Dennis Walker, but I'll do my best." Laskin lowered his eyes. "Sorry, that slipped."

"That's all right, partner. Now let's go get that son of a bitch Muller."

Chapter Sixteen

Janet followed Laskin to their table. Her breath quickened when she saw that David Muller and his date were already seated. "Excuse us." Laskin grabbed Janet's hand as he maneuvered to their seats, which were on Muller's right hand side.

"Hi there," Laskin beamed, quickly picking up the placement cards and sliding them into his pocket. "John Carry. Pleased to make your acquaintance. And this is my girlfriend, Elizabeth Simmons."

Janet attempted to mask her surprise with a cough: they had not discussed aliases. "It's a pleasure to meet you."

Muller looked at them with open indifference. "David Muller. The pleasure is all mine, I'm sure." Then, with a quick glance at his date, he added, "And this is my girlfriend, Aileen Finnegan."

"Pleasure to meet you, Aileen," Laskin said.

"Wasn't it just a wonderful ceremony?" Aileen gushed.

"Indeed," Laskin confirmed. "It's a good thing that Elizabeth is the maid of honor. Had she been sitting next to me instead of standing by the altar, she would have seen me shed a manly tear or two. Oh, well, I guess I gave myself away now."

"There's nothing shameful about a man shedding a tear or two. In fact, I think that it takes a true man not to be afraid of expressing his emotions," said Aileen with a pointed glace at Muller.

"Personally, I find weddings dull," said Muller. "I'm sure it must all be very exciting for the bride and the groom, but why should the rest of us be forced to sit through it?" An expression of hurt passed over Aileen's face, and, as if catching himself, Muller added, "But Aileen just loves this sort of thing. I'm glad you're enjoying this, honey." Muller patted Aileen's hand.

"You would too," Aileen replied reproachfully, "if you would only just give it a chance."

Janet watched this exchange with fascination. It was clear that Muller was anything but attracted to his date. It seemed like he did not even want to be at the wedding, so why did he come?

"Darling." Laskin pulled out Janet's chair and motioned for her to take a seat. Janet thanked him and slid into her seat.

Janet and Laskin turned their attention to the rest of the guests at the table. Everyone smiled politely as introductions were made. There were two more couples who were friends of the groom. Being seated next to Lisa's friends from college or high school would have presented serious problems for Laskin's planned cover-up. Janet gave Lisa mental kudos for excellent attention to detail, a skill that Lisa had never before been famous for and Janet used to excel at but now seemed desperately to lack. At least Lisa and Laskin were both on their game. Now all Janet needed to do was figure out to get close to Muller or his date.

Janet cast a sideways glance at Muller who was examining the menu as though it were the most fascinating thing in the world. His date was leaning on his shoulder in a clear attempt to elicit a token of affection from Muller, but he clearly preferred to focus his attention on the menu.

"So, what are the choices?" asked Laskin, looking over Muller's shoulder.

Muller looked at Laskin. "I think I see a waiter coming. I'll ask him to get you a menu."

"Oh, I didn't realize that I've got one right here!" exclaimed Laskin, reddening under Muller's icy glare.

So much for Laskin's bravado, Janet thought. He might be good at laying out a plan of action, but he was not particularly good at executing one. She had to come up with some icebreakers pronto. Her anxiety was interrupted by the announcement of the bride and groom's first dance.

Accompanied by loud applause, Lisa and Paul walked to the center of the dance floor. Paul offered his arm to Lisa, and the two of them glided into a graceful waltz. Even from the distance, Janet could see the sparks that were shining in Lisa's and Paul's eyes. Despite everything that had happened to the Bostoffs, or perhaps because of it, Lisa and Paul seemed to be more in love than ever.

The waltz ended. "We now ask the guests to join the bride and groom on the dance floor," announced the deejay.

The chords of "Strangers in the Night" filled the room. Couples began rising from their seats, making their way to the dance floor. Janet inwardly cursed the deejay's selection. She loved this song, but the romantic lyrics did not exactly create a conducive environment for her task at hand. She was about to sneak off to the bathroom to work on some icebreakers for Muller when she felt Laskin's hand on her arm. "Shall we dance, darling?"

Janet's first impulse was to refuse. She certainly did not find Laskin's eyes inviting or his smile exciting, but then she noticed Muller's date eyeing them wistfully, and so rose from her chair.

Laskin took Janet's hand into his and slid into a confident foxtrot step. Janet followed him easily. "Where did you learn to dance like this?" she asked.

"Fred Astaire dance studio," Laskin replied. "It was for an undercover assignment that never materialized, but that's not important right now. We have to change our strategy."

"Agreed." Janet thought it best to omit the fact that they did not really have a strategy, at least not a sound one, as she was mostly to blame for that.

"There's no way in hell Muller will ever open up to me. He clearly thinks that he is a far more superior specimen of the human race than I am."

Perhaps sticking your nose into his menu had something to do with it, Janet thought, but bit her tongue: she herself was not exactly bursting with ideas on the topic.

"You go after Muller and I'll go after his date. She looks bored, so I'll play the sympathy card, and you can flatter Muller with admiration."

"Good idea. Let's switch seats when we go back to the table. That way I'll be sitting closer to Muller."

"I've got an even better idea. Here's our opening."

Before Janet could blink, Laskin's hand tightened on her waist and she felt herself being literally swept off her feet as Laskin galloped across the floor in a surprisingly nimble quickstep. Janet held on to Laskin for dear life as they leapt across the floor, followed by admiring glances. "Ready? Here we go."

"Ready for what?" Janet asked.

Just then, Laskin's nimbleness deserted him, and the two of them nearly tumbled into Muller and Aileen who were slow dancing in the far corner of the floor. "Oops, my apologies," Laskin panted. "I misjudged the distance."

"Oh, that's quite all right," Aileen smiled. "You are a wonderful dancer."

"Wonderful dancers don't smash into people," remarked Muller.

"My apologies," said Laskin.

"Oh, don't worry about it!" Aileen came to Laskin's defense. "They didn't smash into us, honey. It was more of a tap, really."

The music ended, leaving the couples on the dance floor frozen in indecision. "Shall we go back to our table?" offered Muller.

"And now on with our next selection," announced the deejay. The bold notes of "New York, New York" rang in the air.

"May I?" Laskin offered his hand to Aileen.

"I would be delighted," Aileen beamed.

Janet hesitated. She knew that the thing to do was to mimic Laskin and ask Muller to dance, but the man looked so glum that her tongue stuck to the back of her throat.

"Shall we?" Muller surprised her.

"I'd be delighted," Janet replied.

"You are a pleasure to dance with," Muller remarked after several moments.

"Thank you." In spite of herself, Janet was flattered. He might be a scoundrel without principles, but it was impossible to deny that David Muller was a very handsome scoundrel. Janet could certainly see how Muller was such a successful crook: he had an aura of effortless charm about him that made his victims fall under his spell in a matter of seconds.

"And of course this is a beautiful song to dance to. I adore Frank Sinatra. "New York, New York" is my favorite."

"His songs are wonderful," Janet agreed.

"And so are you," replied Muller, tilting Janet back. The motion took her by surprise, and Janet nearly lost her balance.

"Careful there." Muller pressed his hand against her back, pulling her close to him, a little too close for Janet's taste. "So what's a girl like you doing with a guy like Carry?"

"What's a man like you doing with a girl like Aileen?" Janet countered.

"I asked you first."

"John is a good guy, and good guys are hard to find."

Muller's gaze travelled from Janet's lips to her neck, to her breasts, to her hips, and then, with noticeable reluctance, back up to her eyes. "I don't see how you would have difficulties finding a man."

"I don't want just any man. I want a man who is right for me. So what brings you to this wedding? Are you a friend of the bride or the groom?" Janet changed the subject before her conversation with Muller got too heated.

Muller's face tensed for a moment. "Just an acquaintance of the groom. We used to do business together, but I am no longer involved in that."

"Oh? What do you do, if you don't mind me asking?"

"I used to run a hedge fund but I closed that down. My interest in the financial markets now is purely academic. I run a charity dedicated to sponsoring scholarships for young men and women who are interested in pursuing careers in finance. It's called the Phoenix Fund."

"That sounds very noble."

Muller smiled. "Oh, I don't know about that, but I do enjoy it, and I hope to be able to help. I know that I would have welcomed a helping hand when I was starting out in my career. The charity is less than a year old. This year we plan to offer scholarships to ten students to the colleges of their choice, and we hope to increase the number of scholarships each year."

"Sounds wonderful."

The last notes of "New York, New York" faded away, and was followed by "I've Got You Under My Skin."

Janet spotted Laskin and Aileen gliding toward them. "I think it's time that I returned you to your date."

"If you insist."

"David!" Aileen exclaimed, putting her hand on Muller's shoulder. She turned towards Laskin, adding, "John, thank you for a wonderful dance."

"The pleasure is all mine, Aileen." Laskin bowed. He returned his attention to Janet. "Shall we?"

Before she could respond, Laskin whisked her away. "So, what did you find out?" he asked.

"Muller is not in trading anymore. He runs a charity now."

Laskin's eyebrows nearly met his hairline. "What?"

"I know. I don't believe it either. Something is not right. Either Muller lied to me, or he really did decide to become a law-abiding citizen, but I just don't believe the latter. What did you find out from Aileen?"

"Aileen is quite a remarkable woman," Laskin replied. "She owns her own public relations company, and she happens to be a very good dancer."

Janet eyed him dubiously. "Anything else?"

"Of course," Laskin replied. "I can mix business with pleasure, you know."

"At least that makes one of us."

"And very effective at that, I might add. Do you know Aileen's last name?"

"No, why?"

"Finnegan. Sound familiar?"

"Do you mean that Finnegan, the New York State attorney general?"

"Yep." Laskin beamed. "She and Muller have been dating about six months, and she is head over heels for the worm, although for the life of me I can't understand what she sees in him."

Janet decided not to comment. Despite his lack of moral character, Muller possessed a number of attributes that women would find attractive. "Did she know anything about Muller's charity?"

Laskin shook his head. "No, it sounds like Muller keeps his business affairs to himself. I'm surprised he told you so much. Could it be because he wanted you to know?"

"I don't think so. I think he just wanted to show off, but it does sound strange that he keeps it a secret from his girlfriend."

"When I get back to the office on Monday, I'm going to do a background check on Muller's charity. What's the name of it?"

"Phoenix Fund."

"He sure has a flare for names. First Emperial, and now Phoenix."

"He certainly does." Janet frowned. "Something is not adding up. I find it hard to believe that Muller has a charitable bone in his body."

"Whatever his new scheme is, we'll get to the bottom of it."

ഇൗരു

Jon Bostoff took a sip of scotch and checked his watch. The toasts would start soon, and he had to put his happy face on. His little brother was getting married. After the deluge of misfortunes that had assailed the Bostoff family over the past year, they were due for a little happiness in their lives.

Jon had worked hard to make up for all the wrongs he had done, but some things could never be corrected: the pain he had caused his father, the disappointment of his younger brother, and the shame Jon had brought on the Bostoff name. He had wanted to turn his father's company into a financial empire; instead, Jon's reckless actions had resulted in the collapse of Bostoff Securities. The past year had been a veritable hell as Jon was dragged through countless depositions, forced to disclose the details of a market manipulation scheme he had worked so hard to construct. He admitted his guilt, but in all fairness he had not been the mastermind behind the scheme. True, he had constructed the highway that subverted speed limits that the rest of the industry was expected to follow, but he was not the one driving the cars that raced on its smooth runway—the steering was done by his clients. David Muller, the owner of Emperial hedge fund, had been one of Jon's biggest clients. Jon's lawyer had assured him that Jon would get credit with the investigators for his cooperation in providing evidence, and that Muller was the main target of the case.

Jon's shock was impossible to put into words when he learned the investigation's verdict. Bostoff Securities was fined in the amount of one million dollars, and Jon was barred from the financial industry for three years. With the legal fees piling up and the fine hanging over his head, there was no other option but to liquidate Bostoff Securities. Jon's shock had been even greater when he learned that the case against Emperial and David Muller had been dismissed due to lack of evidence.

The hardest part was breaking the news to his father, Hank Bostoff, who had put his life into building the company. Jon had expected chastisement and banishment; instead, his father had surprised Jon with mercy and understanding. "Anyone can slip, son," Hank had said. "What sets the man apart from the rest is how he gets back on his feet. I know that you have it in you to get back on track."

From that moment on, Jon dedicated his entire existence to repairing his credibility. With the ban hanging over him, the financial industry was closed to him. He had to find a new way to make a living. He would have to start over. The answer surprised him most of all. One night, as he was contemplating his options, Jon received a call from his lawyer asking him if he would be interested in providing consulting services to a financial company that had caught a rogue trader among its staff and was looking to strengthen internal controls. "I have not given your name or anything like that, Jon, but I thought that you could provide valuable input to this company from your recent experience."

Thus began Jon's consulting career. He was surprised by how quickly his client list grew. His clients consisted of companies that had already experienced problems with nefarious employees and were looking for ways to avoid a repeat experience, and those that were being proactive and were looking for preventive measures to avoid having such experiences firsthand. Jon understood the needs of his clients, and, most importantly, he understood the motivation of the culprits. Finance was a game of high risk and high reward, and the temptation to seize the reward often surpassed the fear of risk. Emboldened by profits made in a good year, traders often lived beyond their means, certain that each year would be better than the previous one. A trader who had made a wrong bet and was losing money on a stock position could turn into a desperate man, willing to go to great lengths to conceal the loss so that he could get that coveted bonus to pay for the lavish condo or vacation home he could barely afford in the first place.

Lies and cover-ups were a slippery slope: once one started, it was almost impossible to stop. Just recently, Jon had helped a client catch a rogue trader who was forging profit and loss reports. The trader had a programming background, which made it easy for him to break into the firm's systems and manipulate the data, making his losses look like profits. The management began to suspect things, but could not quite make heads or tails of things, and they wanted an independent party to investigate, which was where Jon's expertise came in. Still, the job was no picnic, for as much as he enjoyed the idea of helping his clients, Jon could not help feeling compassion for the culprits. After all, not so long ago he had been one of them. He just hoped that the bad guys he now helped to catch would have the will and decency to transform their lives, as he had done. It had been a long road, with an even steeper road lying ahead of him. To cover his legal fees and settle the regulatory fine, he had to sell his recently acquired beach house in the Hamptons and his mansion in Westbury, Long Island and move his family to a modest three bedroom house in Connecticut. Had it not been for his wife's help, Jon doubted that he would have survived this mortification.

Candace Bostoff, née Covington, had been standing by Jon's side ever since he planted a wet one on her at a party at Duke University over twenty years ago. Candace came from a wealthy family. There were many young men with far more impressive pedigrees than Jon's who were vying for her attention, but Candace chose Jon. They got married right after graduation, by which time Candace was already pregnant with their firstborn, Tyler. The Covingtons had not approved of Candace's choice of husband and had made it clear that the Bostoffs would not partake in the Covington fortune. It had been just as well with Jon who intended to make his own way in the world. Granted, Jon did not exactly come from nothing himself. His father's boutique investment firm generated a steady stream of revenue, which Jon hoped to take to new heights. As a young man, Jon was eager to share his business ideas with his father, but Hank Bostoff liked doing business the tried and true way. So Jon bid his time, waiting until his father was ready to retire and hand over the business to him. By the time Hank Bostoff was ready to hand over the reins to Jon, time had passed, and the business opportunities that Jon had wanted to take advantage of were already taken. Still, he was eager to make up the lost ground and transform Bostoff Securities into a money making machine, so that he could finally provide Candace with the lifestyle she was born to have. Not that Candace had ever made a comment about their comfortable middle-class lifestyle: she had been perfectly content. It was Jon who had wanted more. How reckless he had been! Pride and ambition were valuable qualities, but when left unchecked they often drove men to do unthinkable things. If there were one thing that Jon Bostoff was certain of, it was that he would never let his pride or ambition get the better of him again.

"Are you ready to give your speech, honey?" Candace Bostoff squeezed her husband's hand.

"As ready as I'll ever be." Jon smiled, pressing Candace's hand to his lips. Jon glanced at the bustling reception hall. It was reassuring to see that even after the Bostoff name had been dragged through the mud, true friends remained by their side. Jon was about to turn his attention back to Candace when he felt blood flow to his face. There, among the guests who were supposed to be the closest of family and friends, sat David

Muller, the man whom Jon held personally responsible for all of his misfortunes.

"Jon, what's wrong?" Candace whispered.

He frowned, debating whether he should mention Muller's presence at the wedding to Candace. He was not sure if Candace had seen him, and he did not want to ruin the mood. "Oh, it's nothing. Just nerves I guess."

"Nerves? When have you ever been shy about public speaking?"

"Oh, I don't know. I guess I'm just tired. How about a kiss to give me some courage?"

Jon attempted to steer Candace's attention away from the guest tables, but was too late. "Is that David Muller?" Candace asked, her face turning pale.

"That's the bastard in the flesh," Jon hissed. "I have no idea who invited him. He's got some nerve showing up here." Jon saw the pained expression on Candace's face. This was the last straw. "That's it. I'm going to go over there and throw him out."

"Wait." Candace grabbed his hand. "Who's that woman sitting next to him?"

"The redhead? I have no idea, but I've got to say that Muller has certainly come down in his standards. He used to date supermodels. I guess life's not treating him as well as it used to."

"Jon, I think I know who she is. Her face looks familiar; I remember seeing her in one of those society magazines. I'm pretty sure that's the daughter of the state attorney general."

"You mean Cornelius Finnegan's daughter?"

"I've never been good with names, but I never forget a face when I see one, and I swear I saw her picture in one of the newspapers. She was photographed next to her father, who is this hefty, bulky guy, and her mother who is actually quite pretty, and I remember thinking what a shame it was that the girl took after her father."

"Candace, you are brilliant." Jon pulled his wife close to him and planted a long, passionate kiss on her lips.

Candace blushed. "Jon, what's gotten into you? You are the brother of the groom. There are people watching us."

"What's wrong with a man kissing his wife?" Jon beamed. "Baby, I think you just figured out a way to make Muller pay his due."

"What do you mean?"

"Don't you think it's suspicious that he got away with a slap on his wrist, and I was put through the mill?"

"Jon, do you mean to say that Muller got off the hook because he had the attorney general to protect him?"

"That's exactly what I mean. I've been made a scapegoat, and I don't like being anyone's cat's-paw. I'll show that bastard."

"Jon, please don't make a scene."

"Oh, I won't. In fact, I'll go over there and say hello, being my most cordial self. Sooner or later the bastard will slip, and even his friends in high places won't be able to protect him."

Chapter Seventeen

"Baby, I missed you." David tightened his arms around Mila's lanky body. To say that he missed her was the understatement of a lifetime. His attraction to the woman had reached the level of addiction. When he was not with Mila he was thinking of making love to Mila, and when he was with Mila he was anxiously counting the hours until their separation, already longing for the next time he would see her.

"I missed you too, honey." Mila pressed herself against him, making every muscle of his body ache with desire.

"Oh, yeah? I bet that I missed you more," David whispered, reaching for the zipper on the back of Mila's dress.

"Hold on a minute, honey. I want to show you what I've done with the place."

Ever since David had gotten Mila the lease on the new place, she had gone gung ho on the idea of decorating. Last week it had been a set of art deco lamps for the bedroom and a Roy Lichtenstein lithograph for the living room. True, Mila's taste was expensive, but it amused David to discover that underneath the sexy vixen exterior, Mila possessed the genes of a homemaker.

"It's in your study. I can't wait for you to see it." Mila tugged at David's arm. "Come on!"

"What is it?" David asked, cocking his head sideways to make better sense of the image that hung on the study wall.

"It's a Pablo Picasso lithograph! It's called Cubist Composition. It's a numbered edition and it's been hand-signed by Picasso himself," Mila replied with the air of an art historian.

"Wonderful." David stood back, regarding the image on the wall, wondering how much it had cost. Mila certainly had expensive taste. Good thing that his earlier chat with Finnegan and Magee promised to provide a sizeable bump to his net worth.

"Oh, I almost forgot, this came too." Mila motioned toward a metal cabinet by David's desk.

David was pleasantly surprised by the news. He had been so consumed by Mila's presence that he failed to notice that the safe he had ordered earlier had been installed in his office, three days ahead of the scheduled delivery date. The timing could not have been more perfect—funny how even the smallest things began to turn out in one's favor when one's luck was coming around.

"What do you need this ugly thing for? It's ruining the whole ambiance."

David traced his fingers over the safe lock. "It's a safe, baby."

"I know it's a safe. My question is, what do you need it for?"

"To keep important things safe."

"What things?"

"Things that could make us both very, very rich." David nuzzled Mila's neck.

"In that case, I guess it's not that much of an eyesore," Mila conceded.

"I'm glad to hear that. Now, where were we?" David reached for the zipper on Mila's dress, undoing it in one swift tug. "I think we'd better move into the bedroom," he whispered.

An hour later, after he had his fill of her, David rose from the bed. "I have to work for a bit, baby."

"All right," Mila mumbled into the pillow.

With one last, longing look, David tore himself away from her and walked toward the study where he had established a work camp. Mila's apartment had been rented under an alias, which would make it difficult to trace it back to him. Besides, he felt confident that the records he kept at Mila's place would never get into the wrong hands.

It was hard to concentrate on business with the knowledge of Mila lying naked in the bedroom, but it had to be done. David forced himself to focus on the market charts on the computer screen. So far, the information Magee had given him had worked like a charm. Magee was on the board of Rover Industries, a giant manufacturing conglomerate. Rover had a number of different divisions that manufactured commercial equipment for a variety of industries. Some of their products included commercial chillers, engines, and even construction cranes. But the best part about Rover, the part that interested David, was that Rover often subcontracted projects to other companies. A multimillion dollar contract from Rover could easily result in a three- to four-dollar jump in the stock price of the company that received the contract. Of course by the time the news reached the market, it was impossible to take any advantage of the price jump, but if one had advance notification one stood to make quite a profit.

Rover had a tiered approval process for its business: smaller contracts were approved by senior management, but the most substantial contracts were presented for approval to the board of directors. So far, Kevan Magee had given Muller two leads. The first one had been Orion, a mid-size publicly traded manufacturing company that was to receive a fifty-million-dollar three-year contract from Rover for the manufacturing of engine components. When Magee had given David the information, Orion's shares were trading at seven dollars a share. According to Magee, the news of the contract award was to be announced in a week's time, which gave David plenty of time to load up on the option positions for Orion's stock. At seven dollars a share, purchasing a physical stock position would have required a significant capital commitment; instead, David purchased stock options that would enable him to purchase Orion shares at nine dollars a share. The beauty of option contracts was that they did not have to be exercised: one could simply buy an option for a stock and then sell it at a later time without having to acquire the stock position. Orion was a quiet stock without anything in the company fundamentals indicating shift in revenue or growth, so Muller had been able to snap up the options for less than a dollar per contract. With the money wired to him by Magee and Finnegan and the addition of his own funds, David had acquired option contracts for close to a million shares of Orion's stock. This time he decided not to trust any particular brokerage firm to execute his trades, but split the orders between several brokers. All the trades were placed in the name of Phoenix Fund, a charity that sponsored scholarships for young men and women who were interested in pursuing careers in finance. Who would ever question a charity? Hell, David had even gone so far as to dole out a few thousand bucks in scholarships to several lucky buggers to make it look legit. Once the news of Orion receiving the contract from Rover was publicly announced, Orion's stock jumped to ten dollars, making the options jump two dollars in price. David sold off his option position at a hefty profit, which made Finnegan and Magee two very satisfied customers.

Magee's second lead involved a similar setup where Hudson Steel, a piping manufacturer, had been awarded an eighty-million-dollar contract by Rover. Prior to the announcement of the contract award, Hudson's stock had been trading at ten dollars per share, which was when David had acquired a large number of option contracts to buy Hudson's stock at eleven dollars. Once the news of the contract was made public, Hudson's stock jumped to thirteen dollars per share, leading the option price to appreciate from the two dollars David had paid for it to five dollars.

Already the bank account for Phoenix Fund had over ten million as its balance. Granted, the amount would have to be split three ways between David, Magee, and Finnegan. David had considered claiming all the spoils for himself—after all, it would be unlikely for either Finnegan or Magee to protest once they learned that David possessed several recordings of their conversations that clearly implicated Finnegan and Magee in an insider trading scheme—but then decided against it. Three million and change was a good cut, but it was not good enough to get out for life, at least not for David. Magee was the golden goose, and for now David did not intend to slay him or his owner, Finnegan. Instead, David would wait for a tip that would ensure that he would never have to worry about money again. Then, he would leave Finnegan and Magee high and dry. And if Magee's latest tip were to materialize, David would not have to wait long.

During their last meeting, Magee had mentioned that Rover wanted to branch out into the automobile industry and was looking to acquire an automobile parts manufacturer. So far, the choice had been narrowed to three companies: Stork Enterprises, Richardson Inc., and Valley Metals. The three companies were publicly traded, with their stock prices hovering in the ten- to fifteen-dollar range. David was certain that once the merger target was announced, the target's stock price would appreciate significantly while Rover's stock would decline, reflecting the costs associated with the acquisition, as was always the case with the acquiring company. The trick was to get in on the action before the news became common knowledge. David planned to load up on the stock options for the company that Rover would choose to acquire and go short on Rover's stock. After he claimed his windfall, David would not need to concern himself with either Magee or Finnegan any further, but for now David had to ensure that he retained the trust of the two men. This in itself would not be that much of a burden, except for the fact that remaining in good graces with

Cornelius Finnegan required David romancing Aileen Finnegan, and David was getting sick and tired of the arrangement.

Aileen's latest antic had irritated David immensely. Attending the wedding of Jon Bostoff's brother was the last thing David would have chosen to do of his own volition, but he had been forced to indulge Aileen's request: the stupid woman jumped at any invitation, even when it was to the wedding of a man whose entire family hated David's guts. In all fairness, Aileen was most likely ignorant of David's history with the Bostoff clan since David had never told her of the ordeal, but David was not inclined to be fair to Aileen. To his mind, it was not fair that he was stuck dating the woman, so he felt no obligation to be fair to her.

Aside from being unbearably boring, his attendance at the Bostoff wedding had been mercifully uneventful. In order to compensate for Aileen's lapse, David had written a check in the amount of two thousand dollars as his gift to the groom and bride. The Bostoffs must have been counting the money, because Jon Bostoff approached David during the reception and thanked him for attending, without so much as a word regarding their past. David had been equally cordial: as far as he was concerned, this was going to be the last time he saw Jon Bostoff or any of the Bostoffs for that matter. From now on he would be screening his mail much more carefully.

Still, he needed to keep his growing annoyance with Aileen in check. Until his dealings with Finnegan were complete, David could not afford for Aileen to suspect that his affection for her was not only diminishing but had never really existed in the first place. His last outburst had been expensive: he had had to shell out some major cash for a pair of gold aquamarine earrings as a peace offering. He would have much rather spent the money on Mila, but one could not always do as one pleased.

"How is my favorite workaholic?" Mila appeared in the doorway of the study. She was wearing a lace negligee and black stilettos. Slowly she approached David while he sat back devouring her every move with his eyes. "I have to go to work soon, but I have a spare half an hour," Mila purred, wrapping her arms around David's neck.

David inhaled the intoxicating smell of her skin. "You still working at that job of yours?" he asked. "I told you that you could quit. I want to take care of you, Mila."

"Oh, I don't mind. I kind of like it. I get to meet new people. Besides, what would I do? Sit around all day long and wait for you to come over?"

"I'm sorry, baby, you know that I want to see more of you, but at the moment things are really hectic. Just give me a little bit of time. Soon, neither one of us will ever have to work again. Then, we'll be together all the time."

Mila sucked on his earlobe, biting it playfully. "Promise?"

"I swear," David groaned. "Now come here, you."

෫oൽ

Mila Brabec hurriedly wriggled into her pantyhose. Today was going to be her first day at her new job, and she did not want to be late. Sure, David's offer to quit working sounded tempting, but for now she was not ready to abandon her independence. Besides, she made sure that David made ample contributions to her lifestyle. Her clothes, her meals, and her rent were all taken care of by David. All the money she made from her waitressing job, Mila saved.

Since the commencement of her waitressing career, Mila had changed jobs several times. Each time she had moved to a more upscale restaurant, and her earnings grew along with the prestige of each new employment. Her latest job had been at a steakhouse in the theater district. It was amazing how much a good waitress could make in tips. An average tip for a party of four ran upwards of fifty dollars, and that was being conservative. Being a good waitress required having a good understanding of people. As long as you gave the customers what they wanted, they were bound to repay in kind. If she smiled just right and showed her cleavage at a revealing angle, Mila almost always managed to get a minimum of seventy dollars, but usually she scored eighty or more. Couples were tougher, especially married couples. First dates, on the other hand, were the best: there was no easier target than a guy who was trying to impress his date.

Mila ran her fingers along the expensive material of her uniform for her new job. At the Panther Restaurant and Lounge Club, the waitresses wore formfitting shifts cut of luxurious black cloth. The dresses were custom-designed by Rodrigo Calos, a Spanish designer whose clothes Mila's had longingly eyed in the windows of expensive department stores. Calos's dresses started at five thousand a piece, and Mila did not even dare to broach David for one. But now she would be wearing one of Calos's creations. So what if the dress were a uniform? It still made her look stunning, and if things continued progressing in the same vein as they had been recently, Mila hoped to one day be able to buy one of Calos's creations with her own money. Mila knocked on wood, which was a custom from the old country to avoid jinxing one's luck. She was not superstitious but she did not want to risk things unnecessarily, especially not when she was convinced that her luck was changing for the better.

First, David had rented this wonderful apartment for her, and then, a few weeks later, she got the offer for her new job. It happened when she was waitressing at the steakhouse, which was a pleasant but otherwise unremarkable establishment patronized by a middle-class clientele and occasional corporate suits. When it came to sizing up her customers, Mila never missed a beat. Right away her ears caught the sound of the Czech accent emanating from the party of three men that were seated in the far corner booth. Despite the fact that the men were impeccably dressed in expensive designer suits, Mila could tell that they were not expatriates residing in New York but were here on a visit, most likely a business visit.

As she took the order from the other table, Mila glanced casually at her compatriots. The man who looked to be the boss of the group was in his mid-fifties. Even when seated, it was obvious that he was a man of short height, but his build was that of a taller man, enabling him to make up for the space he lost with his height with his width. He was the kind of man who looked in control no matter where he was. His face looked familiar, but Mila could not quite place her finger on where she had seen it. Then it came to her: the man was Petr Kovar, one of the richest men in Eastern Europe. The press called him a self-made billionaire, but it was whispered that his fortune came from appropriating government property after the Soviet influence over the region ended. Petr Kovar's business interests spanned from manufacturing to fast food to real estate. Mila's heart quickened, as she imagined the kind of influence one could get by knowing a man like Petr Kovar, or any of his associates for that matter. Petr's other companion was of the same age as Petr; a balding, average-looking man, he was entirely preoccupied with sucking up to Petr. Mila dismissed him from her attention almost immediately. The youngest and the most handsome man in the party looked to be in his early thirties. He addressed the two men with dignified deference, and Mila wondered if he was related to Petr—there was a definite similarity in their features although the younger man was clearly the handsomer of the two as well as much taller.

As she walked over to the table, Mila deliberated whether she should address the men in Czech. People were funny creatures—some might consider the choice of the native tongue an overly familiar gesture, so she chose to speak in English, leaving it up to the men to decide on the language choice. She did not have to wait long. "Where are you from?" Petr asked.

"Prague," Mila replied concisely.

"I knew it. Prague has the most beautiful women."

"Thank you," Mila said shyly.

"You're welcome. It's the truth. I am Petr Kovar."

"I know," Mila replied. "It's a pleasure and an honor to meet you, sir."

"An honor? I'm not sure I like the sound of that—makes me feel like an old man," Kovar chuckled.

Mila cursed herself inwardly. Usually she never lost her cool around men, but this was Petr Kovar, a man who was pretty much considered to be on par with God in her native country. "I'm sorry, sir, I only meant that ..."

"It's all right. I was just ... what is the American expression? ... busting your balls. So what's good here?" asked Petr.

"Steak for four is our best dish," Mila replied. "We can cut it for three if you'd like," she added.

"No need. We're pretty hungry."

For the remainder of their meal, Kovar and his companions did not pay much attention to Mila. It was a busy night, so Mila had plenty of tables to serve. Every now and then she would cast a hopeful glance at the Kovar table, but the men were engrossed in conversation, and she dared not interrupt.

When she picked up the bill from the Kovar table, she was surprised to find as her tip two one hundred dollar bills. She quickly hid one of the bills in her pocket: there was no way she was sharing the entire hoard with the busboys. There was a note on the receipt: One Mercer Street, tomorrow at 1 p.m.

Mila shoved the note into her pocket and went about her work. She was no prude, but she was no prostitute either. Under the right circumstances she would certainly welcome a roll in the hay with Petr Kovar, but she would expect her compensation to exceed two hundred dollars and not be presented to her in such a crude manner. Well, at least she got a two-hundred-dollar tip, which so far was her record.

The next day, the youngest man from the party showed up at the restaurant at six p.m. The hostess was not at her station, so

Mila had to greet him. "Do you have a reservation?" she asked in the coolest voice she could muster.

"Why didn't you come today?" the man asked.

"I have no idea what you're talking about." Mila stared at him icily. "You must have me confused with someone else."

"Do you remember the two hundred dollars I left you?"

Mila pressed her lips together. The last thing she needed was a scene that would cause her to lose her job. "Look, I don't know what you're after, but if you don't leave me alone, I'm going to call the police," she hissed.

"Relax, lady. My uncle is opening a new restaurant, and I'm going to run the place for him. We're looking for waitresses, and you look the part, so if you're tired of working in this dump, the offer is still on. Come to this address tomorrow at two p.m." The man handed his business card to Mila.

Mila prided herself on having an excellent poker face, but now her control abandoned her as a profuse blush spread over her cheeks. "I'm so sorry," she mumbled. "It's just that we get all kinds of people coming in here ..."

"You won't have all kinds of people coming into our place, so I hope to see you tomorrow. By the way, my name is Anton Kovar."

"I'm Mila Brabec. See you tomorrow, Anton," Mila whispered.

The next day Mila got a job at Petr Kovar's restaurant. The restaurant was called Panther Restaurant and Lounge Club and was serving American cuisine prepared by some fancy chef she had seen on one of those TV culinary shows. Mila thought the name was tacky, but who was she to judge? She would be getting paid ten dollars an hour plus tips. If the Kovar tip were any indication, she was bound to make plenty of money. And who knew, with the kind of clientele that was expected to frequent the place, her job might bring in an added benefit of a loaded boyfriend; eventually, maybe even a husband. Sure, Mila liked being with David well enough, but her current lover was not in any rush to get to the altar, and Mila's U.S. visa was not likely to be extended.

Chapter Eighteen

Dennis Walker was having a rotten Monday. Granted, Mondays were designed to be rotten, but this one positively stank. The same could be said about Dennis's weekend. He had had a fight with Shoshanna on Sunday. The two of them had barely patched things up when another quarrel erupted. Not that he was particularly upset about that bit, but he was upset about the cause of it: Janet Maple.

"Who is it?" Shoshanna had demanded after Dennis declined to join her on a Caribbean getaway she had planned as a celebration of their getting back together. "Who is this other woman standing between us?"

"I'm just really busy at work right now, and I can't get away."

"You mean you don't want to leave her," Shoshanna snapped.

"It's not true, Shoshanna. There's no one else. I just can't take off from work right now, that's all."

"Oh, please. Do you really expect me to believe that you can't take a few days off from work? That's never been a problem for you before. There has to be something else, or someone else."

In Dennis's opinion, Shoshanna had her many vices: she was needy, flighty, and downright selfish, but her worst quality was that she was insanely jealous. Her only redeeming quality was her smoking hot looks, but then there were many women with smoking hot looks.

Dennis had been extremely careful not to give Shoshanna any grounds for suspicion. The most ridiculous part of it all was that he had been faithful to Shoshanna, at least physically, not because he was in love with her but because the woman he wanted did not want him.

"You told me that you hate your job at the Treasury," Shoshanna added imploringly. "Why don't you just quit? I've got enough money for the both of us."

Dennis shook his head. Why was it that he always ended up with the wrong kind of woman? The mere fact that Shoshanna thought him capable of leeching off of her made it clear that she knew nothing about him; to her, he was just a boy toy she would grow tired of in a matter of months, just like she had grown tired of all her other boyfriends. The only difference with Dennis was that, by being emotionally unavailable, he had not allowed her to grow tired of him. A logical question to ask was why had Dennis been putting up with Shoshanna in the first place? Unfortunately, when it came to women, Dennis Walker was not the most logical man.

"My situation at work is complicated right now, but quitting is not an option. I have to see things through, which is precisely why I can't take time off."

"You mean you can't take time off because you don't want to be away from her."

"Who?"

"Whoever you think of when you get that faraway look in your eyes. Because I know for sure that you aren't thinking of me."

"There is no one else. No one else but you," Dennis protested vainly.

"Save it, Dennis. If there is one thing that I won't stand for, it's lying. I could forgive infidelity, but I will not be lied to."

The clicking of Shoshanna's heels echoed in Dennis's ears like bullets. For all her self-absorption and vanity, Shoshanna had seen right through him. For indeed there was someone else between then, or any other woman Dennis had tried to date since he had met Janet Maple. It pained him to admit it but Shoshanna was right: he was a liar, and the person he had deceived most was himself. Instead of going after Janet when he'd had the chance, he elected to take the safer road of being friends. And now Janet was taken by none other than Kingsley—the man who had ruined Dennis's career and his love life.

Dennis got up from his desk. He needed the distraction of human interaction. He headed to the junior analysts' section where there were several pretty specimens of the female gender who were always glad to see him.

The downside to his plan, which he only realized when it was too late, was that his route included passing by Peter Laskin's office. Walking by Laskin's office, Dennis heard the sound of busy typing. Typical Laskin, Dennis thought, no matter what happens, the man keeps plowing along. Deep down Dennis knew that Laskin was good at his job, but right now Dennis was in no mood to admit it. Truth be told, lately Laskin was probably far more productive than Dennis, not that Dennis was eager to admit this point either. In his defense, Dennis had a reason to be in a slump. Ever since he had spotted Janet with Alex, he had been unable to think of anything or anyone else but her. For all his hatred of Alex, Dennis was doing very little to get back at the man. Oh, sure, Dennis had spent plenty of time fantasizing about how he was going to expose the sneaky maggot. But first, he had to come up with a definite plan of action, or any plan for that matter.

"How is it going, Dennis?" Laskin's voice carried through the open doorway.

Dennis stepped inside Laskin's office. Even talking to Laskin was better than being alone with his thoughts. "Rotten," Dennis confessed.

"Too much partying over the weekend?" asked Laskin while his fingers continued to flutter over the keyboard.

"Something like that. What are you working on?" Dennis switched the conversation away from himself.

"Something that Janet and I uncovered when we were at the Bostoff wedding."

"You were Janet's date for the Bostoff wedding? I didn't even know Jon Bostoff was getting married. I thought he was already married. Did he get divorced?"

"Wow, slow down, Dennis. It was Jon's brother who got married—Paul. Paul Bostoff was engaged to Lisa Foley, or have you forgotten?"

Dennis rubbed his chin. He was losing it. "That's right, I remember now. So what did you guys find?"

"I think that you'd better ask Janet. She's the one taking the lead on this," Laskin replied with his eyes glued to his computer screen.

"Very well. I'll ask her."

Dennis kept walking in his initial direction until he heard the click of Laskin's office door. Then he turned around abruptly and headed for Janet's office. He was going to have it out with her once and for all.

When Dennis reached Janet's office he saw that its door was closed. He was about to walk in when he heard that Janet was not alone. Dennis would have recognized the smug notes of Kingsley's voice anywhere, but it was particularly disturbing to recognize them in Janet's office. Suppressing his impulse to fling open the door and punch Kingsley right in his arrogant mug, Dennis flattened his back against the door frame, straining his ears for the conversation that was taking place on the other side of the door.

※※※

"Have you got any interesting news for me, Janet?" Alex asked as he leaned against Janet's desk, eyeing her with a cool, penetrating glare.

"Not that I can think of," Janet managed. Alex had burst into her office unannounced, and now she literally felt pinned to her chair under his stare, like one of those insects in a glass display.

Alex's hands let go of Janet's desk. He walked closer to her chair, taking her hand into his. "So I take it that the Bostoff wedding was uneventful?"

"Oh, that. It was fine; nothing special," Janet replied. "You know, as weddings go."

"Did Laskin prove to be an adequate escort?" Alex asked, still holding Janet's hand.

"Yes. I'm very grateful to him for being my date. As you know, there's nothing more humiliating for a girl than showing up at a wedding without a date."

"Janet, I told you before that you needn't ever be worried about not having a date." Alex squeezed Janet's hand. "All you need to do is pick up the phone and call me. Or just walk over to my office and ask me in person," Alex added huskily.

"Thank you, Alex. I'll be sure to keep that in mind." Janet tried to free her hand from Alex's fingers, but his grip was firm.

"And what about Jon Bostoff?" Alex switched the conversation abruptly. "Have you noticed anything funky about him?"

"No, nothing funky. As we discussed, he's opened a white collar crime consulting firm and seems to be doing fairly well. I don't think there's anything suspicious there. I am glad to see that he is now on the right side of the law."

"Is he?"

"That's what it looks like."

Alex tightened his grip on Janet's hand. "Your leniency surprises me, Janet. A leopard never changes his spots. We'll keep our eyes on him, and if he strays we'll be there to put him back where he belongs."

Janet nodded, wondering when Alex was going to let go of her hand. She was a grown woman, so why was she enduring this humiliation, with her tongue glued to her throat? She imagined using her free hand to grab the paperweight from her desk and smashing it into Alex's balls; this action did not require any spoken words and would undoubtedly produce the desired results.

"How about meeting me for a drink after work?" Alex asked.

"I, um, I'd love to, but I can't tonight. I'm meeting a friend after work." Janet could have kicked herself. She was too much of a chicken to even tell Alex off, let alone kick him in the nuts.

"Very well. But you know that you won't be able to put me off with excuses forever." Alex pressed Janet's hand to his lips. "I'll see you later, Janet."

ꗝꛥ

At the sound of Alex's footsteps, Dennis Walker had barely enough time to jump away from the door of Janet's office and leap into the office supplies pantry, which was just around the corner. Luckily, the hallway was empty, and Dennis was saved from the embarrassment of having to explain his behavior. This was a true stroke of luck, for the usually cautious and levelheaded Dennis would not have been able to produce a plausible explanation of his antics to save his life.

Dennis leaned against the supply closet and waited for the sound of Alex's footsteps to fade away. Then he smoothed his jacket and headed toward Janet's office.

"Cup of coffee, you and me, right now," Dennis said in a tone that was more an order than an invitation.

For several moments Janet stared blankly at him. The words that followed after she recovered her capacity for speech made Dennis wish she had remained silent. "I don't hear from you for days and you think can just barge into my office and expect me to drop everything? Thank you for the invite, but I'm quite busy at the moment, so I'll have to decline."

"Busy with what? Romancing Alex?"

Janet reddened, and Dennis knew that he had hit bull's eye. "How do you know about that?" she snapped.

"I'm an investigator, remember? I saw you together last week when you were walking Baxter together."

"It's not what you think, not that it's any of your business…" Janet began, but stopped in mid-sentence. "You spied on me?"

Now it was Dennis's turn to flush. "I didn't spy on you. I came by to see you, but learned that you were otherwise occupied. The least you could do is be decent enough to let me know where I stand. But for God's sake let's get out of here. This is no place to talk: the walls are paper thin here."

"Where you stand?" Janet rose from her chair with self-righteous vigor. "I'll tell you where you stand: you are in no position to ask me such questions." She grabbed her coat. "Where are we going?"

Dennis barely managed to suppress his smile. Despite the elaborate display of anger, Janet still agreed to talk to him, which meant that she had to care about him at least a little bit.

A few minutes later, Janet and Dennis were seated behind the stained table of the coffee shop Dennis frequented whenever he needed a secure place to talk. Located on one of the side streets that ran like a maze in Downtown Manhattan, the place was a dive, but the good part was that no one from the office knew about the coffee shop's existence. "So what's going on between you and Alex?" Dennis asked.

"I told you that nothing is going on between me and Alex."

"Oh yeah? Then how come he is walking Baxter with you? And why is he asking you out for a drink?"

148

"How did you—" Janet broke off. "You know, Dennis, I thought that you were too mature to eavesdrop on people's conversations. But if you must know, I'm no happier about Alex's attention than you are. I told you that I hate the dirtbag, and nothing has changed since then. I still can't stand him, and I sure hope that we'll be able to come up with a way to expose him for what he is: a lying, cheating scoundrel. But if you continue acting the way you are acting, I doubt we'll be able to succeed."

"Acting the way I've been acting? Why didn't you tell me about the Bostoff wedding? I should have been your date, not Laskin."

Janet lowered her eyes, a barely perceptible smile lurking on her lips.

Dennis cursed his outburst. Making Janet aware of his attraction to her was not part of his intention, at least not at the moment.

"If you must know, I was going to ask you," Janet replied. "But you seemed to be otherwise engaged, so I asked Laskin."

"Otherwise engaged?"

"I believe her name is honey boo."

Dennis could not help smiling. Apparently, he was not the only one with a penchant for eavesdropping. "Guilty. But it's over now, and it was never anything serious. For what it's worth, if you had asked me to be your date for the Bostoff wedding, I would have been glad to be there."

"Thanks, Dennis, I appreciate that. Now, if you'll let me finish, I'll tell you what Laskin and I learned when we were there."

After Janet had finished giving the account of the wedding, Dennis stared at her from across the table. "Muller actually had the nerve to show up at the wedding? And he is dating the state attorney's daughter?"

"Yep. Now do you see why the case against him got dismissed?"

"Crystal clear."

"Wait, it gets better. Finnegan used to run the Manhattan DA's office. He was Alex's boss's boss. The three of them used to be real chummy, with Finnegan calling Alex 'my boy' and inviting him for drinks after work, that sort of thing."

"Did they ever invite you?"

Janet shook her head. "It was boys only."

"And now Finnegan is state attorney general and Alex is our boss," Dennis concluded.

"Call me paranoid, but I think there's a connection between Finnegan, Ham being fired, and Alex being put in charge of our department."

"It certainly does not seem farfetched to me. Alex must have served his master well, and now Finnegan has placed him at the Treasury as his trusted watchdog." Dennis drummed his fingers on the table. "And Muller told you that he is a philanthropist now?"

"Yep," Janet nodded. "But I don't believe it for a second. This whole thing stinks to high heaven. Alex's interest in the matter makes it even more suspicious. Laskin and I are determined to get to the bottom of it. You're welcome to join if you're interested."

"If I'm interested? Of course I'm interested, Janet. You know that there's nothing I'd like more than to see Muller face justice."

"Then, you trust me again?"

Dennis hung his head. "Yes. I'm sorry about what I said earlier. It was uncalled for."

A flicker of a smile passed over Janet's lips. "All is forgotten. No apologies needed among friends."

"So what's the plan?" Dennis could scarcely believe his own words. Usually, he was the one giving instructions, but in this case he had to give Janet her due—she had kept her cool while he had let his emotions get the better of him.

"Laskin is running the check on Muller's charity as we speak. He has also alerted the Market Watch department to keep him posted of any unusual stock moves. Sooner or later Muller will make a mistake, and we'll be there to catch him."

80C3

Alex sat back at his desk, mulling over his conversation with Janet. He was good at reading people, and he was certain that Janet had told him the truth. There was a reason he had pulled a Romeo routine on Janet: he'd held her hand during the entire conversation and if she had been lying, her quickened pulse would have given her away.

Besides, Alex was not merely relying on Janet's words. He had done some checking on Bostoff himself and had come up empty. He understood that Finnegan wanted Bostoff shut down, but as long as Bostoff was not doing anything illegal, Finnegan would just have to back off. So far, Bostoff had limited his business engagements to giving speeches on the evils of corruption and white collar crime. There was nothing any regulatory agency could do to sanction him for that. Now, if Bostoff cheated on his taxes or began poking his nose into matters that were outside of his purview, such as, for instance, gathering evidence against Muller, there would be ample grounds to shut Bostoff down. But until Alex became aware of such conduct, he was going to steer clear of Bostoff. Sure, Alex wanted to keep Finnegan happy, but Alex was not stupid enough to do it at the expense of his own skin.

Alex dialed Cornelius Finnegan's private number. "Cornelius, it's Alex."

"Always glad to hear from you, my boy. I trust you have some good news for me?"

Alex ignored the insufferable "my boy." He was sick of Finnegan's patronizing ways. "Yes, sir," he replied pleasantly.

"I ran the check on Bostoff's new business venture, and I am glad to report that everything is in order."

"You mean you shut him down? That's my boy! I knew you were perfect for this job."

Alex shook his head with annoyance. For such a sharp man, Finnegan could be unbelievably obtuse. "No, sir. I meant to say that Bostoff is not doing anything wrong. He's just trying to make an honest living by giving speeches on how to catch crooks like himself."

"And you're glad about that?"

"Forgive my poor choice of words, sir, but Bostoff is not doing anything illegal, and until he does I don't see what I can do about it."

There was a brief pause on the other end of the line. "It certainly sounds like you've done your homework. Continue keeping an eye on him and notify me as soon as you see anything foul."

"I will, sir."

"And how about that Walker reprobate? No more rogue investigations?"

"Not that I am aware of, sir. I've told him to focus on analytics to get him away from fieldwork."

"I like that. Good thinking. I'm counting on you, Alex. Don't disappoint me."

Have I ever? Alex was tempted to retort, but bit his tongue. He did not have a career death wish to get snippy with Finnegan. "I won't, sir."

"Good." Finnegan hung up.

Alex put down the receiver. He had been faithfully carrying out Finnegan's orders, but everything had its limit. He had checked out Bostoff and put a muzzle on Walker, but Finnegan was starting to become unreasonable, and Alex was not going to be a blind tool in Finnegan's hands. Even Finnegan was not invincible, and if he were replaced, Alex did not want to be left out in the cold. From now on Alex was going to temper the reports he gave to Finnegan.

Chapter Nineteen

Aileen Finnegan checked her reflection in the bathroom mirror. She had just closed a very important contract with a new client, and she felt like a winner. She had dressed carefully for the occasion, choosing a tailored sheath and a matching jacket in periwinkle. The color of the cloth highlighted her blue eyes, and the smart cut of the clothes showed off her newly slim figure. She had been working hard at being pretty for David, and all the hard work was finally paying off. Over the course of the past six months she had lost almost twenty-five pounds, which resulted in her getting a whole new wardrobe, but this was the kind of expense she was glad to have. Sure, she was still no model, but she liked the way she looked, and more importantly she felt good. Things were definitely looking up. It seemed that good things, just like bad things, came in phases, and finally, for the first time in her life, Aileen could say that things were going well for her.

Her recent transformation had also improved her professional life. No matter what anyone said, one's appearance mattered, especially in a business like public relations. Aileen's clients paid her for representation, and they wanted someone who looked the part for the job. Aileen had always been good with people. In fact, up until recently the only feature she liked about herself was her voice, which was why she had chosen public relations as her occupation in the first place. A large part of her job was done over the phone, and she was really good on the phone. She had good people skills as well and was pretty good at in-person meetings—God knows, she had to compensate for what she lacked in looks with a cheerful personality—but now she was even better. Over the past month, Aileen had secured three new accounts. She had already accumulated a good nest egg by living with her parents, and now she was doing even better. It was time to make one last change: it was time to move out of her parents' house. Yesterday, she had signed the lease on a one bedroom apartment in West Village. She would be moving in on the first of next month. The reality of the change was still sinking in, and she was yet to break the news to her parents who were bound to object, especially her mother.

Aileen's mother was the president of the local women's club and was on the board of several local charities. It was her dream for Aileen to one day succeed her mother as president of the women's club. While Aileen's high school friends were out dating, her evenings and weekends had been occupied with helping her mother with charity auctions, dinners, and other social functions her mother organized. At first, Aileen had not minded—her calendar was far from being booked up with dates—but as the years went by, these occasions became more of a burden than a joy. Sure, she wanted to contribute to all the good causes her mother supported, but it bothered her that most of the women in the club, including her mother, cared more about the social status that their involvement with the charities gave them than the causes they so ardently rallied to raise awareness of. And now that she had David in her life, Aileen refused to surrender her evenings and weekends to her mother. Her mother had already chided Aileen for not being available for several events, but Aileen stood her ground. She was as charitable as the next person, but that did not mean that she had to sacrifice her social life at her mother's whim.

At the thought of David, a smile appeared on Aileen's face. She could not wait to tell him the news about her apartment. Deep down she hoped that the two of them would not have to reside in separate apartments for too long, but at the same time she did not want to go straight from living with her parents to living with David. She wanted to live on her own for a while. Not for too long—a year would most likely suffice—and then she would marry David. The prospect of becoming Mrs. David Muller made Aileen's heart flutter; she would do anything to make it a reality. At first she had not even dared to allow such thoughts into her mind, but as the months went by and David remained by her side, the previously unreachable possibility began to seem feasible.

If only things would not change, Aileen thought, suppressing a frown. For as much as she hated to admit it, things had changed. Lately, the previously attentive David seemed to grow more distant. On several occasions David had canceled their dates, and his behavior at the Bostoff wedding had been downright atrocious. David had apologized to Aileen afterwards, presenting her with a lovely pair of gold aquamarine earrings. "They will go nicely with your eyes, lovey," David had said. "I am sorry for losing my temper, Aileen, and I'm sorry for not being around as much. It's just that I've been so busy lately. The charity fund is a lot of work, but once I have it set up, it should pretty much run itself."

The earrings' blue stones had sparkled with icy shine, and Aileen nodded, deciding not to remark on the fact that David always found the time to meet with her father. Indeed, the two of them met on a regular basis, and at times Aileen wondered whom it was that David really wanted to date. "Don't you like them?" David had asked.

"Yes, I like them." Aileen nodded. The earrings were beautiful, and David's voice was so tender, just the way it used to be when they had first met.

"Am I forgiven?"

"Yes."

"Well, are you going to try them on?"

Aileen did as David asked. The cool blue stones did go with her eyes, but it was not the earrings she yearned for David to give her; it was a ring with a solitaire diamond. Still, the earrings were a good start, and they had brought her luck. She had been wearing them to client meetings and she had closed every deal since then.

Aileen checked her watch. It was six p.m. She had planned to stop by her new apartment to measure it for furniture. From a bed to a kitchen table, she would need to furnish the entire place from scratch, and she only had about two weeks to do it. But, on the bright side, moving out of her parents' house would be a breeze, as she would only be taking her clothes. Well, at least the physical process would be a breeze, for Aileen could already foresee the emotional ploys her mother would use to get Aileen to stay.

Aileen navigated her way down the convoluted West Village streets. The neighborhood was new to her and, unlike Midtown Manhattan, one could not figure out one's way by street numbers. In the Village the streets had names, and unless you knew the sequence in which each name followed after the other, you were lost. But Aileen was not worried. She would learn her way around the neighborhood soon enough and there was no better time to start like right now.

&ɔœ

Janet Maple paced the floor of her apartment while Baxter observed her curiously from the couch. It was seven p.m. and she was expecting visitors—two visitors to be precise: Dennis Walker and Peter Laskin. Needless to say, the prospect of Dennis being in her apartment made Janet jittery with apprehension. Still, this option was far better than the alternative of meeting at Dennis's place. At least Janet would be on her own turf, and Laskin would be there to prevent her from making a fool of herself. The three of them needed a safe place to discuss their plan of action for nailing Muller. Speaking at work was out of the question, and even meeting at coffee shops or bars was risky.

So far, Alex remained completely unsuspecting of their extracurricular activities. The majority of the credit for this feat belonged to Janet, as she had endured several lunches with Alex and even one after-work drink. During their rendezvous she fed Alex with elaborate lies as to the activity of the department, assuring him that the Bostoff and Muller case had long been forgotten. She repeatedly assured Alex that Dennis Walker was nothing more than a pompous womanizer whose only concern was increasing the number of female conquests, and that Laskin was nothing more than a mindless data mining machine. Alex seemed to eat these figments right out of Janet's hands, an outcome that she had achieved by allowing Alex to believe that they were indeed headed for reconciliation. She herself greatly doubted that Alex's intention to get back together with her was genuine. In fact, Janet was certain that the only motivation behind Alex's rekindled interest in her was for Alex to be sure of the truthfulness of the information that Janet was supplying him with. If the two of them were to get back together, Janet would undoubtedly be on Alex's side, or so Alex believed.

But if Alex thought that she was foolish enough to fall for this lame ploy, he had another thing coming. Of course Janet had to admit that she had been flattered when Alex had first showed up unexpectedly during her evening walk with Baxter, proclaiming that leaving her was the biggest mistake of his life. What girl wouldn't feel flattered hearing such a speech from her ex? But the flattery wore off quickly once Alex showed his true colors by unleashing on Baxter for something as minor as biting off a piece of his trouser. While Baxter had not been on his best behavior, Alex's reaction was downright pathetic, just like the man himself. The image of Alex's frightened face as he jumped away from Baxter's scowl brought a smile to Janet's face. Alex was nothing more than a bully with a tough exterior that contained cowardly insides.

"You are my knight in shining armor, Baxter," Janet complemented Baxter, patting him behind his ear.

The doorbell rang and Baxter jumped off the couch, heading for the door.

"Wait up, Baxter!" Janet rushed for the door, sincerely hoping that Laskin would be the first to arrive, for despite all her talk about being impervious to Dennis Walker's charms, Janet could not vouch for her conduct if she were to be left alone with Dennis Walker for too long.

"Hi there, Janet."

"Good evening."

Both Laskin and Dennis stood at the threshold of Janet's apartment.

"I thought you guys were going to arrive separately to maintain cover and all that," Janet replied, stunned by the look of her guests: both men were panting for breath.

Dennis shrugged. "That was the plan, but our timing overlapped."

"I see. Come on in."

"I thought we might get hungry." Dennis motioned at the pizza box he was holding under his arm. "And thirsty." He handed Janet a beer six-pack.

"Wonderful. You must have psychic powers because my fridge is empty."

"Nah, I just remember it from last time."

Laskin cast a questioning glace at the two of them, and Janet flushed. The last time Dennis Walker had been a guest in her apartment was when they were investigating the Bostoff case together. In fact, there had been several last times, as the two of them had made Janet's apartment their meeting spot to discuss the evidence they were gathering for the case. And then there had been one occasion when Dennis had spent the night on Janet's couch. She still remembered the sound of his breathing while she lay unable to fall asleep in her own bed. When she woke up the next morning, Dennis was gone, leaving her with nothing more than speculations as to what might have happened had she acted differently.

"Have a seat on the couch," Janet offered. "I'm going to get plates from the kitchen."

A few moments later they were gathered on Janet's couch, digging into Dennis's pizza. "This is what we've got so far," Laskin began. "While attending the Bostoff wedding, Janet and I established that Muller is dating Aileen Finnegan." Laskin paused to chew the last bit of his pizza slice.

"Peter, didn't your parents teach you that it's rude to talk with your mouth full?" asked Dennis, tilting the beer bottle to his lips.

"Dennis, I think that you will forgive my faux pas once you learn what Janet and I have discovered." Laskin paused for emphasis. "Aileen Finnegan is the daughter of New York Attorney General Cornelius Finnegan."

"Janet already told me about that."

Laskin continued unperturbed. "Excellent. Nonetheless, this important piece of information warrants repeating, as it is vital to the premise of our case. From Aileen Finnegan I learned that Muller has established a charity, Phoenix Fund. Apparently, all proceeds go to funding education efforts in the area of finance."

Dennis yawned. "How noble of him."

"That was precisely the reaction Janet and I had. Muller does not strike me as the charitable type. So, I've begun the process of looking up trading activity for Phoenix Fund. The analytics will take some time, but I hope to have some data for us to look at in about three to four weeks."

Dennis groaned. "Three to four weeks? For all we know, Muller could be brewing something this very moment. In two weeks he could be gone to the Bahamas or Mexico."

Laskin threw up his hands. "You've got a better idea?"

"Tell me more about this Aileen Finnegan character. What's she like?"

"Average-looking, not the type of girl that Muller usually dates," Janet cut in. "And I don't think he likes her very much. I'm pretty sure that the only reason he's dating her is her father."

"What makes you so sure?" Dennis asked.

Janet paused; she didn't exactly feel comfortable about summarizing Muller's attempts to pick her up.

"Muller was flirting with Janet," Laskin offered. "It was quite obvious, and in my mind extremely rude to his date.

Dennis's eyes lit up. "Oh, was he?"

"It was nothing like that, Dennis." Janet had had it with Dennis's sarcastic comments. After all, Laskin and Janet were the ones who had found the information about Muller, and Dennis was just being sore for having missed out on the action. "We danced to a couple of Frank Sinatra songs, but that was it. Muller told me about his charity. His overall demeanor made it clear that he did not really care for his date." Janet halted, reluctant to reveal the more sordid details of her conversation with Muller.

"The two of them danced for quite a while, so I had to keep Aileen occupied," Laskin added.

"Excellent. And did you by any chance get Aileen's phone number?"

"As a matter of fact I did. I told her that I had an information security consulting business, and that I was looking for PR representation."

Dennis rubbed his forehead. "Jeez, Peter, couldn't you have come up with something more upbeat? An online pet supplies store would have been a far better choice."

"Janet didn't think there was anything wrong with an information security consulting business cover."

Dennis glanced at Janet, and she shrugged. She really did not see a difference either way and thought that Dennis was just gloating.

"Never mind. Have you called her yet?" asked Dennis.

Both Janet's and Dennis's eyes focused on Laskin who had suddenly turned crimson red. "Well, no. I thought it would be best for us to meet first and decide on the course of action."

Dennis shook his head. "I can't believe we're even discussing this. Look, Peter, it really is quite simple. When you get home tonight, dial Aileen's number and ask her out."

"What if she refuses?" Laskin asked feebly.

"If she refuses, we'll explore a different avenue. But right now this seems like our surest bet." Dennis eyed Laskin suspiciously. "You're not actually attracted to this girl, are you, Peter? Because if you are, we'd better come up with something else. We can't afford to botch this."

Laskin straightened up with indignation. "Unlike you, Dennis, I don't run after every skirt that walks by."

"Then what are you waiting for? Get out there and find out everything you can about her!" Dennis clasped the lapels of Laskin's jacket and steered him toward the door. "We'll reconvene here in a week's time," he added as he shoved Laskin out the door.

"Well, I think that went well," said Dennis after Laskin was gone. "We're off to a great start."

"Sure, but I think we could have discussed a few more details, like where should Laskin invite Aileen, as well as make sure that he has a sound cover."

"Laskin is a pro at this kind of thing. He'll be fine."

Janet raised an eyebrow. "Didn't you tell me that Laskin sucked when it came to field work? And that his best strength is being stuck behind the desk?"

"He used to suck, but he's learned a lot from me, and he is a lot better now. I mean he has to be, or why would you pick him over me as your wingman?"

Janet groaned. "Is that why you kicked Peter out? To bicker over this nonsense with me? I already told you why: I thought you'd be otherwise engaged. And, as it had turned out, Laskin is pretty good in the field."

The hurt expression on Dennis's face made it clear that Janet's remark had hit him hard. "Better than me?"

"Do you really expect me to answer that? Come on, Dennis, you know better than that. Right now is not the time for us to fight among ourselves. Alex is breathing down our necks, and Muller's got Finnegan in his back pocket. Unless we act together, we don't stand a chance."

"What was that about Alex breathing down your neck?" Dennis took a step closer to Janet. "I don't think I like the sound of that," he added, taking another step closer to her, too close for Janet's taste.

"Enough, Dennis! I thought this was important to you. I thought you wanted to get back at them for what they did to Ham, for what they did to our case and our careers."

Dennis straightened up, taking a step back. "Of course I do. But I need to know that you're with me, Janet. I need to know that you're not falling in love with Kingsley all over again."

"Are you kidding me? Is your opinion of me that low? I might have been a fool for falling for him once, but not twice. I thought we've been over this already."

"We have, but I need to be sure." Dennis rubbed his forehead. "I need to know ..."

Dennis halted, and Janet held her breath. Was he going to say it? Could it be that he too felt the same way as she did? "I need to know that you're my partner, Janet," came Dennis's words.

Doing her best not to sound disappointed, Janet reassured him. "I am your partner, Dennis. You know that."

"I do now." Dennis stood up. "I'm sorry about this. I didn't mean to make a scene."

"That's all right. I've got your back, Dennis, and now I know that I can trust you with mine."

"You mean to say that you doubted me before?"

"Let's just say that I wasn't sure about your priorities, but I'm sure now."

"Good night, partner."

"Good night, Dennis."

Janet shut the door behind Dennis and pressed her back against it. Then she groaned with exasperation. "Good night, partner" were not exactly the words she wanted to hear from Dennis Walker, but apparently that was all she was going to get out of the man.

Chapter Twenty

Peter Laskin stared at his watch. He was supposed to meet Aileen Finnegan for drinks in exactly one hour. How hard could it be to take a woman out? The answer of course depended on who was being asked the question. If the question were directed at Dennis Walker, the answer would most likely be "a piece of cake" or something to that effect. But if the question were addressed at Peter, the answer would be "nerve-wracking," especially when the outcome of the said invitation could impact Peter's career. Peter had never been a ladies' man, so the idea of using his male magnetism on Aileen Finnegan in order to get the needed evidence on Muller was as appealing to Peter as getting his chest waxed, not that he had ever waxed his chest, or planned to. He would rather spend hours behind his desk, analyzing rows of data, than take his chances romancing Aileen Finnegan.

"Damn you, Walker," Peter muttered. Despite the constant jabs, both Peter and Dennis had mutual respect, at least Peter hoped so. While he might not approve of all of Dennis's investigation techniques, Peter recognized the results that Dennis achieved—the man had great instincts, and he had closed more investigations than anyone in the department. Still, Walker's laurels did not give him the right to pressure others into adopting his tactics. Peter was particularly pissed off at Walker for putting Peter on the spot in front of Janet. But then the reason for Walker's behavior was only too obvious: despite his numerous conquests, Walker had been pining for Janet ever since Janet had joined the department, and probably from even before then, since the time Walker had been assigned to an undercover job at Bostoff Securities. An assignment that was supposed to be Peter's but had been snatched from under his nose by Walker. Not that Peter held a grudge against Walker, at least not for this particular incident. Despite the fact that most of the time all the attention was undeservedly lavished on undercover specialists, Peter liked working behind his desk. His analytical skills were his strongest point, and he was quite content with shining behind the scenes.

So why on earth had he allowed Walker to bully him into romancing Aileen Finnegan? Peter did not really have an answer to this question—at least not the answer he was willing to admit. The embarrassing truth of the matter was that Peter liked Aileen, and part of him actually wanted to take her out, albeit under a different set of circumstances. True, she was no supermodel, but to Peter's mind supermodels only looked good on TV, and even that was not always the case. But when it came to real women, Peter liked them to be, well, real. And Aileen was most definitely real. Some would argue that she was a bit too plump, but Peter liked it when a woman had some meat on her bones. He also liked it when a woman was genuine and sincere, and Aileen seemed to encompass all of these characteristics. In fact her only flaw was that she was foolish enough to fall for David Muller. Had Peter been left to his own devices, he would have liked to ask Aileen out, and he certainly would not make David Muller the subject of their conversation. But as things stood, Peter would be forced to do just that. Even worse was the fact that he had lied to her about his name: John Carry—what an idiotic moniker! Unfortunately that had been the combination that popped into his mind when he had to come up with an alias for himself at the Bostoff wedding, and now he was stuck with it. The lying made Peter feel even guiltier about using Aileen in order to get to Muller, but that was not the end of his worries. What if he grew to like Aileen even more? And, even worse, what if she grew to like him? What was he to do then? Manufacturing elaborate cover-ups was not Peter's forte; in fact, the prospect of such activity seemed torturous to him. That's it, Peter thought grimly as he rose from his desk, I'll have this one date with her, and after that, Walker can date her himself if he wants to.

☙❦

Aileen Finnegan applied a powder puff to her face with trembling fingers. What was she doing going on a date with another man when she was in a relationship with David? She for one did not have an answer to this question. It all had happened so quickly that she barely had time to think. In the middle of a busy work day, her phone rang. The number on the caller ID was unfamiliar, but she picked up, thinking that it might be a new business prospect. Her guess had turned out to be correct; well, sort of.

"Aileen?" the voice on the phone asked tentatively.

"Yes?"

"This is John Carry. We were sitting at the same table at the Bostoff wedding."

And we also danced two foxtrots, Aileen thought, her memory of the occasion springing up with crystal clarity, in fact too much clarity for her taste. She had been upset by David's abominable behavior, and she had wanted to do something, anything, to spite him, so she had danced with this John Carry character who kept pressing her against him rather closely, too close in Aileen's opinion, but she had not resisted. Had in fact gone along with it, allowing this stranger she knew nothing about whisper pleasantries in her ear, and had given him her business card to boot. The next morning David apologized to her for his behavior, blaming it on work-related stress, and Aileen's world became perfect again—well, almost perfect. She had forgotten all about John Carry but, apparently, he had not forgotten about her. "Yes, of course, I remember," Aileen managed.

"You are probably wondering why I'm calling. I was wondering if I might ask you for a bit of professional advice."

"Yes?"

"I remember that you mentioned that you run a public relations company. I recently started an information security consulting business, and I was wondering if perhaps you could share some PR pointers with me."

Aileen resisted the irritation in her voice. When it came to her job, people often thought that she was the jack of all trades; to most, PR was PR was PR, but in reality public relations was a specialized trade just like any other profession. Aileen's specialty was with non-profit and cultural institutions. Her clients ranged from kindergartens to boarding schools to universities to foundations, but never once had she represented an information security consulting business. She literally would not know where to start. "John, I'd love to help you, but unfortunately my specialty is in a different area. I don't know much about information technology or computers. Heck, sometimes I can't figure out even my own computer," Aileen exaggerated, eager to bring this conversation to an end.

"Well, I could certainly help you there. And while I appreciate that you may not work with information technology companies every day ..."

Try never, Aileen thought.

"I would greatly appreciate any kernel of insight that you could spare. Dinner will be my treat."

How presumptuous, Aileen fumed inwardly. To think that she would agree to have dinner with a man she barely knew, but the invitation was also flattering. It was not as though men were lining up to ask her out on dates, but then this would not even be a date, but a business meal, not that Aileen would have anything valuable to contribute to the business matter at hand, but that was irrelevant, as John was clearly eager to see her, her lack of expertise on the subject notwithstanding. Come to think of it, her evenings looked pretty empty: David had said that he would be working late and had cancelled their dates for the week. Apparently, he had time to see her father: a disconcerting detail that Aileen had learned from her father when he told her that he had dinner plans with David. Lately it seemed that David spent more time with her father than he did with Aileen. "Very well," Aileen agreed. "But don't be surprised to leave the dinner none the wiser, as I am afraid that I won't be able to provide much insight for your venture."

"Oh, I think you're being overly modest. In fact, I'm sure of it. Do you like steak?"

"Yes," Aileen admitted. She had been staying clear of red meat for the past few months, but suddenly the idea of a splurge seemed like a good one. If she was going to sneak behind David's back, she would do it while eating steak, not munching on some low-fat crap she had been living on for what now felt like an eternity.

"So, how about seven p.m. on Wednesday at Del Frisco's?"

"Are you sure? Their steak is not cheap, and I do like meat."

"Positive. I have a feeling that it will be well worth my while."

"You said it; just don't be disappointed if it turns out to be otherwise. See you on Wednesday."

"Until Wednesday."

But now that Wednesday was actually here, Aileen did not feel nearly as confident as she had been while chatting up John Carry over the phone. But then this was hardly surprising to her. The phone had always been her favored means of social interaction: engaging in flirty banter over the phone was one thing, but acting with the same cool, collected demeanor while staring into the man's eyes from across the table was quite another.

Half an hour later, Aileen walked into Del Frisco's. It was seven p.m. on the dot. She inwardly cursed her ingrained punctuality. It was a professional habit of hers to always be on time for client meetings, but this meeting was not exactly a client meeting. In fact, she did not know how to categorize it. Please be here, she sent a mental plea to John Carry. The reality of meeting a man she had shared an overly close embrace with while dancing at the Bostoff wedding was bad enough; the prospect of waiting for him by the bar alone was mortifying.

"Aileen, I'm so glad that you could come." John Carry intercepted her before Aileen reached the hostess.

"Hello. I said I'd come." Aileen smiled, instantly relaxed by John's eagerness.

"Thank you. I promise you won't regret it."

"Oh, I'm sure I won't. The steak here is delicious."

The hostess escorted them to a window table. The dining room was crowded, and Aileen noted with a mark of approval that they were given a table that could seat four; at least John Carry was not skimping on the details.

"Would you like to start with a cocktail?"

Aileen almost blurted out that she would stick with water, which was what she had been doing in her relentless weight loss crusade, but then changed her mind. This morning, the scale had showed her the lowest number ever, and she thought that it was time for a little break. "I'll start with an apple martini."

"Sounds excellent. I'll have the same."

"So, John, how can I help you?" asked Aileen after the waiter had taken their orders.

"Well, Aileen, it is really quite simple. I have been an information technology professional for almost fifteen years. It has always been a dream of mine to branch out on my own, and now I am finally ready to go out and do it."

170

Aileen frowned. "Ready to go out and do it? I thought that you already had an IT company?"

John smiled apologetically. "I might have exaggerated a bit. I do have a company, that is on paper, but that's as far as I've gotten. It turns out that the whole business of getting clients is much more complicated than I anticipated."

"Do you at least have a website?"

"I'm working on it."

Aileen's frown grew deeper. Either this John Carry character was not giving her the whole picture or he was a complete imbecile, and he just looked too intelligent to be an imbecile.

"Perhaps I should be completely honest with you ..."

"That would be a good start."

"It is true that I have always wanted to start my own business, but my decision has been ... how should I put it ... a bit precipitated. You see, I got laid off from my job."

Aileen felt an immediate pang of remorse. The poor guy had come out on a limb, springing for a swanky dinner at Del Frisco's in hopes of getting some pointers from her, and there she was, giving him a hard time. She would tell him everything she knew, and she would pick up the tab.

"I'm so sorry, John. I didn't mean to sound condescending or anything. Please, go on. I think there are a few things that I'll be able to help you with after all."

"This pretty much sums it up. I'm still job hunting, but there seems to be nothing out there, so I thought I'd try to get my own business going instead."

"And what company did you work for before?"

"Oh, just a mid-size IT company. We pretty much offered services to clients across all industries. Of course the big firms that have their own IT departments would never hire us, but the smaller firms that outsourced this sort of thing did. I've worked on systems for small financial firms, marketing agencies, and even some non-profits."

"Non-profits? I think I could help you there. Non-profit organizations are my specialty; I could recommend you to my clients. But first we need to get the basics set up."

Over dinner, Aileen proceeded to explain the importance of having a company website and gave John ideas on affordable advertising such as reaching out to the local newspaper and contacting the local Chamber of Commerce representative, for which Aileen happened to have the contact information. To her, these pointers were the basic postulates of a marketing plan for a successful business, but to John Carry they seemed to be pearls of wisdom, a reaction that Aileen found very flattering.

When Aileen reached for the bill at the end of meal, John refused to hear of it.

"I invited you, Aileen, and I intend to take care of the check," he replied solemnly. "I may be out of a job but I have not sunk so low as to be forced to forsake my manners."

Aileen blushed. "Thank you, John. I only hope that the information I gave you will be helpful enough to cover the cost of this dinner."

"Oh, I am sure it will be. But to me, that is irrelevant."

After John settled the bill, he helped Aileen with her coat, and they headed toward the exit.

"Thank you for a wonderful dinner," said Aileen once they were standing outside.

"Thank you, Aileen." John paused, suddenly looking hesitant. "I don't suppose you would be free to see me next week?"

"Why ever not?"

"I thought that your boyfriend might object."

"My boyfriend? I have lots of male clients," Aileen replied gaily. "If my boyfriend were to object, he would have been driven mad with jealousy by now. But he seems to be too busy with his own affairs to pay me much mind, but somehow he always finds time to see my father."

"Your father?"

"Yes, my father, the famous Cornelius Finnegan."

"The state attorney general?"

"That's right. I might as well put it out on the table since that's the question everyone asks me when they meet me for the first time."

John coughed embarrassedly. "Oh, excuse me. I didn't mean for it to come out like that. I was merely trying to point out that it's a good thing that your boyfriend is getting along with your father."

"Oh, they get along all right. Sometimes I wonder which one of us David is really dating," Aileen halted, cursing her uncontrolled blabber. It was the apple martinis combined with the bottle of red that followed afterwards sneaking up on her.

John smiled, not at all abashed by Aileen's frankness. "So are you free this Friday night?"

Aileen considered her options. Her Friday evening loomed wide open, courtesy of David cancelling another one of their dates. She could spend the evening organizing some silly social event for the club with her mother, or she could do something fun. "I'm game if you are."

"Excellent, so I'll see you Friday."

Chapter Twenty-One

Peter Laskin stared at the data on his computer screen: there was enough evidence to launch an insider trading case against David Muller and his sham of a charity, Phoenix Fund. Normally, Peter would have been pleased. Right now, however, he was not happy about this fact in the least. Instead, for the first time in his life, he wished he had failed at his job.

Over the course of the past two weeks, Peter had had three dates with Aileen. To be fair, their meetings were not exactly dates. Nothing of a physical nature had happened between them: Peter had not tried to kiss Aileen or even so much as hold her hand. But there had been flirtation in their conversations, and he enjoyed spending time with Aileen much more than he liked to admit. The latter realization was now causing him great conflict and discomfort.

In an hour's time, Peter was due at Janet Maple's apartment to share his findings on Muller with her and Dennis. Already, Peter had more than enough information on the trading activity of Phoenix Fund to prove that David Muller was acting on insider information. Phoenix Fund had been actively investing in options positions in manufacturing stocks, a strategy that in and of itself would hardly raise suspicion had it not been for the specific investment choices favored by Phoenix. The two companies that Phoenix invested in, Orion and Hudson Steel, were obscure mid-size firms that had experienced a sudden jump in earnings and stock value after winning large manufacturing contracts with Rover Industries, a major industrial conglomerate. Both times Phoenix had reaped enormous profit on its investment. Phoenix also had investments in other sectors of the market, such as the S&P index and the Dow Jones, as well as several blue chip stock and some bonds, but those were generating very modest returns. It was almost as though these additional investments were meant to act as decoys, and Peter had caught the drift right away. Granted, had he not been spending as much time with Aileen Finnegan as he had been, it might have taken him a bit longer to solve the puzzle, but with Aileen's unwitting aid he had been able to get to the heart of the matter in no time.

The minute Aileen had mentioned that Muller was spending a lot of time with her father, Cornelius Finnegan, Peter's ears had prickled with suspicion. Cornelius Finnegan was a very powerful man—what reason could he possibly have to spend so much time with Muller? There had to be more weighty reasons than the mere fact that Muller was dating Finnegan's daughter. The Treasury Investigations department had a background search software that could find links between people based on common factors. The search process, however, was far from easy: the software produced many false positives that one had to sift through before unearthing relevant results, if any at all. Most investigators, including Dennis Walker, eschewed the software due to its tediousness. Peter, on the other hand, was of a different opinion. Over the years he had perfected his search skills, and there were many times when he had unearthed key evidence for investigations through the background search software. That was the tool he turned to this time as well. The way he saw it, he had three leads: David Muller's investments in Orion and Hudson Steel stocks through the Phoenix Fund, David Muller's connection with Finnegan, and Orion's and Hudson's connection to Rover. If Peter's hunch were correct, there had to be a link connecting the three leads.

Peter's first step had been to identify the top executives of Orion and Hudson Steel and see if there were any links between those individuals and Finnegan or Muller. The search had come up empty, but Peter had half-expected it to be so; he had simply started with Orion and Hudson because these companies had a smaller universe of executives to search than Rover. Peter's next move was to search the backgrounds of the top executives of Rover. After the search of the company executives did not produce any results, Peter's zeal was beginning to cool, as he began to wonder whether he had indeed been mistaken. Just to dot all the i's and cross all the t's, Peter did a search on the board members of Rover. His last search had been on the newest board member, Kevan Magee, and that was when Peter struck gold: it just so happened that Kevan Magee and Cornelius Finnegan had gone to the same Catholic school. Finally, Peter had the connection he had been looking for: Magee was Finnegan's and Muller's informant.

The data that Peter had gathered so far would certainly provide strong evidence to prove the insider trading link between Magee, Finnegan, and Muller, but Peter would be first to admit that the evidence was far from being ironclad. It could take years to prove that Muller's trades on behalf of the Phoenix Fund were indeed based on Magee's tips, and it would be even harder to prove Finnegan's involvement. If only there was a way to show evidence of interaction between the three men ...

The worst part of the matter was that Peter knew just how to procure such evidence, but the fact that he had learned of it from Aileen made him reluctant to use it. During their last meeting, Aileen had mentioned that Muller was going to have a meeting with her father this Saturday. She had mentioned the matter jokingly, but there had been bitterness in her voice when she remarked that she had again been stood up by Muller in favor of her father. What matter could Finnegan possibly have to discuss with Muller on a Saturday night? Peter had wondered. When he attempted to broach the matter with Aileen, she had replied that it was business related and that she kept out of Muller's business affairs. It had taken all of Peter's self-control not to press the subject further.

Peter's usual course of action would have been to share his findings with Dennis and Janet, but when it came to his meetings with Aileen, he had done no such thing. Instead, Peter had done the unthinkable: for the first time in his life he had concealed information from his colleagues. Oh, he had shown Dennis and Janet the trades that Muller had run through the Phoenix Fund, but he had said that the background search on Rover's executives did not produce any leads to Finnegan or Muller. Deep down he knew that he was doing something wrong. He did not want to obstruct the investigation, but neither did he want to help it along at the expense of his own happiness. He liked Aileen, and he could tell that she liked him too. Each time they met, the chemistry between them seemed to grow, and who knew what it could lead to eventually? From what she had told him, Aileen had been head over heels in love with Muller at the beginning, but Peter could tell that she was starting to become disheartened by Muller's negligent treatment. Peter, on the other hand, was lavishing Aileen with attention. True, he could not compete with Muller's riches, but he could make Aileen feel like the most beautiful woman in the world. Why should he lose what he could have with her because of some stupid investigation? He had solved hundreds of cases, and what did he get as a reward? Being called a geek by Dennis Walker, who received all the accolades for Peter's backbreaking work behind the scenes. No, he had decided, if Dennis wanted to solve this case he would have to get his hands dirty and do the background search on Rover's executives himself. Rationally speaking, Peter knew that his protective attitude toward Aileen was compromising his duty. In his defense, he did not intend to hinder the investigation, but he liked Aileen and he did not want to hurt her.

෬⊙രൠ

Alex Kingsley leaned back in his chair and propped his feet on his desk. His new job as the head of the Treasury Investigations department was turning out to be a very nice gig indeed. He got to boss people around all day, and the best part of it was that there was no one to boss him around. Aside from having to report on the department activity to Finnegan every other week, Alex did not have to answer to anyone. And this was only the beginning. Finnegan was bound to move up the political ladder, and as his trusted protégé, Alex would follow Finnegan's trail. Who knew, a few years from now Alex could very well be the next attorney general—he certainly had the credentials for the job. The key was to keep Finnegan satisfied, and that meant not questioning Finnegan's motives, even in Alex's own thoughts. To say that Alex did not find Finnegan's keen interest in the doings of the Treasury Investigations department odd would be an understatement, but at the moment Alex did not see a way of gaining from his suspicions. "At the moment" was the key element in the current state of things: a few years from now, should Finnegan fail to reward Alex's loyalty, Alex might very well remind Finnegan of the rendered services. But for now Alex had to focus on supplying Finnegan with the requested information. And that meant keeping a watchful eye on each and every investigator in the department.

Alex was fairly certain that he had gauged the characters of the majority of his employees. There was, however, one exception: Dennis Walker. The so-called star investigator of the department was the only possible rebel and the source of Alex's worries. Alex was certain that the others were too mousy to defy him; even Janet, who had been so defiant at the beginning, had seen the light and became his informant. Alex smiled at his victory: subjecting Janet to his will gave him a new thrill that exceeded that of sexual attraction. It pleased him to know that she was within his grasp once again, and he could do with her as he pleased. It amused him to play the game of cat and mouse with her: he would ask her out, she would refuse, he would ask her again, and so on. For now he accepted her excuses, content with her usefulness as the office spy, but he would reclaim his prize soon enough, not because he wanted her but because he could have her.

Still, one must not get drunk on power. While he was ninety-nine percent certain of his influence over Janet, there was still that one percent of doubt that Alex reserved in all of his personal dealings. To check for any possible omissions in Janet's reports, Alex had requested Georgiana to run a report on the log-ins into the department's background search software. The background search software was a nuisance to use; Alex had used a similar version at the onset of his investigative career at the DA's office but had quickly abandoned the use of this cumbersome tool. But just because the system was a nuisance did not mean that Alex could not use it for his advantage.

Alex examined the report on his desk that summarized the employee log-ins since the time Alex assumed his position at the Treasury: Alex figured that anything that happened before his arrival was not his responsibility, but if anything went amiss afterwards, Finnegan would be sure to skin Alex alive. Alex was looking for any unusual spikes. He quickly leafed through the log-ins for Laskin and other data analysts who used the software on a daily basis. The list was structured alphabetically, and Alex's attention turned to the letter w. Dennis Walker was the last employee on the list. A deep crease appeared on Alex's forehead. The log-in history showed that Dennis had hardly been using the system previously, but for the past few days he had been logging in for several hours at a time. Alex flipped to the section of the report that showed the subjects of the searches. Apparently, Walker had a keen interest in the backgrounds of the board members of company called Rover Industries. The name was vaguely familiar, and Alex typed it into the search engine on his computer. He soon learned that Rover was a major industrial conglomerate. Alex's lips drew into a sharp line: Janet Maple had not mentioned anything about an investigation into Rover in her report to Alex that morning.

"That lying bitch," Alex muttered, groping for the phone. He was going to get to the bottom of this right away. But before he could unleash his anger on Janet, the door of his office opened, revealing Georgiana on its threshold. Alex slammed the phone receiver down. "What is it?"

"Are you happy with the report that I got for you earlier?" she asked. "I must say that that system is a real pain to use."

"Huh?"

"I said that that system is a real pain to use, and you haven't even said thank you," Georgiana pouted.

Normally, Georgiana's pout never failed to elicit a smile from Alex, but right now it produced nothing but annoyance in him. For all her time working as his "assistant" this was the only job-related task he had asked of Georgiana, and the girl had the nerve to complain. Meanwhile, he did not see her complaining about her fat salary.

"I'm sorry to hear that, Georgiana. Perhaps you should try to become more proficient with the system, so that future requests would take less time to complete."

Georgiana's eyelashes fluttered. "Future requests?"

Suddenly, Alex felt very tired. A few moments ago the world had been his oyster, but now he felt that he was in over his head. The truth of the matter was that he had taken on a job that he had no idea how to do; he was hated by the majority of his direct subordinates, with maybe a handful being indifferent toward him; and with no one but a dumb hooker to back him up. Alex rubbed his forehead: he had to get his act together, fast.

"Alex, what's wrong?" Georgiana dashed across the room and was now kneeling by his chair, her hands groping for his fly, ready to do what she did best.

Alex pushed her away. "Not now, Georgiana. This is an office; we could get caught."

"That never stopped you before."

"We'll have to be more careful from now on."

But Georgiana was not easily deterred. Her nimble hands undid Alex's fly, sending a jolt of pleasure pulsating down his legs. The tension oozed from his mind, replaced by a pleasurable sensation that filled his limbs. Oh, what the hell, Alex thought. It was almost five o'clock anyway. He would deal with Janet Maple in the morning, and after that he would decide if the matter was worthy of Finnegan's attention.

ँ

It was five thirty, and Janet had one more task before leaving work for the day. The task involved visiting Alex's office, and she had been deliberately putting it off until after five in the hope of not finding Alex in his office. Earlier in the day she had given Alex another report on fictitious investigations that she and Dennis were supposed to be working on, and Alex had requested that she bring over the case files. Janet had spent several hours putting the files together (without any help from Dennis Walker, who was off doing who knows what who knows where, but that was another matter entirely), and now she hoped she would be able to leave the files with Alex's assistant without actually having to face the man himself. She grabbed the heavy binders and headed for Alex's office.

When Janet reached Alex's office, she saw that his assistant, who usually guarded the access to Alex's office like a sphinx, had already left for the day. The door to Alex's office was closed. Janet was about to leave when she noticed that there was light underneath the door. Janet sighed: she had promised to give the files to Alex today, and the last thing she wanted was for him to accuse her of not doing her job.

"Alex?" Janet knocked on the door. When she didn't hear a reply, Janet was about to walk away discreetly but the door gave way under her knuckles, cracking halfway open.

What she saw next made Janet wish she had imagined it. Georgiana was sitting on Alex's lap with her arms around his neck. At the sight of Janet, Alex pushed Georgiana off his lap, catapulting her several feet across his office.

"That will be all, Georgiana," said Alex in a voice that sounded as though Georgiana had just been performing some kind of benign clerical task for him, like taking shorthand.

"Yes, Mr. Kingsley." As she sashayed out of the office, Georgiana smiled at Janet.

"I didn't mean to interrupt," Janet stammered. "I can come back tomorrow."

"Interrupt what?" Alex stared her down. "You didn't interrupt anything. As a matter of fact, it's a good thing that you stopped by. I have a few questions I'd like to ask you."

"By all means," Janet said, struggling to keep the apprehension out of her voice. Questions from Alex at five thirty in the afternoon signified only one possible outcome: trouble. "I hope that I have the answers for you."

"I hope so too," said Alex, smiling.

Perhaps it was her imagination, but Janet thought that Alex's smile looked more like a scowl, as though he were taking a cue from the animal world, baring his teeth in the gesture of a threat. "What's going on?" Janet eyed Alex with what she hoped was cool nonchalance.

"What's Dennis Walker been up to?"

Janet felt an inner tremor. She had been feeding Alex with reports of fictitious investigations that Dennis and she were supposedly working on while in reality both of them had been spending most of their time gathering dirt on David Muller; or, to be more specific, trying to gather dirt on Muller, but unsuccessfully so. "As far as I know Dennis's caseload has not changed since the update I gave you this morning," Janet replied coolly.

"Are you sure about that?"

Janet felt Alex's dark eyes burrowing into her. It was almost impossible to believe that there had been a time in her life when she had found Alex's gaze to be sexy. Now, it filled her with a mixture of alarm and repulsion, akin to the sensation one felt when facing a cunning and dangerous beast, for in the world of the corporate jungle, Alex was the equivalent of a wolverine. Still, she could not very well give into her fear. "What makes you think otherwise?" Janet made a conscious effort to look straight into Alex's eyes, keeping her hands calmly pressed together on her lap.

"Oh, I don't know. It could be this." Alex flung a piece of paper across his desk.

"What is it?" Janet asked without reaching for the paper.

"It's a report on log-ins from the background search software. I had Georgiana run it for me this morning."

You mean to tell me that your assistant is actually capable of performing other functions than wearing revealing outfits and sitting on your lap? were the words on Janet's tongue, but she knew better than to voice them—she was in deep enough trouble already. Both Laskin and she had specifically cautioned Dennis against doing background searches on Muller. Instead, Laskin was to perform that part of the job, as Laskin was the only employee in the department who was on Alex's good side, if such a thing was possible. Most likely, it was just that Laskin's bland looks and boring personality had fooled Alex into indifference. But now Dennis had jeopardized the entire project with his pigheadedness.

"Why is Dennis Walker doing research on board members of Rover Industries?"

"Rover Industries? The name does ring a bell," Janet improvised. "Let me just check here a moment." Janet flipped open the folder that kept her past reports to Alex. There was no information there that she could use, but she made the gesture to give herself time to invent a plausible lie. "Oh, yes, I have it in my notes here. This is a new case. Dennis has just told me about it this afternoon. We received an anonymous complaint accusing Rover Industries' executives of tax evasion. Dennis is investigating it."

"An anonymous complaint? Are you telling me that you're squandering company resources on anonymous complaints?"

"The department policy has always been that all complaints have to be investigated. It's in the procedures manual."

"That's been changed effective immediately. No complainant, no inquiry, which means no investigation." Alex rose from his chair. "I want to see the Rover file closed by tomorrow morning. I trust you will take care of this, Janet."

"Yes, Alex."

"That'll be all for now. And Janet, going forward, I expect you to notify me of any new investigations immediately."

"Yes, Alex."

Her heart beating like a sledgehammer, Janet shot out of Alex's office. At the moment her only desire was to get her hands on Dennis Walker's neck and squeeze really, really hard. In her enraged state she stormed down the hallway, ready to storm the bastard's office. Most likely the bugger had gone home already, but she would give it a try anyway. A few steps before Dennis's office, Janet felt a male arm grip hers and almost screamed from the shock.

"Easy there, Janet. It's me, Dennis."

"You!!!" There were several words Janet would have liked to use to address Dennis but at the moment her mind went blank, and all she could manage to say was, "What are you doing here?"

"I work here, remember?"

"Do you?" she fumed.

"Easy there. What's eating you?"

"What's eating me? I've just been reamed by Alex and I had to stand there and come up with excuses for you."

"Shhh, calm down." Dennis grabbed her arm and pulled her inside his office, closing the door behind them. "Lower your voice. Now, what are you talking about?"

"What are you doing poking around Rover executives' backgrounds?" Janet hissed. "Didn't Laskin and I tell you to keep your hands off the background search system? Don't you know that the log-ins are traceable?"

"Actually, I didn't. I wish you would have told me that."

"I told you not to use the software!"

Dennis patted his chin. "That means I'm really on to something. Just wait till I tell you what I found—I bet you'll change your tune then."

"Change my tune? Now you listen to me, you …" Words failed Janet as she found herself powerless under the gaze of Dennis's triumphantly shining blue eyes.

"I'll listen later. Come on, we're going to see Laskin." Dennis grabbed her shoulders. "We don't want anyone to see us leaving together, so I'll meet you on the corner two blocks over from the office. Wait ten minutes before you leave."

"Enough! I won't go anywhere unless you tell me what was it you were hoping to discover through that search, Dennis. Laskin had already run the background search on Rover execs, and he did not find anything. He is the guru on dealing with that software. Do you seriously think that you could find something that Laskin did not?"

Janet might have been mistaken, but it seemed to her that a look of hurt flashed in Dennis's expression. For a moment she thought she might have been too tough on Dennis, but only for a moment. After the grilling Alex had just subjected her to, she deserved an answer.

"What were you looking for, Dennis?" she demanded.

"You'll find out soon enough, Janet. Now meet me outside, as we agreed," was all Dennis said and shut the door behind him.

Chapter Twenty-Two

"He'd better be there," Janet muttered as she walked over to the spot where Dennis had told her to meet him. And why was he calling the shots anyway? As if a ten-minute difference in their arrival was a major decoy. This had better not be a ploy to get rid of me, Janet thought, already regretting having let Dennis Walker out of her sight. The man was an irresponsible, cocky know-it-all, and that was putting it mildly. Whatever it was that Dennis had uncovered by running the background searches on Rover executives was not worth the jeopardy he had subjected his colleagues to by drawing Alex's attention to them. And it certainly was not worth Janet putting herself out on a limb to save Dennis's inconsiderate behind.

Janet eyed the street but saw no sign of Dennis. Typical, she thought, inconsiderate as always. Suddenly, a nasty thought crept into her mind. What if Dennis had indeed stood her up? What if the whole thing was a ploy for him to slip through her fingers so that he would be free to pursue his plans for the night undisturbed? By now he was probably at some bar, romancing the next soon-to-be ex-victim of his charms.

A cab pulled up next to the curb and the passenger door opened. "Get in."

"Dennis?"

"No, it's Prince Charming. Get in already!"

Janet climbed into the cab. "Don't you think we could have taken the train? Laskin is all the way down in Brooklyn."

"There's no time for the subway. The cab fare is on me."

"That's the least you could do after Alex chewed my butt out because of you."

Dennis frowned. "Chewed your butt out?"

Janet blushed. "You know what I mean."

"No, I don't. Did he make a pass at you again?"

Janet resisted the impulse to roll her eyes. For reasons unknown to her, Alex had been making passes at Janet since the day he became her new boss. As much as it would have pleased Janet's ego to think that Alex had recognized the error of his ways and wanted her back, she knew better. Besides, she would not take the two-timing bastard of a snake back if he begged her on his knees, not that he did, incidentally. But at any rate, Alex's sudden lust for her was not the issue at hand; rather, it was the motivation that drove Alex's attention back to Janet. What did the man want?

"No he didn't. But he really wanted to know what the hell you were doing running background searches on Rover's execs. And as a matter of fact I'd like to know as well. In fact, I think I have the right to know since I was the one who had to save your ass."

"You'll find out in due time." A grin of self-satisfaction glinted on Dennis's face, making Janet seethe with irritation.

"And when, pray tell me, might this due time be?"

"When we get Laskin to tell us what he's found out so far. And you won't even have to wait that long since we're already here," Dennis added smugly, handing the cab fare to the driver.

Dennis swung open the car door and jumped out on the pavement, holding a hand out for Janet to lean on. "My lady."

This time Janet permitted her eyes to roll, pushing his hand out of the way. If Dennis thought that his lame attempts at gallantry were going to get him off the hook, he had another thing coming.

This had better be worth it, thought Janet as she followed Dennis toward the stoop of the brownstone where Laskin lived.

Dennis pressed the intercom button. A few moments later, a tentative "Who is it?" was heard in response.

"Hey there, Peter. It's Janet and Dennis. Let us in."

Agitated shuffling erupted from the receiver. "I wish you would have called me. This isn't a good time for me, guys."

Dennis winked at Janet, as though implying that he knew something she did not. "We won't take long, Peter. Come on, you're not going to leave your colleagues standing out in the cold, are you?"

The intercom buzzed, and Dennis pushed the front door, holding it open for Janet. "Which is Laskin's apartment?" Janet asked.

"Six A. Up to the sixth floor we go." Dennis pointed to the staircase.

"No elevator? Great."

"Trust me, if my instinct is correct, and it usually is, the exercise will be well worth it."

"Trust you? That's the one thing that's becoming increasingly difficult to do," Janet retorted.

"After you, my lady." Dennis beamed, pretending not to have heard her.

Five minutes later Janet was panting for breath, unpleasantly aware of the perspiration mist on her back.

"Ready?" asked Dennis, who somehow managed to look as cool as a cucumber.

"I need to start doing more cardio," Janet gasped.

"See? There are benefits to this little excursion already."

The sign on the wall listed the location of the apartments by letters. A was on the right side of the floor.

Dennis rapped his knuckles on Laskin's door.

"I think we'll get a quicker response if we use the bell." Janet pushed the doorbell button.

"Have it your way."

189

There was a sound of hurried footsteps on the other side of the door, after which the door opened slightly, revealing Laskin behind it.

"I told you this isn't a good time!" Laskin mumbled, keeping the door half closed. "Can't this wait till tomorrow?"

"Procrastination is the mother of all vices."

"Huh?"

Before Laskin could react, Dennis jammed his foot in the doorway and shoved the door to the side with Laskin still clinging to the doorknob.

"Thank you for your hospitality, Peter." Dennis took off his jacket and hung it on a coat hanger. "Please, allow me," Dennis took Janet's coat off her hands.

"Take off your shoes!" Laskin demanded. "I just vacuumed."

Dennis strolled into the living room, ignoring Laskin's request. "Your obsession with cleanliness is unhealthy, Peter."

Janet had expected Laskin's apartment to reflect the man's personality, and in many ways it did. From the simple couch that occupied the majority of the living room, to the TV stand, to the small bookcase in the corner, everything was in pristine order with not a single object out of place. What Janet did not expect to see was a dining table romantically set with candles and crystal champagne flutes.

"Planning a party, are we? Or perhaps a tryst?" Dennis lifted one of the flutes and twirled it in his fingers.

"Put that down! It belonged to my grandmother." Laskin leapt across the room and attempted to pry the crystal out of Dennis's hands.

Dennis nimbly averted Laskin's grasp. Turning his back toward him, Dennis lifted the flute to his eyes. "Indeed, the workmanship is remarkable," he added, still holding the glass in his hand. "So, who is the lucky lady?"

"No one of any interest to you," Laskin snapped.

"You are being extremely rude, Peter."

190

"I'm being rude? You're the one who barged into my apartment, and now you're threatening to ruin my date."

Janet felt bad. From the amount of hours that Laskin spent at the office, she knew that he rarely got out. He was always taking on extra projects or volunteering to help other analysts on their cases. Janet guessed that Laskin did it so that he would not have to go home and be alone, and now that the poor guy had finally gotten a break, they were ruining Laskin's chances. "I'm sorry, Peter. We didn't know you were so busy. We'll come back later." Janet grabbed Dennis's arm. "Let's go."

Dennis took Janet's hand into his own and slowly loosened her grip. "Hold on, Janet. Tell me, Peter, why did you say that the search on Rover executives did not produce any leads?"

Janet was still recovering from the sensation of Dennis's hand holding hers, so it took her a moment to notice the crimson color of Laskin's face.

"Because ... Because it didn't," Laskin replied.

Peter Laskin was an excellent analyst who had many skills, but bluffing was not one of them. Janet glanced at the triumphant grin on Dennis's face—the man definitely knew something that she did not.

"Do you really like her that much, Peter?" Dennis glared at Laskin. "Is she more important to you than your friends?"

"Who?" Laskin's voice cracked. Obviously these two knew something that Janet did not; her eyes dashed from Dennis's stern face to Laskin's flabbergasted one.

"You are insulting my intelligence, Peter. But I'll spell it out for you if you wish. Aileen Finnegan."

"What about her?" Laskin whimpered.

"You've got the hots for her, that's what, and you're willing to jeopardize this operation to get laid. But I won't let that happen."

Janet eyed Dennis dubiously. Perhaps the man was getting paranoid. To think that the straight-laced, do-it-by-the-book Laskin was dating Aileen Finnegan was too much to believe.

"How did you guess?" Laskin croaked.

"It was not that difficult, Peter. The background search on Rover's executives showed that Kevan Magee and Cornelius Finnegan went to the same Catholic school."

"You ran the background search?" Laskin's voice was filled with reverent awe. "But you hate that software. You never use it."

"So you thought that you could hide the fact that Kevan Magee went to the same school as Finnegan?"

By now Janet had had enough. The entire situation was beginning to sound like an Agatha Christie mystery. "Who is Kevan Magee?"

"Kevan Magee is on Rover's board of directors," Dennis announced triumphantly. "Every single large contract that Rover signs has to be approved by the board of directors. Magee is leaking tips to Finnegan, and Muller is trading for them through his charity."

"But how do we prove that Magee is actually leaking the information to Finnegan and Muller?" Janet cut in.

"The timing of Muller's trades, for one," Dennis replied. "Phoenix Fund made killer profits on every single trade in stocks of companies that Rover awarded big contracts to."

"That's not enough," Janet argued. "We had far more evidence on Muller's shenanigans through Emperial and the case still got thrown out for lack for evidence. And now we won't just be going after Muller, we'll be going after Finnegan too, and we'll need bulletproof evidence."

"Precisely. And I think that Peter can help us with that."

Laskin threw up his arms. "What do you want me to say? I can't tell you anything more than you already know."

"Perhaps we should wait for your date to get here. She might have something to contribute to the matter." Dennis sat down on the couch. "Make yourself comfortable, Janet," he added, patting the seat next to him, "it's going to be a long night."

"Fine! I'll tell you," Laskin sighed. "But you have to promise to get out of here. And you have to promise not to hurt Aileen."

"Oh, man up, Peter! Do you think you are the only one who ever had to make a decision like that? How do you think I felt when I was doing undercover work at Bostoff? Janet was the assistant general counsel there. Do you think I liked the prospect of her being hurt by the investigation? No, siree, I didn't, but I did what I had to do, and things worked out in the end. You have to do what's right, Peter, even if it goes against your personal wishes."

"I'll tell you everything tomorrow. Aileen is coming over in less than half an hour. You've got to leave."

"So you'll have to make it quick then." Dennis clasped his hands behind his head. "What did she tell you so far?"

"Muller is being really mean to her. I think he's using her to get to her father. She said that sometimes she's not sure whether Muller is dating her or her father." Laskin slapped his mouth, looking like a man who said something he should not have.

"Really? How interesting. Did she by any chance say when they will be meeting next?"

"I don't know."

Dennis frowned. "Don't lie to me, Peter."

Laskin sighed with resignation. "Yes, she did. Her father is supposed to meet Muller this Saturday."

"Do you know where?"

"I don't know exactly, but I suspect that it might be at Keens since Aileen had mentioned that it's Finnegan's favorite restaurant."

"Do you think you could confirm that with her tonight?"

"I don't know. I'll try, but I can't promise anything. She might not want to talk about it."

"Now, Peter, have a bit more faith in your powers of persuasion. If she doesn't want to talk about her father, convince her to."

"I'll try."

"If you really like this woman, I hope that you'll be persuasive. On the other hand, we could forward the investigation to the Feds, and they will most definitely subpoena Aileen Finnegan for evidence."

Janet regarded Dennis with a shocked glance. He sounded so cold-blooded, so indifferent that she found it hard to believe that this was the same man she thought she knew.

Laskin hung his head with the look of a resigned man. "You'll get your information, but you have to promise me that you'll spare Aileen the indignity of being questioned by the Feds. She has no idea about the scheme that her father and Muller are running, so leave her out of this."

"I will do my best, Peter. But you have to get us the information that we need to solve the case."

Janet shifted her seat across the couch to be as far away from Dennis as possible. She did not want to be a part of any of this. As far as she was concerned there was no "us" when it came to her and Dennis Walker.

Laskin shook his head. "I guess I should have seen that one coming. In our line of work there are never any concrete promises. Serves me right for signing up for this charade in the first place."

Dennis got up from his seat and patted Laskin on the shoulder. "Cheer up, Peter. Things have a funny way of working out. There was a time when I had thought that Janet would hate me forever, but now we are not only colleagues but friends."

"I'm sorry, Peter," was all Janet could manage. She wanted Muller and Finnegan to get the punishment they deserved. Even more so, she wanted Kingsley to get his. But as much as Janet longed to bring these scoundrels to justice, she did not want to do it at the expense of an innocent woman.

"Oh, forget it. Once Aileen finds out the truth she'll never want to see me again. If you want to get the information you're after, you'd better get out of here and let me go on with my fake date."

Dennis squeezed Laskin's shoulder. "I appreciate your help, Peter. Believe me, I understand how difficult it is for you, but no one ever said that our job is easy."

Silently, Janet slunk after Dennis as he headed for the door. The emotions inside her were too conflicted for her to speak.

"I think that went rather well," Dennis remarked once they were standing outside of Laskin's building.

Janet's eyes flew wide open. "I think it was a horrible thing to do."

"A horrible thing to do?"

"Yes, a horrible thing to do. And even worse, you dragged me into it. If I knew about the stunt you were going to pull in there, there's no way I would have come with you."

"Are you telling me that having Muller get his justice served to him is a horrible thing to do? And let's not forget Cornelius Finnegan and his honcho, Kingsley. Do you think that these crooks should be allowed to remain in public office, free to do whatever they please?"

Janet felt Dennis's stare burrowing into her face. When she looked up, she was stunned to see that his eyes were filled with genuine bewilderment. Up until now, she had thought those blue eyes to be sexy, playful, and warm, but now she thought them calculating and hateful.

"I want Muller to get justice served to him as much as you do, probably more so. And God knows I have enough reasons to want to see Kingsley and Finnegan kicked out on their butts, but unlike you I still have some decency left."

"Decency left?"

"Yes, decency. Don't you think it's wrong to use that poor woman? Don't you even care about—" Janet cut herself short before she could blurt out what was truly on her mind.

"Care about what?" Dennis moved toward her, standing so close that she could feel the heat emanating from his skin.

Janet stared back at him. Don't you care about me? She wanted to scream. Didn't you care about me when you had me procure evidence for you for the Bostoff case? Or was I nothing but a source of information to you? But instead she said, "About the people involved."

"Of course I care. But Janet, one must consider the good of many versus the good of one person."

There, she had her answer. Janet hung her head to hide the tears that suddenly sprung up in her eyes. She felt like such an idiot. Why was it that she always ended up being attracted to the wrong guy? As it turned out, Dennis was no better than Alex. Dennis was just as ruthless and just as unprincipled. The only difference was that Dennis happened to play on a different side of the law—the side that just happened to be the right side—but the techniques that Dennis was willing to use to achieve his aim could hardly be called right.

"Do you think I like the idea of praying on the emotions of a lonely woman in order to get the evidence?" Dennis continued, oblivious to Janet's turmoil.

"I don't know. Do you?"

Dennis's expression darkened. "That was uncalled for. I think you know me better than that."

Do I? Janet wondered. At the moment, she had no idea who Dennis Walker was. "Do what you want, Dennis, but I no longer want anything to do with this case."

Chapter Twenty-Three

Dennis Walker pushed his laptop away and checked his watch. Instead of enjoying his Friday night, he was cooped up inside his apartment, waiting for Laskin to call. It was getting close: if Muller was indeed going to meet with Finnegan this Saturday, Dennis would need to know the place of their rendezvous right about now in order to make all the necessary preparations. Laskin was sure taking his time, but Dennis would be damned if he made the first move. This was just like playing the stare game: whoever blinked first, lost.

Laskin would call—Dennis was sure of it. Or at least he wanted to believe that he was sure of it because right now there were too many matters that he was unsure about. Like his investigation methods for one, and the reason he was in his profession for another. But right now was not the time to dwell on his doubts, just like it was not the time to think about the woman who had caused them: Janet Maple.

Is there nothing you would stop at to solve a case? she had asked him. Janet's outraged voice still rang in Dennis's ears, and the repulsed expression on her face hung before his eyes. The honest answer to Janet's question was no. No, he had stopped at nothing to solve a case until ... until he met Janet Maple. If Dennis had known about the havoc Janet would bring into his life, he would have run in the opposite direction from the Bostoff Securities undercover assignment. Laskin had wanted the job, but Dennis had snatched it from under his nose, and now Dennis was paying the price—had been paying the price ever since Janet Maple crossed his path.

Is there nothing you would stop at to solve a case? How could she ask him that when he had gone out on a limb in order to secure immunity for her and her friend Lisa during the Bostoff investigation? How could Janet doubt him when he had done everything he could to ensure that Jon Bostoff would receive credit for his cooperation with the investigation? Another investigator would not have cared, but Dennis had put his neck on the line because he wanted a just outcome for the investigation. Jon Bostoff's biggest offense was that he had been stupid enough to become Muller's pawn. And as for Janet and Lisa, they were simply in the wrong place at the wrong time. Muller was the true culprit.

Dennis had even gone as far as putting in a good word for Janet with his boss at the Treasury. After all, Dennis felt responsible for Janet losing her job as assistant general counsel at Bostoff Securities, so he had gotten her a job at the Treasury Investigations department—a job that he knew she would be good at. Was it easy for him to come to work every day and see the woman he wanted to do a number of things to in the bedroom but instead having his interactions with her reduced to no more than a handshake and an occasional kiss on the cheek? No, but he did it anyway because he was a decent guy. And what was his reward? The case against David Muller was thrown out for lack of evidence, and Jon Bostoff was made the scapegoat. Hardly the career-making achievement Dennis had hoped the Bostoff / Muller case would be. Not to mention that Dennis's boss was later fired to be replaced with the arrogant— and, as was now known, corrupt—Alex Kingsley. If this was not enough to make one go on the war path, Dennis did not know what was. He had thought that Janet was his wingman, but now that they were a mere hairbreadth away from getting the evidence they needed, Dennis learned that his wingman did not have his back.

Is there nothing you would stop at to solve a case? Dennis shook his head. At the time, his plan had seemed perfect. How could he have ever predicted that Laskin would lose his head over Aileen Finnegan? Laskin who was Mr. Do-it-by-the-book and was always so eager to get out into the field? And what did Laskin do the moment he got into the field? Messed up the entire case. But apparently Janet thought it forgivable for Laskin to compromise the investigation, accusing Dennis of being in the wrong.

The sound of Dennis's ringing cell phone jerked him out of his reverie. He looked at the caller ID and could not resist a grin of satisfaction when he saw Laskin's number. "Yes," was all Dennis said when he answered the phone, deciding to make Laskin squirm a little.

"Dennis, it's me, Peter."

"I know. I've got one of those caller ID things. What is it you want to tell me on a Friday night, Peter? Or are you calling to ask me out on a date?"

"I have the information you asked for, and I'd appreciate it if you'd put your sarcasm on ice for the duration of this conversation," Laskin said, his voice cool as a cucumber.

"You sure took your time getting me the information I need, so let's hear it before it becomes irrelevant."

"Muller is going to meet with Finnegan tomorrow at eight p.m. at Keens steakhouse. They will be sitting in a private dining room on the second floor."

"Excellent. Now why did you have to wait until Friday evening to tell me this valuable information?"

There was silence on the other end of the line, so Dennis furnished the answer to his own question. "Because you thought that if you waited this long I wouldn't have enough time to get the evidence I need. But you're wrong; I'll still get it. Thank you for your help, Peter." Dennis was about to hang up when

Laskin's pleading voice erupted on the other side of the receiver.

"Promise that you'll leave Aileen out of this!"

"I promise, Peter. If everything goes as planned, after tomorrow we'll have more than enough evidence for the case."

Dennis hung up the phone. Then he pulled up Janet's number and pressed the dial button. One, two, three rings—could it be that she was avoiding him? Of course Dennis could have called from a private phone line, but he was not going to use that option. If he was going to get Janet's help, he was going to get it with full disclosure, as she had requested.

"Why are you calling me?" Janet's ice-cold voice cut like a knife.

"Whoa, Janet. Good evening to you too." Dennis managed not to lose his cool. He had never heard her with such a tone of voice before. "Can you talk?" Dennis listened to the background noise in the receiver. Was she out with her girlfriends, being flirted at by some guys at a bar, or worse, out on a date?

"The question is not whether I can, but rather why should I want to?"

Fine, have it your way, Dennis thought. "Because, your royal ice highness, I have some valuable information that will help us solve the case, and I need your help."

"The amazing Dennis Walker needs someone's help. I never thought I'd see the day."

She was teasing him, and she was enjoying it. Dennis, on the other hand, was not enjoying this in the least; he hated it when people had fun at his expense. "Cut the crap, Janet. Do you want to put Muller away or what? Or perhaps you like the idea of working for Kingsley?"

"No, I don't. But neither do I like your unprincipled evidence-obtaining techniques."

"That's a long-winded phrase. Now, listen up. Here's the deal: Finnegan is going to meet Muller tomorrow at eight at

Keens. We need to get our behinds over there tomorrow to set things up."

"What is it you want me to do?"

"Nothing much; just wear a pretty dress and smile a lot. I'll take care of the rest. Do you think you could do that?"

"I can do a lot more than that. But before I agree to do anything, you have to tell me your plan. Assuming you have one, of course."

"Well, then, this should be a piece of cake. See you tomorrow in front of Keens at five p.m. sharp." Dennis hung up before Janet had the chance to unleash another one of her nasty remarks, which had been peppering her speech lately.

Chapter Twenty-Four

Janet surveyed her reflection in the mirror. She had on a red knit dress with a surplice neckline and a flared skirt. Her feet were clad in black high-heeled boots. She had spent close to an hour with a curling iron, cajoling her hair to fall down her shoulders in soft, voluminous curls; the process had been tedious but the result was definitely worth it. A coat of cherry gloss shone on her lips, and her eyelashes looked lush and long, courtesy of Estee Lauder mascara. She liked what she saw, even if she did say so herself.

With the amount of care she had put into her looks, one would think she was primping for a date. Instead, she was preparing for a work assignment, or at least she thought that she was going on a work-related assignment. Dennis had said that he had a plan, and Janet hoped that her efforts would pay off. The possibility of success seemed slim, but she had said yes nonetheless. To be more specific, she did not get a chance to say yes or no, as Dennis had hung up on her before she could reply. She had considered standing him up, which she was fairly certain would be a new experience for Dennis and would serve him right, but then decided against it. Her opinion of Dennis's tactics had not changed, but she worried that if left on his own, the man would ruin the investigation. At least this way, Janet would be there to contain him.

What a load of crap, Janet thought. The real reason she had spent close to two hours primping herself for her meeting with Dennis was because she wanted to see him, and she hated herself for it. Despite his questionable ethics—or to be precise, lack of such—she still turned to jelly every time she heard the man's voice or saw his unbearably handsome face. Janet puffed her cheeks with air and blew it loudly out of her mouth. Dennis Walker was the bane of her existence. Not only was the man endangering the investigation with his reckless attitude, he was clouding Janet's judgment with his good looks and smug yet somehow charming and irresistible demeanor. The man was a bona fide hazard.

Janet checked her reflection one last time. She could not remember the last time she had looked this decked out, which was another disquieting example of the power that Dennis Walker held over her. "This is for a work assignment. Our meeting will be purely professional," Janet assured herself. "Work assignment, my ass," she muttered, admitting the futility of her words. Sure, Dennis had asked her to look pretty, but there were many levels of pretty, and she had pulled out all the stops. Her heart was beating wildly, and her cheeks were flushed with anticipation. The truth of the matter was that, at the moment, she did not give a rat's behind about both Muller and Finnegan combined. All she could think of was that it was Saturday, and she was about to see Dennis Walker.

It was five minutes past five when Janet approached the entrance to Keens steakhouse. She eyed the dark, old fashioned façade, failing to find any signs of Dennis Walker. She looked around, unsure what to do. Dennis had said five p.m., and she had been purposely late by five minutes to ensure that he would be the first one to arrive.

Suddenly, she felt a hand on her shoulder.

"You're late," a familiar voice whispered into her ear.

The jolt that Janet felt pulsating down her spine was anything but work-related. "You're late yourself," she snapped at Dennis. "I got here first."

"I was waiting for you behind the corner. Being conspicuous is not my style."

Janet's cheeks grew warm. She was still a novice when it came to this whole undercover thing, and Dennis never missed an opportunity to remind her of the fact. Here was his chance to show her his skills. "So, are you going to tell me your plan?"

"Just follow my lead."

"Follow your lead? Dennis, you've got to tell me more than that!"

By way of an answer, Dennis grabbed Janet's hand and pushed the door open. "After you, my darling."

Bewildered, Janet almost slipped down the stairs that led into the dimly lit foyer. She felt Dennis's grip tightening to steady her, the effect of which was the opposite of the intended. It was bad enough that she was literally walking into another one of Dennis's questionable schemes blindfolded, his proximity was making it very difficult for her already unnerved brain to function.

"Let me help you with your coat, dear." Dennis placed his hands on Janet's shoulders while she shrugged out of her coat. "Stunning." Dennis eyed her dress as he took her coat from her.

"Thank you." Janet hoped that the surge of satisfaction Dennis's reaction had elicited in her was not written all over her face.

"Shall we?" Dennis nodded in the direction of the host's desk.

"Lead the way."

"Good afternoon," Dennis nonchalantly addressed the restaurant host. "My girlfriend and I would like to enquire about private dining."

The middle-aged, bespectacled host smiled at them benevolently. "Certainly, sir. We offer a number of banquet rooms ranging in size. May I ask the size of your party?"

Dennis glanced at Janet. "Oh, I'd say about twenty people."

The host nodded. "We have just the perfect room for you, sir. The Lilly Langtry Room. It seats twenty-five people comfortably, so you'll have some room to spare."

"Sounds wonderful," Dennis approved. "Would it be possible to see it today?"

The host scratched his head hesitantly. "There's an event taking place there tonight. I wish you would have called us to schedule an appointment."

"Oh, but couldn't we possibly see it tonight?" Janet managed in response to Dennis's hand squeezing hers. "You see, we drove all the way from Long Island. We are joining my aunt and uncle for a Broadway play later in the evening, so we thought we'd come into the City extra early to stop by here on the way. That's what the room is for—for my aunt and uncle's thirtieth wedding anniversary. They don't have any children, and we've always been so close. I so much want to make this a special occasion for them." Janet clasped her hands in a gesture of appeal, stunned by her ability to improvise. She was just as good as Dennis Walker.

The host shot them a sympathizing glance. "Very well. I suppose we could arrange for a quick walk through." He waved to one of the waiters standing nearby. "Fred here will give you the tour."

"Good evening. Please follow me." Fred smiled at them politely.

"Well done," Dennis whispered into Janet's ear as they followed Fred into the oak-clad interior of the restaurant. "Now, when we get inside the room, I want you to stick this into the wall paneling." Dennis shoved a metal object the size of a watch battery into Janet's hand.

Janet's earlier bravado evaporated. With the last bit of self-control, she placed her arm around Dennis's shoulder as though reaching to nuzzle his ear with her lips. "You want me to bug the room?" she hissed. "Are you insane?"

"Trust me, with that hot number you've got on, no one is going to notice. Besides, I'll distract them with questions."

"Distract them with questions? Are you out of your mind? Where did you get the bug in the first place? Is this even legal?"

"From Feds friends. We'll deal with the legal issues later."

Just then Fred turned around, and Dennis wrapped his arm around Janet's waist, pressing his lips against Janet's.

"Excuse me, but here we are," Fred announced, embarrassed.

"Thank you," Janet managed after Dennis's lips finally lifted away from hers.

The nerve of the man! What did he think this was, a James Bond movie? Oh, she was going to give him a piece of her mind the moment they were alone. The adamant, cocky, bastard who also turned out to be such a good kisser ... Her head was spinning with a mixture of vexing indignation and the intense pleasure that Dennis's kiss had sent ringing like bells throughout her entire body.

"After you, my dear." Dennis motioned at the room entrance with the ease of an experienced imposter.

"Thank you," Janet nodded, clenching the tiny metal bug in her fingers.

She had to get her head together. She'd be damned if she would let Dennis think that he had gotten to her. She was far from being a fan of Dennis's investigative techniques, but at the moment it did not matter. If she failed to do what he had asked her to do, he might think that she did so because of his kiss, and that was a much more mortifying possibility than the prospect of being fired or possibly even arrested for illegally planting a bug in a public place.

Janet stepped into the room. It was medium in size, with a large round table set up in the middle of the room.

"Do you like it, honey?" Dennis asked.

"It's lovely!" Janet exclaimed as she twirled her way around the room, fully aware of the skirt of her dress spinning around her legs.

"Excellent! She likes it!" Dennis repeated Janet's verdict as though it were an honor of great distinction. "And what is your earliest availability?" he asked Fred.

"Oh, I'm afraid you'll have to check downstairs regarding that," Fred answered. "They keep the schedule."

"Very well. And is there access for the handicapped? You see, my grandmother, she can only get around with a walker ..."

While Dennis peppered poor Fred with questions, Janet traced her hand against the wooden paneling. Then, ever so casually, she pressed the bug that she had been holding between her fingers into a tiny crack between the panels.

Mission accomplished, she thought as an intense torrent of emotions rushed through her. It was a mixture of excitement, fear, and triumph. She had just planted a bug in a restaurant, and she was as cool as a cucumber. Now she understood why Dennis did things the way he did. This was so much more fun than being stuck behind the desk in the office. Not that that made this kind of blatant disregard for the rules permissible, especially when their job was to uphold the rules, but she decided that she would think about that later. Right now she just wanted to enjoy the rush. Ever so discreetly she continued the languid motion of her hand to conceal her heart thumping with triumph.

"Honey, I think this is it." She linked her arm through Dennis's. "We'll be calling you shortly," she smiled at Fred.

"Wonderful."

Janet could barely contain her urge to jump up and down as she followed Dennis to the host's desk. I did it, I did it, I did it! Dennis Walker might have many faults, but there was no denying that he drove her to do things that she normally would never dare to do. Most of the time he drove her crazy but sometimes, like right now, he made her feel really, really good.

"Did you like the room?" asked the host.

"Very much so," Janet replied.

"Would you like to place a deposit then?"

Her composure was about to abandon her but Dennis came to the rescue. "We'd love to, but we have to be off or we'll be late, and my girlfriend's aunt and uncle are very punctual. We'll call you to finalize all the details."

The host nodded approvingly. "It's so nice to see close family ties. Whenever you're ready, but please be sure to give yourself plenty of time in advance. This place books up quickly."

Once outside of the restaurant, Dennis shot Janet a congratulatory glance. Her entire being wanted to shout hurray, but she knew better, and followed Dennis silently along the street.

"That was really great work in there, Janet." Dennis patted Janet's shoulder once they were several blocks away from the restaurant.

"Thanks." Janet had to exercise all her self-control to keep the disappointment she felt out of her voice. Was that all it was to him? Work? The intensity of his kiss still lingered on her lips and in her thoughts. A kiss like that could not have been just work, but then maybe to a man like Dennis Walker it was precisely that.

"You were pretty good in there yourself. So what do we do next?"

"We wait and listen."

"Wait for what?"

"Wait to see if our plan has worked. And if it has, we listen to what we're going to be able to hear through the bug that you planted. I have to say, when you made your skirt spin around you back there, I thought that poor Fred fella's eyes were going to pop out. Excellent move. I think you're a natural."

What about your eyes? Janet wanted to ask, but instead she remained silent and merely nodded in agreement.

"So, your place or mine?"

"What do you mean?" Janet blurted out before she could catch herself. Of course she knew what he meant. Your place or mine to listen to the stupid bug she had planted. Suddenly, she did not give a hoot about Muller, Finnegan, or even Kingsley. As far as she was concerned, the whole case could go down the drain; but she could not very well say that to Dennis, so instead she said, "Mine. This way I won't have to worry about finding a dog sitter for Baxter."

"Sounds good. I'll bring snacks."

Janet finally remembered the question she had been dying to ask Dennis all along. "How can you be sure that we got the right room?"

"I can't be sure, but it was our safest bet with the amount of time we had to get it done. Laskin had mentioned that Finnegan usually books a private dining room, and this was the smallest room at the restaurant. Granted, if you or I tried to book a room that seats twenty-five people for a dinner of three, we'd be told to get lost, but Finnegan holds far great clout than we do. Still, there's a chance that I was wrong, and he'll end up sitting in the general area, in which case we're screwed. But we could not very well go running all over the restaurant planting bugs. Besides, I only had one bug. The Feds are real stingy when it comes to sharing unauthorized resources."

"I hope you picked the right room. Otherwise, I've just put on the greatest performance of my lifetime planting that bug for nothing."

"It wasn't for nothing, Janet." The tone of Dennis's voice made Janet look up, but he quickly switched topics. "I'll see you tonight, partner."

"See you later."

Partner. The word made Janet want to seal her ears shut. To be fair, there is nothing offensive about the word partner in general, but when a man a woman likes a lot more than just a work partner uses it to address her, it is downright infuriating.

ෂාශ

As he watched Janet walk away from him, Dennis Walker was a knot of conflicting emotions. Part of him wanted to rejoice in the successful operation Janet and he had just pulled off, while another part of him wanted to kick himself for being such an idiot. Partner? Why on earth did he call her that when partner was the last thing he wanted her to be, especially after that kiss.

He would have liked to say that the kiss had been part of the cover-up, but he knew better. There were pretend kisses with lips barely touching, and then there were sexy, passionate kisses that swept you into a tide of desire. The kiss he had shared with Janet Maple was of the latter kind. The truth of the matter was that he had wanted to kiss her for a while—ever since he had first laid his eyes on her in the office of Bostoff Securities, to be precise—and today marked the limit of his longing. When he saw her in that red dress, her lips juicy and shiny, her eyes demurely lowered under her long, rich lashes, he snatched his moment. Of course there had been a risk of her slapping him and ruining their entire operation, but he had counted on Janet's work dedication, and he had been right. In fact, he was quite certain that the reason that Janet allowed him to kiss her stemmed from motivation that had to be greater than just work dedication. After all, not only had she allowed him to taste the softness of her lips, she had let his tongue caress her mouth and had answered him with equal passion. He had barely had the presence of mind to pull away from her and remember the task at hand. But now there was no danger of him jeopardizing their mission. After the way he had just acted, he was certain that his chances of getting closer than partner distance to Janet were close to nil.

But then maybe it was all for the better anyway. Dennis knew how to live his life the way it was: he worked hard and he partied hard. As long as a woman wanted to have a good time, he was up for the ride, but if she wanted more, he was out. Ever since his attempt at monogamy had failed, he considered that road closed for him. The trouble with Janet was that he wanted more than a good time from her, and he doubted he would know how to give or receive it.

Chapter Twenty-Five

David Muller placed his arm around Mila's warm, slender shoulders. To think that soon he would no longer have to part from her was almost too delicious a prospect, and the knowledge that it would soon be true made it even more wonderful. One last score, and I will be free, David thought to himself, running his fingers through Mila's silky hair. Tonight, he would meet Finnegan and Magee for dinner, and if there was one thing that David was certain of, it was that socializing was not the purpose of their get-together.

During the past few weeks David had finally found one thing in common with Finnegan: both of them had been waiting for Magee to tell them which automobile manufacturer would receive the contract from Rover. Magee had said that the pool had been limited to three companies: Stork Enterprises, Richardson Inc., and Valley Metals. But three was too big a number to gamble on, and David wanted specifics. He was fed up with both Finnegan and his needy daughter, but David could not cut his ties with either of them until he had the information he needed. After that, he would be set for a lifetime, and Aileen Finnegan along with her fat, controlling father would be history.

Then, just as David was about to lose his patience, Finnegan called him with good news. Magee had requested a meeting. Since the commencement of their partnership, David had met with Magee only a handful of times; each time, Magee had delivered vital information, which meant that this time, just like all the others, Magee would have big news as well. David was all set to act on Magee's information. He had opened numerous brokerage accounts for the Phoenix Fund, which would execute the trades according to his instructions, and the offshore bank accounts he had opened for himself would hide his proceeds along with those of Finnegan and Magee. For David did not intend to play fair. The pie was too large to divide it equally. Rather, he would have it all for himself. And if either Magee or Finnegan were to demand their share from him, the recordings of their previous meetings would guarantee David's security.

David checked his watch. It was seven o'clock. Just enough time to get himself in order before his meeting with Finnegan and Magee.

"Mila, I have to go."

"Um," Mila murmured, her face pressed into his chest. "I have to go to work too. Wake me up before you leave."

"Mila, wake up. There's something I have to tell you before I leave."

"What is it?" Mila mumbled.

"It's important, so listen up."

If there was one quality in Mila that David admired more than her looks and lovemaking skills, it was her ability to be constantly attuned to everyone around her, particularly her ability to be attuned to him. This time was no different. Noticing the ever slight change in his tone, Mila shot up in the bed.

"What's going on?" she asked without a trace of drowsiness in her voice.

"Mila, you know that safe that I had ordered for my study?"

"That ugly metal box?"

"Yes, that ugly metal box," David confirmed. "Although once you learn about its valuable contents, you may not think it so ugly."

David took Mila's hand into his and pressed it to his lips. He needed a moment. He was about to entrust Mila with information that without exaggeration would put his life into her hands. He had never trusted a woman or a man that much before. There he was, about to put his life into Mila's hands. He had deliberated his decision to tell her for weeks. The upcoming deal with Finnegan and Magee would be big, too big to go into it alone. David needed someone to have his back. Mila was the woman he wanted to spend the rest of his life with, so it only made sense that he should be able to trust her with his life. The realization of what he was about to do filled him with agony that bordered on pleasure, akin to the adrenaline rush he had felt when he had tried bungee jumping during college spring break. But now, unlike with a bungee jump, there was no safety cord tied to his legs.

"Mila, you know that I work with investments," David began.

"Yes, David. I know. If you need my help, I think I should be able to follow along. You may not remember, but I did major in finance back in Prague." Mila's deep blue eyes looked straight at him, as though accusing him of perceiving their owner as nothing more than a pair of killer tits and long legs.

"Yes, Mila, of course I remember. And I have no doubts that you'll be able to grasp what I am about to tell you."

"Whatever you need me to do, I'll do it," Mila said flatly.

The matter-of-factness of Mila's voice reminded David why he was so crazy about her. Mila might be one hot babe, but when it came to her brains she was more rational than any man. He could trust her.

"There are two business associates of mine who are about to supply me with very valuable information," David began...

About twenty minutes later, after he had finished his story, David searched Mila's face for signs of condemnation as he waited for her reply.

"Not to worry, David. Your information will be safe with me," Mila said simply.

"I knew it would be," he said, kissing her hand. "And when this is all over, we'll be able to go anywhere we want. Anywhere in the world—pick a destination and that's where we'll go."

"With you is the only place I ever want to be."

He had expected her to shriek with delight, sputtering out places like Paris, London, or Milan. Instead, her steadfast response nearly brought him to tears. This was a woman he would get the moon and the stars for.

"Mila, I promise you that once this deal is done, I'm going to marry you."

At eight o'clock sharp, David Muller approached the entrance to Keens steakhouse. Freshly showered and clad in his Zegna suit, he felt on top of the world. Finally, the deal he had been working on ever since his beneficial but highly onerous association with Finnegan began, was about to come to fruition.

"Good evening. I am here for the Smith party." David barely resisted a smirk at Finnegan's alias. One would think that a man occupying the position of the state attorney general should be a touch more inventive, but apparently Finnegan's imagination ran thin. At least he varied his aliases.

The host nodded understandingly. "Of course."

A few moments later, David was ushered into Finnegan's favorite dining room.

Finnegan and Magee were already seated behind the table. In his usual fashion, Finnegan had already tucked a napkin into his shirt collar. He had taken off his suit jacket and hung it on the back of his chair, exposing the sweat spots under his arms.

"David, there you are!" Finnegan heaved his ginormous frame to his feet and extended his hand to David. The buttons on his shirt looked like they were about to pop off from the sudden movement.

"Good to you see, Cornelius." David smiled. For once he was being honest, for tonight even Finnegan's repulsive appearance was not enough to dampen his excitement about their meeting.

"David," Magee greeted him laconically.

"Hello, Kevan," David nodded back.

"Sit down, sit down." Finnegan slapped the back of the chair next to him.

David did as he was told. His eyes darted from Finnegan to Magee in turn as he tried to rein in his anticipation. Come on, get on with it! He wanted to shout at the two idiots sitting on either side of him, but he knew better.

Finnegan cracked his knuckles. "Let's get some chow first, and then we'll talk." He motioned to the waiter who had been hovering by the door. "We'll have steak for six, mashed potatoes, and creamed spinach. Oh, and a bottle of 18-year-old Macallan. And we'll have smoked bacon to start with."

David resisted the urge to wrinkle his nose. As if Finnegan needed to fatten up his ginormous belly any further, but then David was not here to supervise Finnegan's diet. Come to think of, Finnegan dropping dead from a coronary would be a welcome outcome of events.

While they waited for their food, David raked his mind for possible conversation topics. It was not as though he had much in common with either Finnegan or Magee. David had tried his best to make both men like him, and while he was fairly certain about Finnegan's favorable disposition toward him, David was not so sure about Magee—that one was a slippery sucker.

"So, David, when's the wedding?" Finnegan's tiny eyes glistened. "You're not going to leave Aileen in the lurch, are you? The poor girl's got her panties in a knot over you."

David felt his stomach turn. How about never, he was tempted to answer, but instead he said, "Oh, no, sir. Aileen is the love of my life. I just want to make sure that everything is settled before we tie the knot."

Finnegan patted his belly. "That's what I liked to hear. It's going to be a glorious wedding, and you don't have to worry about a thing. I'll pay for everything."

There was a knock on the door, and a waiter bearing a bottle of Macallan entered the room.

"Go on, pour it out," Finnegan instructed. "Leave the bottle here," he added after the waiter finished pouring the drinks.

A second waiter walked into the room. He was carrying a plate of steaming bacon. "Bring it over here," Finnegan demanded, watching closely as the waiter heaved a giant serving onto Finnegan's plate.

Magee's turn was next.

The waiter approached David, and the greasy smell wafted over David's nostrils. He contemplating declining, but after catching Finnegan's watchful eyes, knew better. There were men who bonded through drinking and whoring in strip clubs; Finnegan was the kind of man who bonded through eating.

Sensing Finnegan's eyes upon him, David cut off a large slice of bacon and shoved it into his mouth. He closed his eyes to prevent himself from vomiting. "Delicious," he said after the slippery, greasy substance had made its way down his throat.

"Simply the best," Finnegan confirmed. "How do you like it, Kevan?"

"Very nice indeed," agreed Magee, while his bony hands dragged the knife over the meat on his plate.

"I tell you, there's nothing like a good slice of bacon. Now, while we wait for that steak, let's have a drink." Finnegan raised his glass. "To joint success."

"To joint success." David lifted his glass to his lips and emptied it.

❧❦

At the sound of the doorbell, Janet jumped up from the couch and headed for the door. Baxter followed suit and raced after her.

Without asking who it was, Janet flung open the door. Sure enough, Dennis Walker was standing in front of her. He was holding a box of pizza and a six pack of beer.

"Don't you ask who it is before you open the door?" Dennis asked, making his way inside her apartment.

Before Janet could answer, Baxter pushed by her and started pawing at Dennis's leg, barking excitedly.

"He remembers me," Dennis observed with a note of smug satisfaction.

"I think it's the pizza smell that's getting him excited," Janet countered, snatching the pizza box from Dennis.

"Don't forget the beer." Dennis handed her the six pack. "It's going to be a long night, and the last thing we want is warm beer."

Janet took the six pack from Dennis and headed into the kitchen. She placed the pizza box on the counter, took two bottles of beer and placed the rest of the beer into the fridge. She reached for plates and rolled her eyes: this was going to be a long night indeed.

Janet brought the pizza into the living room and saw that Dennis was busy tinkering with a gadget in his hands. "It's the transmitter for the bug," Dennis explained.

"Is it working?" Janet asked as she placed the food on the reading table.

Dennis adjusted the controls, and distant human voices erupted from the speaker. "It is now. Can you recognize Muller's voice?"

Janet recognized Muller's cocky inflection emanating through the receiver. "Yes, that's him all right!" she exclaimed, straining her ears to make sense of the conversation that was taking place on the other end of the transmitter.

"Now all we have to do is sit back and wait for the evidence to glide right into our hands." Dennis took a bite of pizza and chewed it with relish.

Janet resisted the urge to smack the man. "It would also help if we could actually make out what they are saying," she added pointedly.

"Let them settle in first. They are just shooting the breeze for now." Dennis took a swallow of his beer. He handed Janet her beer. "Here, let's toast to success."

"I don't want to jinx it." Janet took the beer bottle from Dennis's hand and placed it on the table. "And I don't drink on the job," she added because that was all it was—a job. Even though it was Saturday night, and a handsome man was sprawled out on her couch, drinking beer, he was nothing more than a colleague. A colleague who also happened to kiss her earlier but, as Dennis had made clear, that too had been part of the job, and Janet had no intention of disappointing him.

"Fine, be boring." Dennis shrugged, reaching for the beer. "I on the other hand think that there's nothing wrong with combining business with a little bit of pleasure."

Maybe it was the tone of Dennis's voice, or maybe it was the way his lithe, muscular body lay stretched out on Janet's couch only a few inches away from her, but she felt her face growing hot. Actually, she sensed her entire body temperature rising. This will not do, Janet thought, this will not do at all. There she was, on the brink of closing what could easily turn out to be the biggest case of her career, and all she could think about was the tantalizing scent of Dennis's cologne and the sexy, although admittedly smug, smile on his face. She forced herself not to think about the glint in his blue eyes, the faint stubble on his cheeks, and the hollow of his throat that, along with a bit of clavicle bone, was peeking through the open collar of his shirt.

"I am not boring!" Janet snapped, still struggling to tame her disheveled thoughts. "I am professional."

"Hang on a second." Dennis raised his hand. "I think it's starting."

Janet focused her attention on the words coming from the transmitter. "We'll have steak for six, mashed potatoes, and creamed spinach. Oh, and a bottle of 18-year-old Macallan. And we'll have smoked bacon to start with."

Dennis whistled. "18-year-old Macallan. Someone's got expensive taste."

"Shhhh," Janet hissed. "We'll miss the whole thing."

They listened intently for a few more minutes, but the conversation did not mention anything of substance. "I think we can relax for now," said Dennis. "It sounds like Finnegan won't be ready to talk business until he's stuffed his gut."

Janet wrinkled her nose. "Steak for six for four people. Can you imagine?"

"And I wouldn't be surprised if Finnegan ended up eating most of it. He sounds like a man with a big appetite."

"That figures," Janet nodded.

For the next half an hour, Janet and Dennis ate pizza and nursed their beers while listening to Finnegan, Magee, and Muller indulge in their prime steak and 18-year-old Macallan. Finally, there was a sound of plates being carried away and coffee being brought in. "I bet it's going to start now." Dennis leaned closer to the transmitter.

Janet followed his cue, but she leaned in too quickly, brushing her knee against Dennis's. "Sorry," she blushed.

Dennis did not have time to accept her apology because at this very moment they heard Finnegan's voice coming through the transmitter. "Gentlemen, I think now would be a good time for us to talk about why we gathered here tonight. As you know, I always enjoy your company, but I believe that tonight Kevan has some very interesting news that will make this gathering even more pleasant than it already is."

A screeching voice that Janet and Dennis had identified as Kevan Magee's carried through the transmitter. "Thank you,

Cornelius. Yes, indeed, I do have some important news that could be very profitable for us all." Magee coughed. "But before we proceed, I would like to stress the importance of absolute discretion. We have to be very careful in our conduct—"

"Yes, Kevan, we understand that," Finnegan interjected. "That's why we have David here. He's a pro at what he does."

"I just want to make sure that David here does not get us into the same mess that he went through when he ran Emperial."

"With all due respect—" Muller began.

"Calm down, David," Finnegan's voice boomed. "Kevan, I know you're worried, but that whole Emperial / Bostoff Securities mess happened before I knew David, and trust me, I've made sure that those snoops over at the Treasury have been muzzled. Nobody is going to mess in David's affairs now."

"Very well. The instructions are in this envelope," said Magee. "David, please review them once you get home."

"Give it to me," Finnegan snapped with irritation. "Really, Kevan, what do you think this is, some crazy thriller movie?" There was the sound of paper being torn. "Ah, so we have our winners. Rover Enterprises is to acquire Valley Metals. David, I think you know what to do next. The acquisition decision will be announced Tuesday at noon, so be sure to act before then."

"You can be sure of that, Cornelius. The payment will be delivered to the accounts that I have previously indicated. Same goes for you, Kevan."

"Thank you, David," Magee droned. "I suppose this concludes our meeting."

"Not before we drink to our success," said Finnegan.

There was a sound of clinking glasses, and the next thing Janet knew, Dennis's face was only a few inches away from hers, and then he was kissing her with the same deep passion she remembered from a few hours ago.

"Shouldn't we listen until it's over?" she murmured.

"It is over. Besides, it's all being recorded," Dennis whispered as his lips travelled up Janet's neck. "Finnegan should have listened to his friend Magee." Dennis nibbled Janet's earlobe. "Now we've got them all by their balls."

"Yes." Janet barely contained a groan. "We should tell Laskin to run market watch reports on Rover and Valley Metals."

"I'm already on top of that." Dennis began to undo the buttons of Janet's shirt. "We'll call him tomorrow morning."

This was hardly erotic talk, but Janet felt a jolt of ecstasy rushing through her. Dennis Walker was in her apartment, about to make love to her, and he was going to stay until the morning. She had wanted this for so long that she thought it would never happen, and now that it was happening she could scarcely believe it was true. There was no need for false modesty. She wanted him right there and now. She had waited long enough, and she was not going to wait a moment longer.

She ran her hands through his hair, traced her fingers across his face and his neck, reaching for the taut, strong muscles of his chest and arms. She tugged at his shirt, helping him pull it over his head and toss it onto the floor. His lips were kissing her lips, her face, and her neck while his hands were caressing her breasts and her hips. He pulled her blouse off and did the same with her pants, leaving her in nothing but her lacey underwear. A smile spread on her lips as she thought of her decision to wear pretty underwear for his arrival. One never knew. Indeed, one never did. The heat in his eyes showed that he appreciated the gesture. He began to kiss her shoulder, tugging at the strap of her bra with his teeth. She arched her back so that he could undo the hook closure on her back. He pulled off her bra, and she gasped as his lips closed over her nipple. His lips switched to her other breast and then followed the outline of her ribs, as he alternated kisses with gentle nibs. Then he moved down to her stomach, and his hands reached for her lacey thong, pulling it off. Her lips parted with anticipation. She wanted him so

222

much it hurt, but he was taking his time, caressing and teasing, his touch growing from tender to passionate and vice versa.

And then he was inside her, making her groan with a pleasure she did not know existed. She wrapped her legs around his waist, clinging to him, heeding the rhythm of his movement.

"My turn to be on top," she whispered, biting his ear.

"Your wish is my command, my lady." His strong hands held on to her as their bodies turned in unison.

He was on his back looking up at her, and she was on top of him. She gasped with the intense sensation of the new angle, feeling him pressing against her. She began to rock, slowly at first, eager to savor the pleasure he was bringing her. She caught his glance, wild with ecstasy, torn between the desire to prolong the pleasure or taste the climax. Now it was her turn to tease as she alternated her movements from slow and gentle to fast and intense. As she began to rock faster and harder, his grip on her tightened, and their ecstasy rose even higher and finally cascaded into culmination. She collapsed on top of him, their bodies linked in blissful pleasure.

"Miss Maple, I always knew that you are one tough investigator, but I had no idea that you are such an ace in the sack," Dennis whispered.

"You're not so bad yourself," Janet replied.

"Yeah?"

"Yeah."

"And do you still think that my investigative techniques are unethical?"

Janet bit her tongue. She had been so hard on Dennis, but he had turned out to be right in the end. Thanks to him they now had the evidence they needed to nail Muller, Finnegan and their cronies. Not that case evidence was on her mind at this very moment; in fact, it was the last thing she wanted to talk about at the moment. "Shut up, Walker. Just make love to me instead."

"Yes, ma'am. With pleasure."

She was still savoring the pleasure of her last orgasm and had been half-kidding, but he surprised her by being ready again.

This is going to be a very long night, Janet thought. And the best part was that she was not afraid of it ending because there was the morning to look forward to.

Chapter Twenty-Six

The first thing Janet thought of when she woke up the next morning was that she had had sex with Dennis Walker. And not just any sex, but hot, wild, steamy, passionate sex. It was almost too good to be true, but Dennis's face on the pillow next to hers proved that it was true.

She watched him through her lowered eyelashes, not wanting him to wake up. What was going to happen now? Did last night mean as much to Dennis as it did to her, or was he going to just stroll out of her apartment with nothing more than a casual peck on the lips? She did not know, and she was afraid to find out. Instead, she wanted to relish last night's memory for as long as she could. At least while he was asleep in her bed she could pretend that Dennis Walker was her man.

She noticed Dennis's eyelashes moving and promptly closed her eyes. "Good morning," she heard Dennis's voice.

"You're awake?"

"I felt you watching me."

"Did you?" It was useless to pretend. Janet sensed her blush giving her away.

"Yes." Dennis placed his arm around her. "Last night was wonderful."

Janet's heart quickened with delight. "Yes, it was."

"And you know what the best part is?" Dennis asked.

"What?"

"We've got the whole Sunday to repeat it."

Janet was too happy to speak.

"Unless you have other plans, of course."

"Your plan suits me just fine." Janet ran her hand across Dennis's chiseled chest. "Now, where did we leave off?"

"I think I remember." Dennis wrapped his arms around her and rolled on top of her. "Yes, I think this was it." He traced the outline of her neck with his lips.

"Yes, that's right," Janet whispered, as Dennis's hands caressed her, making her body sing with the ecstasy of last night.

An hour later, freshly showered, Janet was rummaging through her kitchen in search of breakfast ingredients. Luckily, she had stopped by the supermarket a few days ago, and there was a carton of eggs and a pack of bacon in the fridge.

Baxter sat on the floor, eyeing her reproachfully. Janet had cut their morning walk short, and apparently Baxter was still mad at her for that. At first he had been too busy gobbling up his breakfast, but now that he was finished he was back to making her feel guilty.

"Sorry, buddy." Janet rubbed Baxter behind his ear. "I promise to make it up to you. But right now I've got to make breakfast for Dennis."

She could hear the sound of water in the shower, and an image of Dennis lathering up his hot, lean, muscular body materialized in her mind. The memory of all the things they did last night and this morning flashed before her eyes, making her hot. "Concentrate," she told herself, as she placed the bacon into the frying pan. The sound of the water stopped, and she heard footsteps approaching the kitchen.

Dennis had a towel tied around his waist, and his wet hair was slicked back. "I'm starving." Dennis wrapped his arms around her.

"You're in luck. I'm going to make an omelet."

"Mmm, smells delicious. How about some pancakes?"

"Pancakes?"

"Yes, pancakes. I make killer pancakes, and I'd love to make some for you."

"I love pancakes," Janet stalled, remembering seeing a carton of pancake mix somewhere in the back of her kitchen cupboards. "Can you watch the bacon?" Janet rummaged through the cupboards, finally locating a worn-looking, but unopened carton. "Here we are!"

Dennis eyed the carton suspiciously. "I think you might want to check the expiration date."

Janet's eyebrows furrowed as she searched for the date. "It's perfectly edible for another two months," she announced triumphantly.

"Excellent. Now I need milk and butter and we'll be in business."

"Milk? I've always made pancakes with water."

Dennis cocked an eyebrow. "By the looks of this carton, it's been a while since you've made any pancakes, with water or milk."

The playful look in Dennis's eyes was the only thing that stopped Janet from snapping at him. He was only kidding, and she knew it. Besides, the best revenge would be to see Dennis actually making those darn pancakes he was harping about. Janet flung open the fridge door, hoping to find a carton of milk that was less than a month old. She was in luck.

"Here you are," she announced, placing the milk carton on the counter. "The expiration date is tomorrow."

"Excellent." Dennis grinned. "I got it from here."

Janet used the opportunity to sneak into the bathroom and check her makeup. Dennis Walker was in her kitchen, making her breakfast. She was so happy, she could float on air.

When Janet returned to the kitchen, she found that Dennis was an ace at manning the stove. Already the first batch of pancakes was ready, and Dennis was expertly pouring the batter for the next round. Just as the batter began to sizzle on the pan,

Dennis turned his attention to the omelet. "Breakfast is almost ready," he announced.

"I'll make coffee," Janet offered.

A few minutes later they were seated behind the table. Baxter curled up by Janet's feet, his nose curiously inhaling the tantalizing breakfast fumes.

Janet ate a forkful of eggs and bacon. "It's delicious." Normally, she limited her breakfast fare to toast, oatmeal or yogurt, but she figured that she had burned more than enough calories last night and this morning to justify the splurge.

"Good. You'd better eat up if we are going to have an encore of this morning."

Janet's face grew warm with pleasure. An encore of this morning meant that he wanted to see her again, which meant ...

"I love it when you blush," Dennis teased her.

"I bet you do. You love making me uncomfortable."

"From what I recall, you were pretty comfortable with me this morning. More than comfortable, actually."

"See what I mean?" Janet felt the blush creeping up her face. "You're doing it again."

"Okay, I'll stop."

"I don't believe you."

Dennis put a forkful of pancakes into his mouth. "You're safe for now. I'm too hungry to embarrass you."

"Good." Janet dug her fork into her food.

Baxter peaked from under the table and placed his head on Dennis's lap.

"He's just had his breakfast," Janet said reproachfully.

"Come on." Dennis made eyes at her. "How can you resist the little fella?"

"Human food is bad for him."

"Most human food is bad for humans too, but we eat it anyway."

"I'm looking out for Baxter's wellbeing. If he gets an upset stomach, I'll be the one dealing with the mess, thank you very much."

Dennis made a face. "Sometimes you can be such a worrywart, but I love that about you too." Dennis blew an air kiss to Janet with one hand, while his other hand disappeared under the table.

"I saw that."

"What?"

"You slipped Baxter a piece of bacon. I can hear him chewing it."

"Guilty as charged. We men have got to stick together."

"What have I gotten myself into?"

"I hope you'll stick around to find out."

This time Janet did not blush. "I intend to."

Finished with his meal, Dennis took a long swallow of coffee. "How about we go for a walk around the city and play Joe tourist?"

"Sounds like a great idea. I'm just going to call my neighbor and ask her to take Baxter for the day."

Baxter was the only one who seemed to disapprove of the plan, as he growled and looked at Janet reproachfully.

Dennis scratched Baxter's back. "We can take Baxter with us. He looks like he's dying to come along."

"Are you sure you don't mind? I can leave him with my neighbor. She is retired and she is always glad to take Baxter for a few hours."

"Me, mind Baxter? We've become best buddies." Dennis began scratching Baxter's belly, and Baxter rolled on his back in pure delight.

"You're going to spoil him." Janet folded her arms on her chest. Not that she was jealous, but ...

As if to reassure her, Baxter got to his feet and started licking her legs. "Yes, I love you too." Janet smiled.

A few minutes later they were exiting the lobby of Janet's building. "That breakfast hit the spot." Dennis rubbed his washboard stomach, which miraculously stayed just as flat as it had been prior to their meal.

"Yes, it did." Janet agreed, conscious of the snugger fit of her jeans.

"How about a walk in Central Park? We could cut across town here."

"Sounds like a great idea. I need to walk off all that greasy food we just ate," Janet replied.

Dennis gave her a once over. "I don't see the need to walk off anything." He pulled her toward him and held her in a long, sweet kiss. "Believe me, I'll make sure that you get plenty of exercise."

"Dennis! We're in the middle of the street."

"So what? Can't a man kiss his girlfriend?"

Girlfriend? Janet's heart jumped like a schoolgirl's. She was Dennis Walker's girlfriend. "You don't mind me calling you my girlfriend, do you, Janet?"

"Not in the least," she murmured.

"Good. In that case, your boyfriend would like to know if you'll grant him another kiss."

"With pleasure."

They spent the day enjoying Central Park, eating hot dogs and ice cream. Baxter was happy to tag along, and Dennis had managed to sneak him bits of food while Janet pretended to be oblivious to Dennis's tricks. Afterwards, Dennis suggested that they go to SoHo, and they took the bus downtown. They stopped by SoHo's many galleries and enjoyed the neighborhood's artistic flair. Baxter received endless compliments as he was welcomed by all the gallery attendants and visitors.

"I've to get going soon," Janet said. "We both have a big day tomorrow." It was close to five o'clock.

"Yes, we could do that, but why waste another wonderful night?" asked Dennis.

"What do you have in mind?"

"My place is just a few blocks away from here."

"Ah, I see you had a plan in mind."

"Maybe. Do you like it? You could stay over."

"I'd love to, but I don't have a change of clothes for the office."

"Ah, I didn't think of that, but I could grab a change of clothes and stay at your place instead."

"That sounds like an excellent idea."

Chapter Twenty-Seven

U sually Janet woke up to the sound of the alarm clock, but the next morning she awoke from a sensation of kisses on her neck.

"Rise and shine, sleepyhead."

She smiled at the sound of Dennis's voice. The details of the previous day came back to her. She had spent two magical nights and one wonderful day with Dennis Walker, and now he was in her apartment, making her breakfast. He was in her apartment! Janet burrowed her head under the pillow, only imagining how she must have looked with her hair a mess and her eyes bleary from the lack of sleep last night. "What time is it?" she mumbled.

"Time to go to work," Dennis whispered. "I'll be in the kitchen."

Twenty minutes later, Janet was ready for work. Her hair was pulled in a French twist. She was dressed in a black suit and black pumps—her usual work attire. The only difference from her typical appearance was the flush in her cheeks and the plumpness in her lips that still tingled from Dennis's kisses.

"Wow, now that's what I call a transformation." Dennis gave her a once over. "Although I liked you warm and sleepy under the covers."

"We've got to go work in a few minutes. Don't get me all excited."

Dennis looked at his watch. "You've got a point there. But you owe me a rain check."

"You can claim it any time after work."

"That's a deal."

"Should we get going?" Janet asked.

"Don't you want to have breakfast first?"

"I usually have breakfast at work."

"But you don't usually have breakfast with me. Don't tell me that you're going to make my cooking go to waste." Dennis motioned at the kitchen table that was set with coffee and toasted bagels.

"Oh, I didn't even notice. Thank you." This was a nice surprise indeed. How hard was it to make coffee and toast bagels? Not very, but none of her previous boyfriends had ever made her breakfast.

Janet took a sip of her coffee. If anyone had told her a week ago or even a few days ago that she was going to spend two steamy nights and one incredible day with Dennis Walker, and that after all of that he was going to cook her breakfast, she would have never believed them. And even though Dennis was sitting opposite her right now, she still found it hard to believe.

Dennis checked his watch. "We'd better hurry. I want to talk to Laskin first thing when we get in. He's got to be on the lookout for trading in Rover and Valley Metals." Dennis finished the last bit of his bagel. "Ready?"

"Ready."

"But you didn't eat anything."

"I ate some." Janet motioned at the three quarters of her bagel.

"You eat like a mouse, Janet. It's going to be one hell of a day today, and you'll need your strength."

"I'll take it with me to go. How does that sound?"

"That's better," Dennis relented. "Do you need to walk Baxter before we leave for work?"

"No. I knew we'd be in a rush to leave so I've asked my neighbor to walk him. She has the key."

"In that case, let's go." Dennis halted. "Janet, you know that this weekend has been amazing ..."

Here it comes, Janet thought. The brush off.

"And I want to see a whole lot more of you. But until we have the case wrapped, I think it would be best if Alex did not see us together. Would you agree?"

Janet hesitated. Alex had insisted on keeping their relationship secret at work, and now Dennis wanted the same. Her common sense told her that he had a point, but her heart literally sank.

"Is something wrong?" Dennis asked.

"I ... No, nothing's wrong. Let's get going."

"Janet," said Dennis, taking her hand. "This is only for the next few days, until we get the case nailed. After that I'm going to stand in the middle of the office and yell that Janet Maple is my girlfriend."

"Promise?"

"I swear."

"I was only kidding. I wouldn't want you to get dinged for disorderly conduct. Just promise that that you won't hide it from people."

"I won't, Janet. I know you've been hurt, but I'm not like him. I will never do anything to hurt you."

"Promise?"

"I swear."

"Good. Then you'd better get of here. I'll follow you in ten minutes."

"See you at the office."

Half an hour later, Janet was at work. She was a few steps away from her office when Alex intercepted her in the hallway. "Good morning, Janet. How was your weekend?" Alex regarded her for several moments. "You look rested," he added.

I look like I've been made love to all weekend, Janet mused. "Thank you, Alex. I took Baxter to Central Park. Being outdoors always does it for me."

"I agree. How is the little fella? No more jumping at people, ripping off trousers?"

Janet swallowed a smirk. "Nope. I believe he reserves that kind of treatment especially for you."

"I see. The next time I go to visit you, I'll make sure to wear combat gear."

What made Alex think that she wanted him to visit her? But she knew better than to argue. If everything went according to plan, Alex would not be her boss for much longer.

"Oh," added Alex, "I meant to ask you about that anonymous complaint against Rover executives—has that been closed out?"

"Yes, Alex. It was closed out right after we spoke, as you requested. I have the file in my office. I could bring it over if you'd like."

Alex frowned. "A file for a nonexistent complaint? I don't believe we should be spending our resources on that. No official complaint, no file."

"I'll shred it then."

"Excellent. I'll let you get back to work," said Alex, stepping aside.

When Janet got to her office her phone was ringing. She shut the door and picked up. It was Laskin.

"Janet, can you stop by my office please?"

"I'll be right there."

A moment later she was in Laskin's office.

"Shut the door behind you," Laskin instructed her calmly.

Janet did as she was told.

"Dennis has briefed me on the situation," Laskin began. "I've requested market watch reports on Rover and Valley Metals."

Just then, Dennis walked into Laskin's office. "Do you really think it's a good idea for you to be seen here? Do you want Alex to walk in on us?" Laskin snapped.

"Relax, I took precautions. Anyway, Alex is busy getting a blowjob from Georgiana."

"How do you know that?" Laskin's voice peaked with interest.

"I heard them from behind his office door. The walls here are thinner than Mr. Kingsley realizes."

"I knew it!" Janet exclaimed. "I saw that floozy sitting on his knee before, and I thought that was funny. But I never thought they would do it in the office."

"If we do our job right, they won't be doing it for long," said Dennis. "Peter, what have you got so far?"

"Option trades in Rover and Valley Metals have spiked through the roof. The trades are broken up into small pieces, but the overall size is almost twice the usual volume. It'll be a pain to trace these to Muller, but we'll get it. He won't be able to get the money before the trades clear, and by that time we'll have the information on the accounts."

Dennis nodded. "Good. I'm going to call Ham."

"Do you think he can help us?" Janet asked.

"I sure hope so. He's been in this business long enough."

"Then why didn't he fight his retirement?" Laskin asked.

"I don't know. I guess he just got fed up, but I know for a fact that he's got friends in high places. I sure hope he won't be fed up now." Dennis halted, about to leave. "How are you doing, Peter?"

"Is that a serious question?" Laskin peered at Dennis over the computer screen. "Other than losing the one woman who could have been the love of my life, I'm doing peachy, just peachy."

"You've got to talk to her, Peter," Janet cut in.

"And ruin the investigation?" Laskin shook his head. "I couldn't do that. I'll just have to find myself a different woman to fall in love with."

"I understand that you can't do it now, but once the investigation is in the open, you've got to talk to her, Peter. Sure, she'll hate you at first, but chances are she'll forgive you later. She'll need a friend, and you can be that friend," said Dennis.

"Yeah, right, a friend who ruined her life. I don't think so."

"Don't be a chicken, Laskin. Take your chances. I'm glad I did." Dennis took Janet's hand.

Laskin's glance shot from Dennis to Janet. "Are the two of you …? Finally! It sure took you long enough, Dennis."

"Better late than never."

"I'm afraid it's never for me and Aileen," Laskin muttered. "Now, if you two lovebirds will excuse me, I've got work to do."

∛∞∝

Back in his office, Dennis grabbed his cell phone and dialed Ham Kirk's number. "Ham?"

"Dennis! It's so good to hear from you! What have you been up to?"

"Ham, can you talk?"

"Of course I can talk. I've got all the time in the world."

The reception grew fuzzy. "Where are you?" Dennis demanded, alarmed by this laidback-sounding Ham who was nothing like Dennis's old boss.

"I'm in Delaware, doing some fishing. I've never had the time for it before, you know, but I've always loved it. It's a wonderful way to de-stress. My wife came up with me, but she is not an early riser, so it works out perfectly. I have the mornings to myself, and then we spend the days and evenings together."

"Ham!"

"What? What's the matter with you?"

"I am trying to tell you that I've got information on Muller that's going to put the bastard away once and for all, and you're carrying on about fishing."

"Do me a favor, Dennis, and let that whole thing go. It won't do you any good to keep digging at that corpse. Sometimes, you just have to cut your losses and move on."

"What if I told you that I have proof of Muller being involved with the attorney general and one of Rover's executives?"

There was a pause on the other line. "You've always been pigheaded, but then that's why you're so good at what you do. I can't promise anything, but I'm listening."

Dennis bit his lip in order to keep himself from cursing at Ham. Dennis spoke slowly and clearly as he brought Ham up to date on everything that had transpired since Ham's departure from the Treasury.

When Dennis was finished, there was a whistling sound on the other end of the line. "Are you sure you want to get into this? It could get really messy."

"Of course I'm sure, Ham. And I was hoping that you would be willing to help me settle the score. Hell, I thought you would want to settle the score."

"Don't get me wrong, Dennis. Of course I want that, but I don't want to put you in any danger. You see, I've got nothing to lose: I'm retired; there's nothing they could do to me. But they could destroy you, and as much as I'd like to, I can't guarantee that I'll be able to protect you. Although I promise to do my best."

"That's good enough for me."

"In that case, I'm going to call my friend on the senate subcommittee."

"You've got friends on the senate subcommittee?"

"I've got one friend there and a very good one."

"Then why didn't you call him when they booted you out of here?"

"I don't like calling in favors."

"But you'll call in a favor for me?"

"Yes I will, Dennis. After everything you've done to bring this case home, it's the least I could do. I hope you brought an extra large umbrella because it's going to be a shit storm. I'll call you as soon as I have an update for you."

Dennis hung up the phone. There were any number of people he could have turned to—his old boss at the FBI, the head of the SEC—but after learning what he had learned about Finnegan, where was the guarantee that they, too, would not be corrupt? If there were one thing that Dennis knew about Ham it was that Ham was honest, and that Ham never made promises that he did not keep. Dennis clasped his hands. It was going to be a shit storm, and he was prepared to face it.

What Dennis was not prepared for was the chaos in his personal life. Not that he had not enjoyed the past two nights with Janet; he had—immensely. What he did not enjoy was the realization of how much he liked her, how much he—dare he think the word?—loved her. Dennis dug his fingernails into his palms. What was wrong with him? He was acting like a schoolboy out on a date for the first time. It was bad enough that he had called Janet his girlfriend after only one night together, he was not about to go professing love to her, even if he did feel it in his heart. But then he had known Janet for far longer than one night, and he had been in love with her ever since he had met her.

ഇൻ

David Muller rang the door of Mila's apartment.

"Who is it?" The sound of Mila's throaty voice made David want to break down the door.

"It's me, baby. Open up."

The door opened, and David was treated to the sight of Mila in a lacy corsage, complete with garter belt, stockings, and black stilettos. She was holding a bottle of Dom Pérignon. Her fingers were on the cork. "Do I open it?" She looked at him meaningfully.

"Pop it, baby."

Mila popped the cork. The champagne began to spill over. David leaned in and licked the foam off the bottle. He kissed Mila hungrily. He had been waiting for this moment all day.

"David! The champagne is spilling!"

"Let it spill," he mouthed. "We can afford it."

He shrugged out of his coat, dumping it on the floor. And then he was holding her, hungry for the taste and feel of her. He scooped her into his arms and carried her into the bedroom.

After he had finished making love to her, David lay on the bed, spent and elated.

"So I take it everything went well?" Mila asked.

"It went swimmingly. One more day and we'll be in the clear."

Mila burrowed her face in David's shoulder.

"What's wrong?" he asked.

"I'm worried. What if something goes wrong?"

"Nothing will go wrong."

"Are you sure, David?"

"Don't you trust me?"

"Of course I trust you. It's just that ..."

"What?"

"Whenever something good is about to happen to me, I'm always afraid that things will go wrong."

"They won't. Not this time."

"But once the merger is announced, the regulators will start digging around. They're going to get suspicious about the trades you placed. What if they find us?"

"You've said it yourself: by the time the merger is announced. By that time we will have gotten our money and be gone. Let the dogs snoop around all they want while we're drinking champagne and eating caviar."

"Mmm, sounds delicious."

"Not as delicious as you are."

David wrapped his arms around Mila, rolling her on top of him. He loved the sensation of her toned body: her soft breasts pressing against his chest and her toned stomach fitting neatly against his. Her hair enveloped him with its silkiness and the warmness of her breath made him feel like he was where he belonged. He loved her. One more day and they would be in the clear. And then he was going to ask her to marry him.

Chapter Twenty-Eight

The next day Mila Brabec and her cousin Ania were sitting at a French brasserie on the Upper East Side. Mila watched Ania consume a pear tart with a side of hazelnut ice cream. Ania could stand to lose a good ten pounds. Instead, she was gobbling dessert, while Mila limited herself to a café latte made with skim milk. But then Mila did not have the luxury of Ania's security. On the contrary, Mila's situation was anything but secure. She had not heard from David since morning, and it was already after two o'clock. That in itself did not sound like such a long period of time, but when put in the context of David usually calling her five times a day at a minimum, it became exceptionally long. Worst of all was that she knew about the risky venture that David was involved in. The man was walking on a wire.

"So," said Ania, pushing the pear tart away and dabbing her lips with a napkin. "When are you and David going to tie the knot?"

"Soon enough."

Ania made a tsking sound. "Soon enough is a very ambiguous time frame, Mila, and you need certainty."

"What do you suggest I do? Go back to Prague and slave away as a bank clerk?" Mila snapped.

"What's wrong with working at a bank?" Ania shrugged her plump shoulders. "It's a perfectly respectable job."

A perfectly respectable job, Mila resisted the urge to mimic Ania. I bet you would just love to see me wasting away in some dump, wouldn't you? I don't see you lifting a finger since you married Daniel. "I want to keep my options open," was all she said out loud.

Ania frowned and placed another forkful of the pear tart into her mouth. She chewed methodically for several moments before she spoke. "I hardly think you're keeping your options open, Mila. If anything, you're limiting them."

"How's that?" Mila asked sulkily. She had made the mistake of arguing with her cousin, but she was not going to back down now.

"It's very simple, really. It's not as though you are gaining experience in your profession here. Instead, you are wasting your life working as a waitress."

Go ahead, why don't you rub it in, Mila thought. Still, as much as she hated to admit it, she knew that Ania had a point. She sure as hell was not getting any younger, and as far as getting a job in her field, the chances of that were also slim. Not that she wanted to slave away as a bank clerk for the rest of her life. "I could go to school here," Mila ventured.

Ania almost choked on her coffee. "Go to school here?" she repeated. "Why, I suppose you could if you qualified for a scholarship. But you'd also need to keep working to cover your living expenses. I imagine that would be difficult."

Yes, I imagine it would, Mila thought. Ania's husband had more money than the Bauers could spend in their lifetime. Daniel was not a stingy man. All Ania had to do was say that her cousin needed help, and he would be happy to oblige, but Ania was too paranoid that Mila might steal her husband and was desperate to get rid of her cousin as soon as possible. Not that Mila wanted to go back to school, anyway. As far as she was concerned she had learned everything there was to learn in a classroom. It did not take Einstein's IQ to understand the world of finance. Hell, David was not any smarter than she was, and he was moving millions of dollars. It was not what you knew, but the proverbial who you knew. If David's scheme worked out, Mila would not have to worry about her future anymore. But if it did not ... Mila checked her watch again. Where was David?

"Are you in a rush?" Ania asked pointedly.

Deciding that she had had enough, Mila finished the last of her latte. "Yes, as a matter of fact I am. I just remembered that I promised to feed my neighbor's cat."

"Your neighbor's cat?"

"Yes, my neighbor, who also happens to be a Calvin Klein model, asked me to feed his cat while he's away on a modeling gig in Milan."

Ania's eyes lit up with jealousy. "You didn't tell me that your neighbor was a model."

"I only just met him." Mila rose from her chair, dropping a twenty dollar bill on the table.

"And he already asked you to feed his cat?" Ania's eyes widened with anticipation of intrigue.

"Yes." Mila nodded, barely keeping herself from bursting into laughter. She had just made the whole thing up on the spot, and Ania was eating it up. No doubt Ania would spend the rest of the day being jealous of Mila and her imaginary neighbor model. Serves the nosy bag right, Mila thought, gleeful of her tiny revenge. "I'd better get going. I wouldn't want to disappoint the cat."

But once Mila got back to her apartment, her mood darkened. Her apartment—she could scarcely even call it that since without David's help she would not even be able to afford the rent—seemed lonely and desolate despite the expensive furnishings and antiques she had acquired on David's credit card. Without David, she had nothing. If he were to disappear from her life, she would indeed have to pack up and go back to Prague.

Enough, Mila thought, willing the grim thoughts away. Most likely David was simply too busy to call her, tidying up his nifty profit and settling with Finnegan and Magee or, more likely, screwing Magee and Finnegan out of their shares. David had told her about his entire plan. It was as simple as it was brilliant, and it did not require a finance degree to execute it, but merely the confidence of a corrupt attorney general and a high-ranking company executive.

"Oh, David, where are you?" she tugged at her hair. "Just call me and tell me that everything is all right."

To give herself something to do, Mila grabbed her phone to browse the Internet. She was about to flip from a CNN page when a headline caught her eyes: "Breaking Story: Charity president arrested in insider trading scandal." Mila felt a chill crawl down her spine. She focused her eyes on the article and began to read: "Today, David Muller, President of Phoenix Fund, was apprehended in his apartment on charges of insider trading. State Attorney General Cornelius Finnegan and Kevan Magee, a member of the board of directors of Rover Enterprises, are charged with collusion in the insider trading scheme."

Mila did not bother to read the rest. Her heart was beating so fast she thought she was going to throw up. Visions of David being dragged through court flashed before her eyes. And then, jail.

No, she thought; she refused to have her life ruined. She had to keep her head clear. If she acted quickly there was still a chance that she might make it. David had rented the apartment under a fake name, which meant that she had a little bit of time before the authorities would link it to him.

She raced into David's study, rushed to the safe, and began to turn the lock dial in the complicated sequence that David had given her. Her fingers were shaking as she counted out the sequence. When she reached the last number on the dial, she held her breath and pulled at the safe door, praying for it to open. The door remained shut. "Damn it!" Mila hissed. Could it be that David had lied to her about the code? "Calm down," she murmured. "Just be calm."

She repeated the sequence. This time her fingers were still and precise, and the safe opened. She grabbed the contents of the safe and shoved them into a backpack.

Then she raced to her closet and pulled out the most practical items of clothing: there was no time to pack her designer dresses and heels.

Twenty minutes later, Mila exited the building. She was wearing jeans, a leather jacket, and a hooded sweatshirt with the hood pulled over her head. She ducked her head and reached for her cell phone. There was only one man who could help her now, and that man was not David Muller. "Anton? It's me, Mila. Can I come over?"

"I thought you'd never ask," Anton's voice boomed triumphantly.

"I am asking now," Mila lowered her voice into a sexy purr. "So, can I come over?"

"You know you can. My door is always open for you, sweetie pie."

"I will be right there." Mila shoved the phone into her purse.

She had all of David's accounts and passwords. Her head spun at the thought of how much money was at stake. There was still a chance, a real fighting chance that this money could be hers, and Anton Kovar was the man who could help her get it.

Anton Kovar was young and handsome. He was just as rich as David—in light of recent events, richer probably. But most importantly, he could give her the protection she needed. Mila pressed her lips firmly together. She could learn to love Anton Kovar just as much as she had loved David Muller.

Chapter Twenty-Nine

A week later, Janet Maple and Dennis Walker stood in the office that used to be Alex Kingsley's.

"What's going on?" Janet asked. "I thought you said there'd be a staff meeting. There's no one here but us. It's after five, so we might as well call it a day."

"It's a nice office, isn't it? Especially so without Kingsley in it."

Janet nodded. Alex's stint as the head of the Investigations department at the Treasury had turned out to be a brief one. He had been relieved of his duties pending further investigation of his conduct at the Treasury as well as his work on the Borrelli case at the DA's office. "It is a nice office, but you still didn't answer my question. What are we doing here?"

Dennis looked around conspiratorially, mischief flashing in his eyes. He took a step closer to Janet so that he was only a few inches away from her. He ran his fingers along her neck, stopping at the collar of her blouse. "Maybe I wanted to see what it would be like to make love to you at the office."

"Dennis! Stop that! Do you want to get us both fired?"

Instead of answering, he slid his hand down to her breast and nibbled on her ear.

Janet trembled with pleasure. "Fine, but why does it have to be in this office? Can't we use your office or my office?"

"We could. But right now you might want to gather your bearings. Ham Kirk will be here at any moment."

"You!" Janet mock punched Dennis in the chest.

"But I do like the office idea though. I think my office will work just fine."

Janet ran her hands over her hair and straightened her blouse. "I'll get you for this!"

"Am I interrupting?" Ham Kirk stood in the doorway.

"Ham! How wonderful to see you!" Janet exclaimed a shade more enthusiastically than she intended.

"It's wonderful to see you too, Janet. It's been a long time, and believe me it was not because of my choosing."

"It could have been shorter if you had been taking my calls," Dennis cut in.

"Cut an old man some slack, will ya?" Ham squeezed Dennis's shoulder. "But seriously speaking, Dennis, Janet, thank you for getting my job back."

"I think we are the ones who should be thankful, sir. Had it not been for your swift action, Muller could have gotten away."

Ham smiled. "I appreciate it, Dennis, but I never take credit for other people's work. You and Janet solved this case. All I did was call my friend on the senate subcommittee to make sure that the case got priority."

"And he was just in time. We raided Muller's apartment the next day, and there were suitcases all over the place. A few more hours and it would have been too late. You should have seen the look on his face. He went all white."

"I wish I had seen it," Janet retorted.

"I was told that it would be too dangerous for you to come," said Dennis.

"But it wasn't too dangerous for you."

"I had the FBI to protect me."

"And they could not have protected me?"

"If I didn't know any better, I would say that the two of you bicker like an old married couple," said Ham, chuckling.

"It's too bad we couldn't find Muller's money," Janet hurried to change the subject. "He agreed to give up his profits in exchange for a reduced sentence. He even gave us his offshore account numbers, but they had all been emptied out. The money is not there."

"And I really believe that Muller has no idea where the money went. He looked ashen when he heard that all the money was gone," Dennis added. "I wonder who took it."

"It might still turn up. Besides, neither Muller, Magee, nor Finnegan will be able to use it now. At least not for a very long time."

"So, are you checking out the grounds before your first day back on the job?" Dennis asked.

Ham rubbed his chin. "I wanted to talk to you about that. To both of you—that's why I came here today. How would you and Janet like to go into a private venture with me?"

"Huh?"

"During my early retirement I started a small consulting business, and it seems to have taken off."

"What kind of business?" asked Dennis.

"A discreet investigations agency specializing in confidential matters. Discreet and confidential are the key words in the job description."

"Do you mean working for Washington?"

"Possibly, and the Feds. That sort of thing. Mostly white collar crime and occasional background checks. Your skills would fit right in. What do you say?"

Dennis and Janet exchanged glances.

"Thank you, Ham. But Janet and I would like to have some time to mull it over," said Dennis.

"Can't we talk about it now? What's bothering you? I assure you that the benefits will be comparable—in fact better—than those at the Treasury."

Dennis rocked back on his heels. "Would dating coworkers be against your policy?"

Ham's eyebrows rose as he eyed Janet and Dennis in turn. "Oh?"

Dennis nodded, and Janet blushed.

"My only policy is to get the job done," said Ham. "Now, are you up for it? It'll be a hell of a lot more exciting than working for the Treasury and a lot less red tape. Oh, I almost forgot the most important part: you'll both get a twenty percent raise, plus a discretionary bonus at the end of the year."

"In that case, I'm in," said Janet.

"So am I," added Dennis.

"Very well. Shall we say you start in two weeks then?"

"Sounds good to me," Janet agreed.

"Works for me." Dennis nodded. "But now, if you'll excuse me, Ham, I've got a date, and I don't want to be late. You'd better come too, Janet."

"Good for you, Dennis. You've made the right choice," said Ham. "I'll see you both soon."

Once they were standing outside, Dennis put his arm around Janet's shoulders. "Where do you want to go and celebrate?"

"Anywhere you chose," Janet replied. There was one thing bothering her.

"What's wrong?"

"It's just that I feel bad for Laskin. Do you think he'll patch things up with Aileen?"

Dennis frowned. "Look, Janet, I know it was a tough decision for him, but he made the right choice, and he knows it. The case will take a while, and Aileen will need all the friends she can get. Laskin can be that friend. And who knows? Their friendship could turn into something more." Dennis paused. "Just like ours did," he added and drew Janet into a long, passionate kiss.

"Yes, it did."

Janet felt a surge of happiness run through her. She had many reasons to feel on top of the world: she had busted a conspiracy involving a top ranking government official with the added benefit of revenge on her ex-boyfriend, and had just been offered an exciting new job. But the joy from these accomplishments paled in comparison to the way her heart swelled from the knowledge that Dennis Walker was her man. Not a coworker, not just a friend, but her man.

Don't want to miss out on other books by Marie?

Go to www.MarieAstor.com and add your email address to the mailing list.

83713775R00158

Made in the USA
San Bernardino, CA
29 July 2018